JINXED

Also by this author

The Potion Diaries

The Potion Diaries: Royal Tour

The Potion Diaries: Going Viral

JINXED

AMY McCULLOCH

SIMON & SCHUSTER

First published in Great Britain in 2018 by Simon & Schuster UK Ltd
A CBS COMPANY

1 3 5 7 9 10 8 6 4 2

Simon & Schuster UK Ltd
1st Floor, 222 Gray's Inn Road
London WC1X 8HB

www.simonandschuster.co.uk
www.simonandschuster.com.au
www.simonandschuster.co.in

Simon & Schuster Australia, Sydney
Simon & Schuster India, New Delhi

A CIP catalogue record for this book
is available from the British Library.

PB ISBN 978-1-4711-6996-0
eBook ISBN 978-1-4711-6997-7

Typeset in Goudy by M Rules
Printed and bound by CPI Group (UK) Ltd, Croydon, CR0 4YY

Simon & Schuster UK Ltd are committed to sourcing paper
that is made from wood grown in sustainable forests and support the Forest
Stewardship Council, the leading international forest certification organisation.
Our books displaying the FSC logo are printed on FSC certified paper.

To Sarah,
Wonder Woman

PROLOGUE

S HE BURST THROUGH THE TREES, cradling the monster in her arms.

The whine of a pulse gun sounded in the wood; she ducked and the shot flew over her head, obliterating the trunk of a beech tree in front of her. Panic rose in her throat. They weren't just out to destroy the monster.

They were going to kill her too.

She kept running, her feet slipping inside the blue plastic overshoes she hadn't had time to remove before bolting from the lab. She'd known this day would come – she'd crossed the line so far, it was no longer even a mark on the horizon. But she still hadn't been ready.

How could you ever be ready to lose what you'd been working on your entire life?

The creature vibrated against her chest, a red light pulsing against its hot metal skin like a heartbeat. It wriggled in her arms, trying to escape – as if it too knew what was coming – but she tightened her grip. She just had to make it to the other side of the ravine, to the emergency car that would take them to safety.

The next shot hit her shoulder and she wasn't sure who screamed louder: her, or the creature. She stumbled, one leg collapsing underneath her as her foot sank into a crevice hidden by a carpet of fallen leaves. She dared to glimpse down and her heart almost stopped: the creature's metal body was smoking, the acrid stench of burnt electronics filling her nostrils. The pulse guns were doing their job, destroying it from the inside out.

She pulled her foot free and pressed on. The bridge was so close she could feel the rumble of trains as they passed underneath. Yet the heavy booted steps of the men behind her were louder still.

'Come on, come on,' said the voice crackling in her ear.

She must have come into range of her partner's communication device. She forced her legs to pump harder, ignoring the sticky wet stab of pain in her side . . .

Barely had her toe crossed the threshold on to the bridge when alarms started wailing, hidden IP protection sensors blaring from the tree line. Traps sprung from the ground, nets that coiled around her legs, tripping her up. 'I'm down!' she screamed into her earpiece. 'Help me!'

'Cutting comms, link destruction in process.' Almost as an afterthought, he added, 'Sorry.' And then the line went dead.

Another pulse thumped her in the back, launching her forward and sending the monster flying from her arms. She had no choice but to watch as the smoking hunk of metal disappeared off the side of the bridge. Her assailants ran past her now, flinging themselves at the railing, leaning out over the edge and watching the blaze of sparks sent up as the metal monster hit the electrified track.

It was gone. Her life's work: destroyed.

The men turned back to her, gun barrels levelling at her head. She closed her eyes and accepted the inevitable.

Down on the tracks below, the monster shuddered with one final pulse of life. As a train thundered down the tracks towards it, it only had the energy for the faintest sound.

It purred.

PART ONE

JINX

CHAPTER ONE

S MOKE RISES FROM THE TIP OF THE soldering iron, my eyes watering as I stare at the motherboard through the microscope. I don't dare to blink, not until I finish melting the silver solder with its rosin core flux into miniature peaks, connecting the loose components together.

I count the seconds in my head as the solder dries. *One, two . . .*

The butterfly lifts its delicate mechanical wings, scalene triangles of filigree metal opening and closing as it runs through system checks. *Whirr-click.* A small vibration signals the 'okay'.

'Yes!' I jump to my feet and dance, swaying my hips in time to the victory music in my head.

Mom rushes in from the kitchen. 'You did it?'

'Why don't you check?'

She nods and says, 'To me, Petal.' It takes a second for the command to register, but the butterfly flaps its wings, lifting up to land on her hand. Mom's face glows, reflecting back

3

the stream of texts and emails that Petal projects on to the flat of her palm. 'Looks to me like she works!'

I grin. 'Okay, just one final thing.' I take Petal from Mom, gently placing her back under my microscope as I sit back down in my chair. My work is flawless: so neat the repairs are barely visible. Taking it to the Moncha vet would have taken days (and cost a fortune), but I've finished in less than an hour.

Satisfied, I snap the casing back over the exposed electronics. 'There. Good as new.'

'Thank you, honey!' Mom wraps her arms around me, planting multiple kisses on my forehead. I groan in mock-mortification, but my face heats up with the warmth of her praise.

It's not *that* big a deal. I've had a lot of practice with Petal. The butterfly *baku* is one of the bestsellers for Mom's demographic and insects in general are the least complex models on the market, offering the bare minimum of functions like text and talk, a browser, GPS. The butterfly is extra popular because of the ability to customize its wings. On the flip side, the wings are flimsy, prone to snapping with the tiniest snag, which in turn damages the internal electronics. Petal is a perfect example. She got caught when Mom unwound her scarf and her projector malfunctioned.

'You're welcome. Remember to unleash her as soon as you get inside next time.'

'I don't know what I'd do without you, Lacey. Your repair

is better than what any of the vets could do.' Mom smiles as Petal flies back up to settle on her shoulder, her hand still lingering on my back. 'You find out today, don't you?'

I cringe. I thought she had forgotten. To my surprise, even I'd managed to forget about it for an hour. Fixing things does that for me. My mind focuses in on the problem – in this case a loose wire and a dodgy PCB connection – and the rest of the world falls away.

Even the fact that any minute now I'm going to receive the biggest news of my fifteen-year-old life.

'Yup.' All moisture evaporates from inside my mouth, and I try in vain to return the smile. I sense hesitation from Mom, her fingers drumming a pattern up and down my spine, so I stand up abruptly from my chair. 'Better put this stuff away,' I say, gesturing to the tangle of silver wire and machinery.

Mom gives me one final kiss on the top of my head. 'Whatever happens, you're still the best companioneer in *this* household.' She heads over to the sink, Petal fluttering up to the leash behind her ear, where she plugs in to charge. Mom bobs her head in time to some invisible music, and I assume Petal has started streaming her favourite podcast.

I wipe the end of the soldering iron with a sponge and pack it away, closing the case with a decisive click. Some people ask for bikes or giftcards or books for their birthday. I asked for a soldering iron. I had researched a store on the outskirts of town that sold refurbished electrical tools and casually added it to Petal's GPS database – and Mom had taken me there on my fourteenth birthday. Hey, Monica Chan – who invented the bakus and lent her name to Moncha Corp, now the largest tech firm in North America – had one when she was a teenager. I'd read that somewhere. If it's good enough for her, it is for me too.

As Zora, my bff, would say, *that doesn't make you special – it just makes you weird.*

She's right.

I carry my kit and microscope back to my room. Mom normally hates it when I solder in the condo – the metallic smell seems to sink into everything, from the pillows on the sofa to the rice in the cooker – but when it's her own baku that needs repairing she makes an exception.

That's too often for my liking. The level 1 insect bakus are renowned for being a bit . . . *buggy.* If I had my choice, I know exactly what baku I would get. I'd go straight for one of the originals. One of the level 3 spaniel models, with cute floppy ears and a tail that works as a selfie stick. If I close my eyes, I picture hanging out with my baku in my room, teaching it to play games, helping me with my homework and cuddling up with it at night. *But you only get a spaniel baku *if* you get into Profectus*, my brain reminds me.

My dream school – Profectus Academy of Science and Technology – founded by Monica herself, and fully owned and operated as a division of Moncha Corp. I need the grant they offer incoming students who can't afford the minimum level 3 baku. Otherwise, the only one I can afford is a puny level 1. Even though I've been eligible to get my first baku for a week (since I finished junior year for the summer), I've

6

put off going to the Moncha Store until I found out about my admissions status.

I take a deep breath.

I've done everything I can to make it happen. I have near-perfect grades, checked off all the extra-curriculars, participated in science fairs and early bird band and volunteered for an environmental charity to pad out my resume.

Zora once told me I was a lock for a place because no one worked as hard for it as I did. If only it was that easy. It's not like I'm Carter Smith, the son of Eric Smith – Monica's business partner and co-founder of Moncha. Carter is also in our grade at St Agnes, and even though I beat him in all our classes, and in two science fairs, I know he'll get in without a fight.

Whereas my dad . . .

I twist the ring on my finger, the only object I have left of him.

. . . is just a liability. I don't let myself think about it any more. Besides, Mom and I, we owe Moncha *everything*. They gave us a place to live when Dad disappeared, gave Mom a job and provided childcare for me while she worked. Without Moncha, I wouldn't have met Zora.

No matter what, I want to work for the company – I'd sweep Moncha floors if I had to, a practical dung beetle baku at my side. But if I truly let myself dream . . . I know what I want to do with the rest of my life. I don't want to work for Moncha. I want to be Monica Chan. I want to be

7

a companioneer, one of the people working on the bakus. I want to design new animals, innovate for existing ones, implement even more amazing features. Every day would be a challenge.

But the first step to get there is acceptance into Profectus. Although in theory, Moncha could hire companioneers from anywhere, for the past decade (since Profectus has been open), every companioneer hire has been a graduate of the Academy.

You'll know soon enough, I remind myself. I gently place everything down on my desk. *But maybe I should just check . . .*

I bounce on to the bed and tap my phone screen to wake it up. No email from Profectus. But I have missed a Flash from Zora. 'BYE BYE!!!!' is scrawled in her fingertip-writing as a boomerang clip plays back and forth of her hurling her phone from the deck of the Toronto Island ferry.

I swipe the screen so I can see the next Flash: a still of the splash her phone makes in the lake, with the caption #PHONEMURDER.

I snort a laugh and collapse back on to the nest of pillows. #PHONEMURDER is the latest craze – the wanton, totally unnecessary (but often hilarious and creative) destruction of your old, government-granted smartphone, filmed by a newly acquired baku and shared online. Things got out of hand when a Flashite committed #PHONEMURDER by dropping his device from the edge walk of the CN Tower and almost caused *actual* murder-by-phone. Still the video got over ten million hits, so he'd probably consider it a win. Thanks to his status as an incoming Profectus student, he was released from police custody with only a caution.

Within the space of a few seconds, I film a video of myself drawing a fake tear dripping down my cheek, select the puppy-ear filter, type 'RIP ZORA'S PHONE' as a caption and send my reply. This is the distraction I need.

If Zora is destroying her phone that means she must have chosen her baku already. My next message to her is a giant question mark. Okay, I send her about fifteen of them.

'I chose ... a dormouse!' Zora's next selfie shows her hugging the cutest baku I've ever seen, a tiny ball of soft matte-grey metal fur, pointed nose and oversized eyes. It's curled up in a ball next to her cheek, its long tail extended to take the picture, her dark brown skin glowing gold from the sunlight reflected off the lake. She looks so happy; I can't help but smile with her. A dormouse is a level 2 baku – higher than I could afford, but not good enough for Profectus – but going there was never one of Zora's goals. She's going to continue at St Agnes for senior year, then apply for programming internships after she graduates.

'His name is Linus and I can already tell we're going to be best friends for life. Well, not better friends than you and me but you'll know what I mean as soon as you get your own. Tell me as soon as you hear anything!!!' reads her next message.

'Of course,' I shoot back. I stare at the photo of her and Linus together a little longer, my throat feeling tight.

Then it comes in. The alert. I can only read a tiny portion

of the subject line and it gives nothing away. LACEY CHU: PROFECTUS APPLICATION STATUS

My heart hammers inside my chest. The slim rectangular device feels so old-school in my suddenly clammy palm but then . . . this is it. The very last time I use it. Before I choose a baku of my very own. Level 1 or level 3.

A single tap opens my email app where, in bold letters, is the message I'd been waiting for.

I click open.

> Dear Lacey,
>   We regret to inform you that . . .

The phone flies out of my hand like it's heated to a thousand degrees. It bounces off the corner of my bedframe and on to the floor, where – just like that – the screen shatters into a million tiny pieces.

Just like my dreams.

CHAPTER TWO

'I'M SORRY, WE'RE SOLD OUT OF THE praying mantis.' The vet doesn't even look up at me as he stares down at the information provided by his retriever baku. They're standard-issue for employees of the Moncha Store (and most service industry professionals), always helpful, with smooth black digital fur that makes reading information off their backs easy.

I feel a twinge of jealousy at the sight, and then a wave of embarrassment for envying a Moncha Store employee. They call themselves 'vets' because they think it's hilarious, as if they have real medical degrees or something, but the actual geniuses behind the bakus are the companioneers, not the faux-hip guys in white lab coats and lens-free, plastic-rimmed glasses with no real understanding of what makes their bakus tick.

But the truth is, this vet is still going to have a better baku than I will.

'This is a waste of time,' I say to Zora, turning away, but she grabs my arm and drags me back around to stare at the screen on the glowing white counter.

11

'No way am I standing in line again,' she hisses. Then she turns her sweetest smile on to the vet. On the counter, one of Moncha's slogans glows into life ... MONCHA: WE ALWAYS HAVE YOUR BAK(U).

Well, it doesn't have *my* particular baku, but that's apparently beside the point.

'So ... no praying mantis and no dragonflies. What *do* you have in stock?' Zora asks. Linus pokes his head out from underneath her collar and twitches his nose at me. I wrinkle mine in response and poke my tongue out. Linus ducks back under the fabric and Zora shoots me a look over her shoulder. I roll my eyes but pay attention to the vet once again.

'We have butterflies and scarabs in the insect department,' he says, bringing up my options on the screen. 'If you want to move up to level 2, small mammals, the selection is a lot bigger ...'

I grimace. Without the Profectus grant, all I can afford with my savings is a level 1 insect. 'I'll pick something another time,' I say, through gritted teeth, not feeling inspired by any of the options.

'You can't, because you smashed your phone, remember? You need something *now*.' Zora grabs my arm again to stop me moving.

I sigh. I know she's right, but my mind is still refusing to accept reality. I rub the sore spot behind my ear where the leash has been installed. I'm committed now, and I have to choose something. *You can always upgrade in a few years, when you've saved more money ...*

The vet stares pointedly over my shoulder at the long line snaking its way out of the door behind me. I take a deep breath and force myself to focus. 'Okay, I'll take a scarab,' I say, pointing at one on the counter's screen. Its carapace is greenish purple, iridescent like an oil slick. It's kind of pretty. Scarabs are known for having flight issues (something about the way the wings fold up) but I don't want the same baku as my mom. That would just be too sad.

'Coming right up. Rolo and I will go get one for you.' He snaps his fingers and his retriever baku follows him obediently to the stock room.

Once the vet and his baku are gone, I turn my back on my counter and fold my arms across my chest. 'Well, this sucks.'

Zora nudges my shoulder. 'Can I give you a hug?'

She knows I'm not normally the touchy-feely type, but I nod – every hug is worth its weight in gold right about now. The sting of the Profectus rejection is a raw hurt, an open wound that refuses to heal over. I keep going over it in my head.

Did I fail a portion of the test?

Which bit?

If I'd studied harder . . .

Or maybe the competition this year was just too much . . .

Yet as much as I want to pretend it was a mistake, or forget the email ever came in, Zora's right; I barely lasted the morning without the internet (is net-withdrawal a thing? Because I was all shaky and sweaty without being able to check my Flashes . . .) and I can't show up to school with a broken phone. I need a baku. It's not even a social standing thing any more. At St Agnes (my high school, where I'll be forced to stay now that I'm not going to Profectus), once we enter our senior year, all our textbooks are stored in baku-encrypted software and homework assignments are sent to our bakus directly. It's the trade-off of living in Monchaville. It's not really called that, but it might as well be. Moncha provides our housing, healthcare and education – it's a corporate mini-city that has grown up within Toronto, spreading beyond the 'discovery district' where Monica first shared a co-working space to occupy almost the entire eastern half of the city. And a requirement of living in Monchaville is that you have your own baku. Not that that's a big deal any more. Almost everyone in the country has one.

Another slogan appears where my elbows are touching the countertop. BAK-UP YOUR LIFE . . . MONCHA'S NEWEST CLOUD SOFTWARE INCLUDED WITH EVERY NEW BAKU. This time, a picture of Monica flashes up, with her signature asymmetrical fringe cut into a diamond pattern, almost like a reverse crown. Mom has a story of when I tried to cut my hair into the same style . . . and that's why I had a pixie cut for half of second grade.

Seeing Monica's face makes me smile. The story behind bakus is ingrained in our cultural history and Monica Chan is its main protagonist. There's even a Hollywood-produced mini-series about her journey, called (WO)MAN'S BEST FRIEND. I stream it whenever I'm feeling low, or uninspired – and I dread to think how many times it's been logged that I watch it.

The story goes that Monica grew up glued to her smartphone – so much so that it began to be detrimental to both her mental and physical health. During her doctor-mandated phone-break, she walked the streets of Toronto and found herself watching people walking their dogs in High Park. She realized what she'd been missing all along: a companion. If her smartphone was going to be by her side all the time, why not have it be cute and interactive? Something she could love and feel comforted by? But that could also be useful – helping her keep track of her life and her calendar, stay in touch with her friends and family, and access her social media, the internet and everything else she needed.

She started work in the storage locker of her apartment building, because her parents didn't have a house with a garage (I bet her mom couldn't stand the smell of solder either). They squeezed their entire family into a two-bedroom condo, just like my family's. She designed a robotic pet with all the features of a smartphone and called it a *baku* because of a story she'd heard from her Chinese grandmother, about creatures made up of the leftover parts of other animals. Her first model, affectionately known as Yi (the Chinese word for 'one'), was built from the screen of her portable gaming device, her old smartphone's motherboard, and metal parts she could scrape together from old toys and electronics. She went door-to-door in her apartment building, asking her neighbours to give her any old bits of tech destined for the scrapyard.

She took her design to a board of reality television investors, who threw money at her and turned her – and her baku – into a viral sensation overnight. Before long, MONCHA was up and running in a small co-working space in Toronto's Discovery District, alongside crowd-sourced taxi services and the latest health tracking software. It opened its first factory in North Toronto and just kept expanding, taking over buildings and multiplying like mould in a petri dish as bakus became *the* must-have device around the world. Monica bought her old condominium building to help provide housing for her employees, then started her own school for her employees' kids, acquired a local hospital to provide healthcare . . . and quickly Monchaville was born.

A loud crash from beside me snaps me from my thoughts. Zora gasps and when I look up, my jaw drops too. On the counter two down from ours is a stunning high level baku – an eagle – its wings spread so wide they've knocked over a display case of customizable butterfly wings. The companioneering work on display is on a level beyond anything I've seen. The feathers are made up of individual filaments of steel-sprayed-gold, giving it a rich, sparkling texture. It tosses its head – so lifelike – and lets out a screech that almost pierces my eardrums. It's magnificent. It's absolutely top-of-the-line. Must be at least level 4, if not level 5.

Who could *afford* something like that?

I get my answer. The eagle folds its wings down and, staring wide-eyed at his new baku, is a guy in a Profectus-branded jersey.

'Lace?' Zora whispers in my ear. 'I think you're drooling.'

'What?' I drop my head and wipe my mouth, just in case she wasn't joking. 'That baku is amazing.'

'That's not the only thing that's amazing. *Damn*, he is fine,' Zora says in a low voice, wiggling her eyebrows at the guy, making me snort.

She's not wrong. I dare one more glance. The guy is older than us and tall – six feet at least – with a smooth high brow and close-shaved black hair that's just starting to lift into small curls. His teeth are bright white against his dark skin as his lips split into a giant grin.

I'd be grinning like that too, if that beautiful bird was destined to be my baku.

'Tobias, my man!' comes a shout from behind me. Another guy – also in a Profectus jersey, but this one so new I see the price tag sticking out at the back – barges past me, knocking me into Zora, and then both of us into the counter.

'Watch it!' I snap. 'There's a line, you know.'

The guy doesn't turn around but his baku does. An ugly pig snuffles at our feet, pawing at the ground. It has two huge tusks and it sways its head menacingly – not a pig, then, but a boar. I leap back, letting out an involuntary yelp.

'Rein it in, Carter,' says Zora, who recovers faster than me.

My neck snaps around so fast, I almost get whiplash. *Carter*?

I don't know why I'm so surprised. Despite the fact that I

17

beat him in almost every class – much to his annoyance – his acceptance into Profectus was a signed, sealed and delivered thing.

He saunters over, smirking at me.

'Zora? Is that you – and Lacey?'

I cringe as he says my name. I wish with all my heart now that I had taken the subway out to some distant Moncha Store where I wouldn't run into people I know. Especially not this particular person.

'Admiring my new baku, are you? When I got my Profectus acceptance last night, I got an upgrade *straight* away.'

'You mean your dad bought you an upgrade,' Zora snaps. *That's* why the boar baku is so surprising. I'm sure the last time I saw him at school, he had a dog baku.

Carter just shrugs. 'Meet Hunter – he's a level 4, don't you know.'

I grimace, despite myself. Trust him to get a level 4 baku without having to earn it. I wonder if he even knows how to operate it properly. His dad probably got one of the companioneers at Moncha to customize it just for him. My body aches with jealousy.

'Choosing your baku, are you?' He leans his elbow on the counter, tilting his head to one side. 'What are you going for?'

'Oh, uh . . .' I try to calculate the time it would take for me to bolt to the door. Internet or no internet, anything is better than the humiliation I'm about to face if . . .

'Here's your beetle, miss.'

The vet's timing couldn't be worse. He sets the tiny

box down on the counter, the beetle baku trapped in a white plastic mould, clearly visible through the transparent opening in the front. Carter's eyes bulge out of his head. I don't know whether he's going to explode from confusion or glee – or both, as the realization dawns. Then he begins to laugh. He laughs and laughs, as my face burns with embarrassment.

I turn away from Carter but not before I notice that everyone in the store is looking at me, including the hot guy Tobias with the eagle baku.

'You didn't get in, did you? Oh, Lace – all those years of being a total nerd, wasted!' Carter says, before laughing even more.

'Come on, Zora,' I mumble, snatching the beetle from off the counter, and this time she doesn't try to stop me.

'Hey, don't you want me to show you how to leash it?' the vet calls after us.

But Zora and I are already out of the door.

CHAPTER THREE

'HE'S A JERK. FORGET ABOUT HIM,' SAYS Zora, once she catches up to me. She slips her arm around mine, forcing me back into a more normal pace. But I don't want to slow down. Everywhere I look in the mall, I see people with their higher level bakus – mechanical dogs and cats either trotting at their heels or leashed up on their shoulders – and it's a constant reminder of what I can't have. I make a beeline for the exit, craving sunlight and fresh air.

I'm still shaking, Carter's laugh a soundtrack to my steps that I can't turn off. I'm simultaneously humiliated and annoyed that I've let him get to me. My new beetle baku is still trapped in the box in my hand; I can't bear to look at it yet. 'Let's go somewhere,' I say to Zora, once we're through the revolving doors and outside. 'Somewhere ... to escape from here.'

'I know just the place. I'll get directions.' She holds her palm out as her dormouse sneaks down her arm, projecting directions on her fingers.

I shove the beetle into my backpack, pushing it right to the very bottom. Zora shoots me a look, but doesn't say anything. I avert my eyes, focusing on the zipper of my bag. I can tell by the gentle rattle of the beads at the bottom of her braids that she is shaking her head at me.

By the time I stand up again though, she's over it. That's what I love best about Zora. She's the least emotional person I know. It's one of the things that makes her such a great coder. She sees everything as if it's an algorithm, including our emotions – 'this is just the body's inbuilt response to stressful stimuli' she told me when we first met, while I was crying in the elevator after getting a B on a test in third grade, and I blinked at her as if I couldn't believe I'd found another eight-year-old as nerdy as I was. She'd just moved into the same condo building with her parents and three high-maintenance sisters. I'd always been the loner kid in class – the one who took everything (especially my grades) a bit too seriously, who was always hungry to learn more about engineering, to see my name at the top of the honour roll. Zora was the first person who was as passionate about something as I was. At first, she was just glad to escape the madhouse of her family, but we quickly became best friends.

She knows when to push and when to leave me alone. We lock together like pieces of a very specific jigsaw. No other person has ever understood me like she does. She pushes; I pull. She codes; I build. My creations would be lifeless without her code and her code formless without my builds. And because we live in the same building, she's always

21

hanging out in my unit – helping me not get too lonely when Mom is at work, and even hanging out with Mom when I'm tinkering in the basement. She's more like a sister than a friend – she calls me a sister that she *chose* rather than was born with – and I don't know what I'd do without her.

There is no specific border for when we leave 'Monchaville', no massive gate or wall, but there's a definite *feeling*. A gentle shift in energy from one side of the road to the other. I think it's because of how clean everything is in the part of town that is run by the company. They took over responsibility from the city for all the maintenance of the ten-block (and expanding) rectangle in exchange for preferential planning permissions and the right to override specific bylaws. I saw an article in a regular city paper once that said the sidewalks and pathways around Moncha are embedded with anti-trademark-infringement alarms that trigger if someone attempts to steal anything, and that there are security bird bakus flying over every square inch of pavement – as invasive as CCTV. I don't know if any of the rumours are true – I've never seen any unusual-looking birds or heard the blare of an alarm, but the Moncha guard – the security team – are ever-present, keeping the streets of Monchaville safe.

Tales of security bakus and alarms go against everything I've read about Monica Chan – she doesn't seem paranoid about copyright infringement. We've had loads of talks in school about how important it is for us to experiment and play – that's how technology takes its great leaps forward. And no company in the world has yet been able to replicate the bakus to any reasonable standard. There was a disastrous version that came out in Germany – the animals were all based on mythological creatures (that part was totally cool) – but they bugged out and started twitching, scrambling text messages and rerouting web searches to illegal dark net stuff. One even attacked their owner. They had to shut down production within a week. Once again, there were rumours that it could have easily been Moncha's ace code-creators that infected the German hosts, but viral code wouldn't explain the weird mechanical tics.

In the decade that bakus have been around, there haven't been any major glitches. The neuroleash technology is no more invasive than an ear-piercing (although the law still makes people wait until they're entering their final year of high school before they can get one). The best part is that even older bakus can be upgraded, incorporating any developments in the technology, under lifetime Moncha warranty. Their spread around the world has been so rapid and prolific, there isn't any need for competition. And if you want to work for a cutting-edge technology company, there is only one choice: Moncha.

There has only ever been one choice for me, that's for sure. Except now, the spark of hope is accompanied by a wave of crashing disappointment. I wonder if that feeling will ever go away, or if I'll be left with this regret for the rest of my life.

When Linus indicates that we should turn left, I realize where Zora is taking us. I grin with delight. The Don River valley trails. The Don River valley splices through the city centre like a river of green, an oasis of calm in the busy metropolis. It's one of my favourite parts of the city. You can look down into it and pretend you are in the middle of the wilderness. I have a blurred memory of being on my dad's shoulders as we hiked down through towards the tracks and—

I immediately curse my brain and scrub it of all mention of my dad. I do not need to go there. Not today. Today has been filled with enough disappointment.

'Everything all right?' Zora asks, and Linus tilts his head in strange synchronicity. He's only been hers for a day, and yet already he's adopting her mannerisms, and becoming as much a part of her as the line of earrings dotted up her earlobe.

'What do you mean?'

She stares down at my hand. 'You're rubbing your ring.'

Heat rises in my cheeks and I snap my hands apart. But she's right. Whenever I touch my dad's old engineering ring – the last piece of him I have left – something is up.

The iron rings are a Canadian engineering tradition. Supposedly forged from the iron of a collapsed bridge, it's a reminder of the immense responsibility borne by engineers, and to keep the safety of their work in mind. It's supposed to be worn on the left pinky, but my hands are much smaller than my dad's. I wear mine on my thumb. Besides, I'm not an engineer yet.

And maybe now you never will be, not for Moncha Corp anyway, says a small voice in my head.

I dash the thought away.

'Oh, I'm fine,' I say. 'This was the perfect place to come. I love it here.' I throw my arms wide and twirl around under the canopy of leaves, hoping to distract her.

It works. She closes her eyes and takes a deep breath. 'It's pretty great. And if we head across the bridge it's a short cut downtown, so we can get some bubble tea.'

There's a suspension bridge in the middle of the park that crosses over the high-speed rail tracks. 'Excellent plan,' I say. I stare down at the pattern of shadows created by the leaves on her face and arms, her skin shining burnished copper where the sun hits it. I feel a twinge of sadness that she's off on an advanced coding course this summer. It's an amazing opportunity for her – Zora's wanted to be a coder ever since she programmed her first 'Hello World' in BASE – and this course will give her a leg-up on the competition before she applies for an actual computer technology degree next year.

'When does your course start?' I ask, wanting to know exactly how many days I have to hang with Zora before she leaves me for two whole months.

'Hmm?' She opens her deep brown eyes and levels her gaze at me. 'Oh ... end of June. Are you going to miss me?'

'Are you kidding?' I stop in my tracks. 'What am I going to do with my summer without you?'

She pokes me in the ribs. 'Maybe you'll *enjoy* yourself. It's the summer. You've worked hard all friggin' year. You're allowed to take a break and relax.'

'Right ...' *Except that you get to do the thing you've been wanting to do your whole life*. The words balance on the tip of my tongue but I don't let them spill off the edge.

Laughter reaches us from behind, the low chuckle of inside jokes and bad puns. Zora looks over her shoulder. 'Oh no,' she says, her shoulders tensing.

'What is it?' I turn around too, and immediately see the source of tension: the twitch of a robotic boar nose coming up behind us. Their bakus must have directed them down the same short cut into downtown.

'Oh look, it's beetle brain and her rodent friend,' says Carter, his voice laced with smugness as he approaches. He's accompanied by a few guys I don't recognize, all with level 3 bakus and also in Profectus shirts, and Tobias. At least *he* has the decency to look ashamed at his friend's blatant taunting, staring off into the trees and refusing to make eye contact. As if I'm looking at him anyway. My eyes drift over to the sight of his beautiful eagle baku, my stomach clenching with jealousy.

'Ignore Carter,' whispers Zora, holding her chin up high. Linus quivers inside the hood of her jacket. We slow our pace, hoping they'll pass us by.

'Now, seriously though,' says Carter, holding his hands up in front of him as he steps in front of us, forcing us to stop. Reluctantly, I hold his gaze. 'I'm kinda disappointed that you're not going to be at Profectus next year. You were by far my closest competition in our class. I guess now I get to see what the *actual* smart kids are like. Guess you flunked the entrance exam?'

Beside me, Zora bristles, all five-foot-nothing of her stocky frame, and she glares at me expectantly, her expression in her deep brown eyes screaming: 'YOU CAN'T LET HIM GET AWAY WITH SAYING THAT!'

But my treacherous brain draws a blank at anything witty or creative. Instead I just mumble non-words, drop my chin and my eyes and keep on walking, speeding up this time. My cheeks burn with shame – I wish I could be half as clever in the moment as the teens on my favourite streaming series.

Zora doesn't immediately follow and I whisper a silent prayer for her to *just drop it*, and a few seconds later, she's hurrying to catch up with me. 'I preferred him without that baku,' Zora hisses in my ear, and – as if he's heard us – we hear a huff and snort from the boar behind.

'He'll probably upgrade him again in no time.' Despite myself, I sneak a glance over my shoulder. It's true: Carter is like a different person with that boar by his side. He's standing taller, his stance wider and his blond hair less lank and greasy on top of his head. The Profectus makeover. It's a thing.

'Come on, guys,' he shouts after us. 'This might be the last time we see you – soon we won't exactly be travelling in the same circles.' He's tossing a ball up and down in his hand – I recognize it as a baku training tool, so owners can play 'fetch' with their bakus, just like with a real pet. 'Unless I need someone to come and clean my house. Isn't that what beetles do? The grunt work of the animal world?'

'What does that make you, a garbage disposal like your

pig?' The words fly out of my mouth before I can stop them. I might hate my little beetle, but that doesn't mean I'm going to give Carter permission to diss him.

A flare of red creeps over Carter's pasty skin, rising up from his collar to his cheek like an angry tide, and his fist closes over the baku ball. We don't want to see his reaction rise any further (satisfying though it is); I know full well I might have just poked an angry bear … or boar. I pull Zora forward.

'I'll have you know pigs are highly intelligent and resourceful creatures!' Carter's screechy voice follows us down the trail. 'Come back! Don't you want to see what a level 4 baku can do?'

We ignore him, half-running, half-walking until we are out of sight and earshot before we relax.

Once upon a time, I would have loved to see a level 4 baku at work – especially something as complex as a boar model – but now I only want to get away. I hate how small Carter can now make me feel. It's less than twenty-four hours since I got the rejection from Profectus, and already it's like my dreams have shrunk down from sky-high to subterranean.

There's a snapping of twigs and leaves behind us, a sinister snarl.

The boar is back. I reach out and grab Zora's hand – the boar baku might be intimidating but he can't hurt us or Linus. If we can get across the bridge and into the city, we can lose them for good. I start to run.

At first, Zora surges forward with me, but then her palm

slips from mine. There are angry shouts from behind us and then a piercing screech from the eagle. I stop and spin around, already halfway across the bridge.

Tobias's eagle soars over the top of Zora's head, so close his wings brush her hairline, and he snatches something too small for me to see out of the air in his talons. She screams with fear, but she's running so fast she stumbles over her flip-flops, skidding out of control, and she lands with a thump on the metal surface of the bridge. Something escapes her collar then bounces once, twice, and over the edge and down into the valley.

Out of instinct, I grab the closest thing I can find – a pine cone – and whip it at the eagle to get it away from Zora. My aim, surprisingly, is good. The pine cone rattles against the eagle's golden wings, sending it off balance.

Then I hear Zora's panicked scream: 'Linus!'

Oh no. My throat drops into my stomach and I race to Zora's side, leaning out over the railing as Carter, Tobias and the rest of his friends run past us on the bridge, disappearing into the forest on the other side. Cowards.

But her brand new baku is absolutely nowhere to be seen.

CHAPTER FOUR

'NO!' CRIES ZORA. SHE'S SHAKING, HER hands clawing at her collar and at the leash around her ear, as if praying to find Linus tucked away in a fold somewhere. 'Linus? Linus, are you there?'

But if he was there, he would have answered. Instead, there's a deafening silence.

She grabs my hands, pulling herself to her feet. 'Lace, I can't lose him! I just got him. All my savings . . .'

'I know.' I take a deep breath. I know *exactly* how hard Zora has worked to save up for her baku and I'm not going to let Carter and his friends take that away from her. I look down towards the valley floor and the railway tracks – then at my feet encased in their sturdy boots and Zora's in flip-flops. I know what I have to do. I turn back to Zora, pressing my phone into her palm. Even though the screen is broken, it still works. 'Call the Moncha guard. Tell them what happened.'

She stares down at the phone through tear-filled eyes, her forehead wrinkling in confusion. It looks laughably old-fashioned in her hand already. But then she sniffs, and closes her fingers tight around the handset. 'Okay.'

'Good,' I say, before pulling my sleeves down so they cover my lower arms and tightening up the straps on my backpack.

'Wait, where are you going?' she asks.

I climb up on to the metal railing. 'I'm going to find Linus.' Without waiting for her response, I swing my leg over and hop down on to the overgrown slope on the other side. Zora hesitates – I can tell she wants to follow – but she does the mental calculations in her head. She can't clamber down into the ravine in her footwear. 'I'll be fine,' I tell her, and after another second she relents.

'Thank you!' she shouts after me.

I start my hike, pushing aside the shrubs, trying not to think about the ticks and bugs that lurk in the long grass. I hear the start of Zora's conversation with the Moncha guard. 'Hello? Yes, I'd like to report a lost baku . . .'

The deeper I get into the ravine, the steeper it becomes, and Zora's voice fades away as I concentrate on my footing. Stupid rational thoughts crowd my brain like *how am I going to get back up out of here?* And *Why did I leave my phone behind?* I push them away again. When I look back up at the bridge to try and make sure I am following Linus's most likely arc, I can barely make out the metal railings. From here, it just looks as if I am in a forest – all I can see are the tops of the trees and the shrubs and the blue sky. It could be peaceful.

Then, I'm almost forced to my knees as there's a loud

screech of iron against iron and a strong gust of wind as a train hurtles by on the tracks below. It intensifies my need to find Linus – I only hope the baku wasn't thrown as far as the tracks. He would be squashed dormouse parts if that was the case, and impossible to fix.

I'm surprised by how quickly Zora has bonded with Linus – it's one of the magic side effects of the bakus that Monica Chan said she never could have predicted. Of course, she had known that having a companion would be part of the robot's appeal – but what started out as a tool to help her overcome her smartphone addiction exploded once it hit that mass market. People really came to *love* their bakus. And Monica was keen that she built each machine to last, with upgrades fully backward-compatible. She herself still had her first gen model – a slinky cat by the name of Yi – and the Moncha marketing machine played on that for their slogans. *A baku is for life – so get one for Christmas.*

My own grandma would tell me stories of how people used to be addicted to their phones, sitting at the dinner table scrolling on tiny screens rather than talking to each other. And they had to be charged every single day, tying you to the wall. Sometimes, if you used them too much, they even lost charge in the middle of the day and you were stuck, phoneless, until you could find a plug socket. When Toronto passed a bylaw that stated you couldn't use plug sockets in public places – because people were sitting there for *hours* waiting for their phones to juice up again – there was almost a revolt.

32

That was the Moncha breakthrough *part two*. She always credited her business partner, Eric Smith for the discovery, even though I'm positive she had more to do with it than him. Still, *together*, let's say, they discovered a way to convert the natural kinetic energy of human movement into battery charge for the bakus. Combined with solar power back-ups, as long as they spend some time being 'leashed' to their owner, they remained fully charged. It was a strange concept to get used to at first, but the procedure to install a leash was no more invasive than an earring. One gun and done. I'd had my leash put in that morning – I just hadn't connected the beetle to it yet. But once I did . . . maybe I would bond with it.

Beetles are the best bakus. They take up hardly any energy; they don't even need to be leashed every night. They're virtually indestructible. They're super customizable. Beetles are the perfect companions.

Yeah, says everyone who can't afford anything different.

I think about Companioneers Crescent, the road we would have moved into had my dad not . . . disappeared. If I'd gotten into Profectus, I could have guaranteed a good life for Mom and myself. A big house. A job for life. Life-long benefits. But once I graduate from St Agnes, I'll have to leave Monchaville, or else get a Moncha job suitable for a beetle baku owner.

The trains are even closer now and the force of the wind they generate is close to knocking me off my feet. They were recently upgraded to super speedy trains from Japan, allowing people to commute from the suburbs much more easily. The ironic thing was, the challenge of addressing Toronto's urban sprawl and population explosion was solved by so many different people at the same time, the trains barely run at capacity. Moncha, for example, had made a difference in urban planning. Since they offered subsidized accommodation for their employees, most people chose to live in Monchaville, the city-within-a-city, making a commute virtually non-existent. You could live an entire life without ever leaving Monchaville. Other companies had started to follow the model, especially as smaller start-ups began to merge into huge monoliths to rival Moncha, Google and Apple. None were as good as Moncha's though.

My foot slips on the muddy ground, and I steady myself by grabbing a branch. The arc that Linus took means that he should have landed nearby – but who knows how far he might have continued to roll down the hill. Zora didn't have him long enough to install a baku beacon – that will be the first thing I'll do once I leash my beetle.

I need to think of a name for him. Anything except 'Beetlejuice' or 'Crawly'. People are so unimaginative. Maybe I'll call him 'Speck'. Because compared to other bakus, he's a tiny bit of machinery.

Bakus do have built-in distress signals for if they're away from their owner's side or if they're broken. My ears prick up as I hear a tell-tale beep – not as strong as a normal signal, but maybe the fall damaged that too.

'Linus?' I call out. The bakus are programmed to respond to their names. Sometimes it doesn't work so well with

34

someone other than the owner's voice, but the beeping speeds up like a chew toy on steroids – I'm sure it must be him. I crash through the overgrown foliage, trying to locate the source.

Then I see him, so small he's caught in the centre of a huge leaf, right where the foliage meets the stem. I push the leaf down and scoop the little mouse up in my palm. He doesn't look in too bad shape – his tail is a bit bent and I'll have to take some test pictures to see if the camera still works, but I'm confident I can fix him.

'There, there, Linus,' I say, even though it feels a little absurd to be comforting a robot. He seems to appreciate it though, twitching his nose before giving a final wheeze and all electronic life leaves his eyes. He needs to be leashed before I can assess him any more. Now to find a way out of here.

I place Linus in my jacket pocket and search for a path back up the hill.

The leaf I'd been leaning on snaps as I shift my weight. Before I can grab anything else, I tumble, my shoulder colliding with the ground as I catapult forward and slide deeper down into the ravine.

I scramble with my feet, trying to stop my fall towards the railway tracks and super high-speed trains at the very bottom of the valley. I grab at every passing branch and plant, slicing my palm in the process, but I can't think about it before I launch off a small concrete wall and land on the stony ground below. Something crashes down beside me.

I wait a beat, then another, my breath coming in hard, fast gasps as I wait for pain. I can't wait too long. I can hear the whine of an approaching train and my feet are way too close to the tracks. I yank them in, curling my arms around my knees, my back up against the wall. I close my eyes as the train whooshes by me.

It seems to last for ever, the scream of the wind and the debris hitting my face, but eventually it passes. I take a deep breath that fills my lungs. I'm not hurt – or at least, nothing is broken – but I'm going to ache like hell in the morning.

CHAPTER FIVE

MY HAND SNAPS TO MY POCKET. I almost don't want to look inside but I do, and breathe a sigh of relief – Linus doesn't look much worse for wear after my fall. He's survived one big drop already – I guess another didn't do him any more harm.

My heart jumps as I see a smear of red on my jeans, my jacket ... everywhere. Blood. It's coming from my palm where I sliced it on the way down. The wound is sharp and clean and gapes like a mouth – my stomach turns just looking at it. I pull out an old gym T-shirt from my backpack, which I awkwardly wrap around my hand to staunch the blood. I need to get home. Now.

The benefit of being by the railway tracks is that I know there are steps for workmen leading down into the valley. I can follow them back up to the main road.

As I swing my bag over my shoulder, I hear a trill of electronic beeping. My instinct makes me think of Linus, but it can't be him – he's powered down.

Then I see it. At my feet is a crumpled pile of black

metal – the thing that fell down next to me. One side is slick with bright red blood – mine, I realize. This is what I must have sliced myself on.

'Stupid piece of junk,' I say, kicking it with my boot. It seems to make a tiny mewl of pain – but I must have imagined it. It rolls over against the concrete, revealing a gaping hole, grey and charred around the edges. It looks like it's been through the mill.

Something catches my eye, and I kneel down to look closer. I blink rapidly, my brain hardly processing what my eyes are seeing. It's the Moncha logo. At least, I think it is – it's distorted and half-hidden by what look like scorch-marks. But Moncha-made metal can be valuable – especially when it comes to doing unauthorized repairs on bakus.

The railway lines hum again and I don't give myself any more time to think. I scoop the metal contraption into my bag, shoving it to the bottom beneath my smelly gym kit and the new beetle baku I've just bought. There might be parts to sell or salvage, if anything.

Then, without wasting any more time, I climb the steps back up out of the valley.

The top is blocked by a gate, but I clamber over it without too much trouble, relieved to be out of the woods. It takes a while to orient myself – without a phone or an active baku, I feel cut off, missing a limb. I've come out on a quiet residential road, towering apartment blocks all around, but the signs mean little to me. I don't normally travel anywhere without GPS.

How did people handle it, before? With physical telephone boxes on the side of the road that needed change to make a call or actual maps that didn't provide automatic directions . . .

My hand throbs where I've sliced it. I swallow and spin around 360 degrees. This can't be too difficult. Toronto is built on a grid. I'm not in Monchaville, so that means that the ravine is east. If I walk away from it – west – I'll find a main road and from there, a subway station.

I adjust the straps on my bag, face what I *hope* is west, and start walking.

'Hey, you there!' A gruff voice sounds from behind me.

I spin on my heels and my heart lurches. Three men are jogging up to me in perfect synchronization, coming from the set of stairs I just climbed up out of the ravine. Three vicious-looking panther bakus are at their heels, sleek and efficient. No attempt has been made to make them look even remotely like real animals. They're all sleek metal plates, exposed pistons and wires, flashing yellow eyes and razor-sharp claws. The men wear full-face masks and black uniforms, but I don't see the distinctive Moncha-logo or the Toronto police badge on their shoulders. One of them lowers his visor enough to reveal dark brown eyes under his bushy black brows.

'Don't move. Moncha guard.' He flashes his badge at me so quickly, I barely register it. It did look vaguely like the logo so I stay put. My feet are rooted to the floor anyway. I've never once been in trouble with the police or the Moncha guard.

The man flicks his eyes up and down, taking in the state

of me. I can't imagine what he must be thinking – the T-shirt wrapped around my hand is blood-stained, I've got bits of tree and dirt stuck in my hair and my jeans are all torn up – not in an artful way.

In an *I've-just-tumbled-down-a-ravine-trespassing-on-train-tracks* kind of way.

'We need to see your baku.'

'I'm sorry,' I stutter out. 'I didn't mean to trespass. My best friend's baku fell down into the valley and I went to find it . . .' I babble.

'Your baku, please.'

'I . . . I don't have one yet—'

'Active baku indicated in—' the man talks over me and the panther baku steps forward.

Then I remember. Linus. I quickly grab him from my pocket. 'This is the baku I have on me! He belongs to my friend, Zora Layeni.'

The panther stalks forward and sniffs at Linus. A stream of information appears on his back, which the dark-eyed man leans over to read.

'Property of Zora Layeni. Reported missing forty-five minutes ago. What's your name?'

'Lacey. Lacey Chu.'

'You're on the approved list.' He steps back and stares at me. 'Did you see anyone else while you were down there? Or see any other bakus?'

I shake my head, my legs trembling. 'No . . . nothing! I just grabbed Linus and came straight out again.'

The panther circles me once, and the man waits for several of my loud heartbeats before waving his hand. 'You're free to go,' he says, dismissing me.

'Thank you, sir.' I nod, then turn and start walking in what I hope is a normal manner. They don't seem to care that I was down in the ravine at all.

I've barely taken ten steps when I hear a snarl behind me.

'Wait, Rex IXX has detected another baku in the backpack.' The unmasked man strides forward, grabbing my bag and forcing me to stop. Before I have chance to protest, he rips it down off my shoulders. He opens the zip and my beetle baku, still in his packaging, tumbles to the floor.

My mouth goes dry. I'd forgotten about the beetle. And even though I don't think I've committed any crime, my heart pounds with fear. These guards look deadly serious, and I don't want to look like I've deliberately deceived them. 'Please – I forgot because I haven't had the chance to leash the beetle yet – I just got him this morning . . .'

'Her story checks out, Jones,' says one of the other guards, and my shoulders slump with relief. 'Receipt from the Moncha Store is stored on the cloud registered to a Lacey Chu. Let's go. Boss has sent us through another lead.'

He grunts, tossing the ruined backpack at my feet, and I drop to my knees to scoop the beetle baku back into the bag. The men take off in the opposite direction, running in sync.

When I touch my face, it's damp with tears. It doesn't seem like this day could get any worse.

CHAPTER SIX

'LACEY, WHAT TOOK YOU SO LONG? I WAS worried ...' Mom's words die in her mouth as she rounds the corner and takes in my tatty appearance. 'What happened to you?'

I drop the backpack with a thud on the floor and don't reply – just groan.

'Let me look at that hand.' Mom leads me through into the kitchen and sits me down firmly by the shoulders. This is when Mom really comes into her own – she is patient and firm and seems to have this untapped knowledge about all things medical. I have vague memories of her talking about going to medical school, but after Dad disappeared, she'd taken a job working for one of Moncha's subsidiary offices that provided baku customer service. It's not her dream job – but it allowed her to provide for the two of us.

Attending Profectus was supposed to be my chance to help ease her burden and maybe allow her to rediscover some of her passions. But that's not going to happen now. The rejection stings as much as my hand as Mom unwinds the makeshift

T-shirt bandage from my wound. She hisses a breath at the sight of it, then clucks her tongue against the roof of her mouth.

'Don't move,' she says, as she disappears into our bathroom.

'Ow!' I cry out as Mom returns and cleans the wound with an antiseptic solution.

She turns my palm this way and that. 'You'll live,' she says with a sigh. 'Any deeper and you might've needed stitches. That would have put an end to your intricate soldering days for the summer – what were you thinking?' She leans forward and pushes my hair off my face, scanning my head for other scrapes or cuts. 'Are you hurt anywhere else?'

'No, I'm fine,' I lean back to push her away, my hand throbbing.

She folds her arms across her chest. 'Well, good. That means you can explain to me how this happened.'

I wince. 'Zora and I ran into Carter.'

'Lacey!' Mom's tone is sharp. While she knows a bit about our rivalry, she's more concerned that I don't piss off the son of the second-most-powerful person in Moncha Corp.

'What? He and his friends were jerks. Zora got spooked by one of their bakus and accidentally dropped Linus down into the ravine. So I went to get him.'

'Oh honey,' says Mom, disapproval warring with admiration on her face. 'And Linus is all right?'

I pull him out of my pocket to show her. 'He's a little bashed up. I'll go downstairs and take a look at him, but he should be fine. I'm just so mad at those guys. And the fact that Carter got into Profectus and not me? Where's the justice in that? I'm twice the engineer he is, my grades are always better . . .'

Mom's mouth draws into a thin line, any residual admiration disappearing. It's disapproval all the way, now. I'm sure the V-shaped frown marks at the top of her nose have been caused solely by my obsession with getting into Profectus. She knows my motives are good, but I think the obsession reminds her of my dad . . . and that didn't end well. All I know is that when I was around five years old, he had some kind of nervous breakdown, leaving Mom and me, never to be heard of again. I don't know the whole story because I've never pressed, but I know my intense drive can be triggering for Mom.

'St Agnes isn't the end of the world, and you'll have Zora with you. You can still be an engineer.'

'Just not for Moncha,' I mutter.

Her expression softens, and she reaches out to stroke my hair. 'No, not for Moncha. And if we have to move, we'll move. Sometimes you have to change your dreams, Lacey. No matter how hard you work, sometimes things won't go your way.'

I want to protest, but I also know better. 'I'm going to shower off and then go to my cave, okay?'

'Okay, honey. But take a plate of food with you. You've had a shock today and you need your brain fuel.'

'Not for St Agnes, I won't,' I mumble, dashing away to the bathroom so Mom can't groan at me.

The heat of the shower scrubs the dirt and leaves from my hair and skin, but leaves me feeling raw. The fact that the choice has been taken out of my hands is what makes it even worse. I sigh. I just have to make an education at St Agnes College my new dream. And if I can't be a companioneer for Moncha then I'll be a . . .

My mind fails to come up with even a halfway decent alternative.

At least I'll be with Zora, I remind myself, as the shower water around my feet finally starts to run clear.

Out of the shower, I throw on an old plaid shirt and some knock-off Lululemon yoga pants, winding my dark hair into a bun to dry naturally. I don't have a phone to text Zora on, so I shoot her an old-school email on my ancient laptop, telling her I've found Linus and I'll bring him around to her unit tomorrow after I've fixed him up.

She responds almost straight away with a series of 'Praise the Lord' emojis. She has a real nostalgia moment whenever we email and fills the screen with as many emojis as she can.

Heading into the kitchen, I pick up a pot of ramen noodles, nuke them in the microwave and pour them into a thermos, then pick up my backpack while yelling goodbye to Mom. The television blasts the theme song to her favourite show as I shut the door and head to the elevator. I press the button for the basement level.

It's time to work.

The elevator doors open into the underground parking lot, but I'm not there for the cars. Every apartment in the building is allocated its own small, rectangular storage locker. Most people keep bikes, tents or hockey equipment down

45

here, but I convinced Mom to let me turn our locker into my own personal workshop. At first it was like being in a big cage, but I've hung so much stuff off the wire mesh fencing, I've created a nice, private space. And I almost never see anyone down here. It's just me and the unwanted clutter. Exactly how I like it. My cave.

Bill Gates, Bill Hewlett and Steve Jobs may have had their parents' garages, but Monica Chan and I have our condo lockers.

'When you have the drive to invent, you find the space to make it happen' – one of my favourite Monica quotes.

I installed a thumbprint scanner in addition to the normal padlock for extra security. Occasionally it's buggy and I have to force my way in, but this time I press the pad of my finger against it and it opens easily.

Home sweet home.

The place is a Little Mermaid's grotto of electronic equipment and tools, including the precious soldering iron I'd used to fix Petal upstairs. I have drawers filled with silver wire and screws of all different sizes, PCBs stolen from broken equipment or rummaged from yard sales (we still call them that, even though none of us have yards – it's mostly people selling unwanted junk on the advertising boards of our building). I have large sheets of thin metal for when I make repairs, rolls of different filaments for my 3D printer, an old TV so I can watch my favourite K-dramas as I work, some computer monitors for Zora to look at code on, and a bookshelf filled with old manuals and scavenged university textbooks.

In the far corner is a camp bed. Mom doesn't like it when I sleep down here, but sometimes I work until my eyes droop and there's no way I can make it to the elevator without nodding off. As long as I'm prepared to grovel in the morning, I can get away with it.

Above the bed is the cheesy vision board Zora made me put up. It was a school assignment that we took to another level – we'd been tasked with creating a collage of images to define our specific goals for the future. We kept our school ones quite generic and boring, but made special versions for ourselves that were much more precise.

Mine had pictures of Hong Kong, Tokyo and Seoul – the dream trip I wanted to take after graduating. I had researched train routes, ferries, accommodation, everything.

It had a photo of a spaniel baku, my dream companion.

It had pictures of Profectus Academy, of students walking through the huge two-storey height doors, into the hallowed hallways and then graduating as new Moncha employees.

It had a picture of the research and innovation lab at Moncha, where I dreamed of working as a companioneer.

And it had a picture of Monica Chan herself, standing, arms folded and looking powerful, signature fringe on point, in front of the next generation of bakus.

I kneel forward on the squeaky camp bed to take the pictures down – even the ones of the trip. I'd never be able to afford to go now, on a beetle baku owner's salary. I blink back tears. It's hard to look at the gaping hole left on the corkboard.

Taking a deep breath to pull myself together, I dump the

clippings in the garbage can and get settled at my scratched-up glass-top desk. I place Linus down on my workstation and pull up the typical schematics for a dormouse baku on the nearest screen. You can find anything on the Moncha-cloud, but most people don't mess with their bakus as Moncha-approved vets will only work on bakus that haven't had any unauthorized repairs. Zora, however, trusts me.

The work takes my mind off Profectus, and it takes me a good hour to get Linus's tail straightened out, manipulating the metal back into shape with the help of a heated clamp and the soldering iron. He looks almost as good as new. I can't check the movement or camera until he's charged, so I leash him to the mains using an old cable of Petal's. It's not nearly as fast as leashing it to his owner, but it will work.

I rub my eyes, the impact of the crazy day finally hitting me. I can't believe I started the day in the Moncha Store, getting my leash and picking my beetle baku. Feels like a lifetime ago.

I suppose I should leash my scarab beetle and give him a name so he can start learning my behaviours and downloading my feed from the Moncha-cloud.

Ringo? Too retro.

Herbie? Too eccentric.

Dune? Too geeky.

I'm stalling, and I know it. I lift the backpack up, groaning at how heavy it is. When it lands on the desk with a resounding thud, I remember the hunk of twisted metal I carried home with me. That's what's weighing the pack down. With a lot more excitement than before, I tear into the already ruined backpack, tossing the beetle up on to a shelf, still in his box. I'll leash and name him later.

I tip out the crumpled metal, pulling away bits of dirt and leaves that cling to the surface. It has no distinguishable form, but my instinct was good: there is something really valuable here. The metal that isn't covered in either my blood or scorched by some sort of burn mark is dark as onyx, a deep, rich black that I can almost see my reflection in it. I stare at it without touching it, trying to figure out where to begin.

The hole has almost torn the thing in two. I can't figure out what would have caused a 'wound' like that. Certainly not being run over by a train, or a falling from a height.

Finally, I realize that the metal is curled in on itself around the hole – I'm going to have to unravel it to see if there are any parts to salvage. Unfortunately the burn means the beautiful black metal itself is pretty useless and will just end up in the garbage.

Junk. I wasted all that time and energy carrying home junk.

No point being delicate with it now. I take the metal in my hands and wrench it apart. It refuses to budge at first and I think about getting a hammer from the toolbox, but then finally it gives.

I gasp.

There, tucked into the burnt space, is a face.

49

CHAPTER SEVEN

NO QUESTION ABOUT IT: IT'S DEFINITELY a face. The eyes are open, one lid dented, the nose is squashed and pointing off to one side, but its little triangular ears are in almost perfect condition.

It's the ears that get me. The rest I might have written off. But those ears are perfect. They're a level up in design I haven't seen before, with tiny filaments spun out into simulation fur, soft but strong, and most likely vital sense receptors just like they are in real cats.

That's what this hunk of metal is. A cat baku.

A very expensive cat baku, if the quality of the materials are any indication.

I run my fingertips over the ears, half-expecting them to twitch in response. But they're lifeless.

Now that I know what I'm looking at, the crumpled heap makes much more sense. My blood is on the tail – that's what sliced my palm when I was down in the ravine. The gaping, scorched hole is on the right side, where the ribcage would be. Also, where a lot of key tech would be stored.

Maybe in real animals it makes sense to have the majority of the 'thinking' tech in the head, but that's not how it works with bakus – the motherboard is in the main body, not the brain. It's a shame, as that probably means the poor thing is unfixable.

My eyes widen as my fingers run over the cat's broken body, gentle now as if I were diagnosing a real animal. The tech on display in front of me is unbelievable. I can barely stop turning it over and over in my hands, finding something new to marvel at each time. The metallic strands that cover its body are so thin they have the smooth texture of real fur. As I attempt to follow the connections down through the body, I can see that each one of them would be charged with gathering different types of data – maybe weather conditions, or solar energy, or measuring information from its owner – like resting heart rate or core internal temperature. A lot of bakus have these sorts of capabilities, but I've never seen them encased in such an elegant shell.

I swallow and take my hands off it, placing my palms on the glass. Someone must be really missing this baku. I can't help but wonder how it ended up down near the train tracks ... or how it got such a huge hole in its side.

I bite my lower lip. I should really return it to a Moncha Store so they can run any tests to see who the owner is. I could go in the morning.

Or, a naughtier voice in my head says, *you could wait to see if anyone comes looking for it.* If there's still a functioning tracking beacon within the baku's shell then someone will arrive to claim it. If not ... then who would know? It's as good as mine, just the same as any of the other tech I've scavenged.

My guilt temporarily set to one side, I get to work.

For the next couple of hours, I clean the baku up, scouring off the scorch marks with a wire sponge and wiping off dirt and dust that has collected around the metallic strands of 'fur'. Every now and then, I gasp. I keep uncovering tiny, beautiful details in the machine's bodywork, elements with an impeccably smooth finish I know couldn't have been accomplished by a machine. No, someone made this by hand. Crafted it. Soldered and manipulated the metal and electronics with the skill of a sculptor. I feel like an apprentice studying the long lost work of a master.

'Got something good in there, kiddo?'

I almost leap out of my chair at the sound of the deep male voice. But I instantly breathe a sigh of relief. It's only Paul. He looks the part of a scary intruder – he's got a scraggly grey beard and a ruddy, often grease-stained face, with piercing bright blue eyes that gleam out from beneath the bushiest eyebrows I've ever seen. But he's harmless. He's my fellow basement tinkerer, hobbyist DIY-er and cave-dweller, always pottering around and fixing things other people throw away. Old technology that they have no use for. He's got the best collection of telephones that I've ever seen. He even has an old fax machine. Positively ancient.

Sure, he scared the living crap out of me the first time we met, sticking his chubby fingers, blackened by dirt and calloused from hard work, through the holes in my wire mesh cage and giving it a shake.

He says he did it to get my attention, since calling my name didn't seem to work. I get it. I dive deep into the zone when I'm working, and it's almost impossible to drag me back to the land of the living. With my safety goggles and headphones on, the rest of the world disappears. It was that focus, laser-like intensity, that was supposed to get me into Profectus. *Oh well*.

Paul and I are comrades in engineering. Still, I find myself turning my back on him as he peers in, blocking his full view of the broken cat baku. I've overlooked some of his ... less than legal, say, DIY jobs, the things I've seen gathered in his locker that I know don't belong to him, so I'm sure he wouldn't breathe a word. But my body is tense and defensive of my find.

I feel protective of it.

'Oh, just a bit of junk I found on the street, you know how it is.'

'Sure do.' His lemur baku climbs up the wire fencing and peers in. George is a pretty advanced baku for a guy like Paul to own – level 4, at least – but he won't tell me what his job was at Moncha before his accident. Paul only has one arm. I assume that George was his upgrade baku once he got on disability. 'That's why I need a baku with opposable thumbs!' is his long-running joke.

'Well, I'm turnin' in for the night. You need anything?' We often remind each other to do normal things – like eat and drink. Tinkerers understand.

I gesture to the thermos, then lift a pair of chopsticks to fill my mouth with cold, slimy noodles for good measure. 'All good,' I say, the words muffled by ramen.

He chuckles. 'Well, all right then. Don't stay up too late now.'

'Night.'

'Night.'

George lets out a series of beeps.

'Wait, did you get your baku today?' He pronounces it the old way, 'back-you' rather than the more modern 'back-oo'.

My heart skips a beat. I don't remember telling him anything about a baku. Maybe George was able to see the cat on the table and showed a picture to Paul and . . . then I remember. The beetle. 'Oh yeah. I'll show you tomorrow as I haven't leashed it yet.'

Paul frowns. 'But George says there's a live baku in there.'

I pause. 'Oh! That must be Linus. That's Zora's new baku. I fixed him up for her and just leashed him to charge.'

'Huh. Always thought you'd be the type to leash yours straight away. Leash it, name it, then take it apart. You're going to run circles around anyone at that school.'

'I . . .' I don't have the heart to tell him I didn't make it to Profectus. It feels like disappointing too many people in one day. 'I'll show you tomorrow,' I repeat.

He pauses for a beat, apprising me beneath those bushy brows, but to my relief, he nods and walks away, George leaping on to his shoulder.

'Goodnight, Tinker!' he calls out as he walks.

When I no longer hear his footsteps, I hunch back down over the desk. I work on the broken baku for another couple of hours, until I straighten out as much of the creature's body as I can without resorting to electronic tools. Now I can do a proper damage assessment.

One of the key finds is that the leash connection is intact. Excitement tingles in my fingers. If this works – if the baku is able to carry a charge, despite the gaping hole in its belly – then that means I might be able to bring it back to life. Holding my breath, I take the leash and plug it into the mains.

I wait for any sign of life. A light. Movement. A hum. But there's nothing. Frustrated, I pull open the drawer closest to me and dig around for my multimeter. I attach the probes to various parts of the baku but, despite it being plugged in, I can see no sign of any response. My shoulders slump with disappointment. It's such a shame. To have something so beautiful go to waste. I pull the leash from the mains, and sigh.

Then an idea strikes me. It's a bit of a wild one – there's no reason why it should work. But bakus are not designed to be charged from the mains. They're designed to work with people. I have a brand new leash hooked around my ear, ready and waiting. Maybe . . .

I lift the end of the cat's leash and hook it up to mine.

As it syncs, my nose begins to tingle, and I sneeze.

At almost the exact same time, the baku's whiskers judder, the first sign of potential electronic life.

'Jinx!' I say to it, laughing. I think all the work is turning me slightly mad.

When nothing else happens for a good few minutes, I wonder if I imagined the juddering whiskers. I poke and prod at it, staring at it, willing it to make another move. But nothing happens.

Eventually, my eyes feel as if they are going to drop out of my head. I slump over my desk, the events of the day hitting me like a punch bag. Slam, rejection. Kapow, forced to buy the beetle. Suckerpunch, humiliated by Carter. Knock-out blow: stopped by those terrifying Moncha guards.

And then the final kick while I'm down: seeing Tobias's eagle baku in action and knowing I'll *never* own a baku that cool.

Knowing they'll be at Profectus but not me.

That *they'll* be living my dream.

I know I have to let it go. But not before I let one single final thought dominate my brain, my throat, my stomach.

It's not fair.

I don't even make it to the camp bed before I'm fast asleep.

CHAPTER EIGHT

A FAINT BEEPING ROUSES ME. IT TAKES A good few seconds to orient myself, and my neck cricks in protest at being moved. I paw for my phone on the desk to check the time, but it's not there.

I blink several times, my body awakening to the world. No phone. No phone because I smashed the screen. No replacement phone because I bought myself a baku. But I haven't leashed it yet, so it can't function as my clock.

The beeping grows louder, echoing around the basement, and – when it's accompanied by loud metallic bangs – I recognize it: the garbage trucks have arrived. And that means I've slept the whole night in the locker.

Crap. Mom is not going to be happy. I quickly pack up my things, unleashing the broken baku and shoving it into a box before throwing it under the desk. Linus is fully charged and a quick selfie proves that his camera and display projector screen are fully functioning. Perfect. His clock read-out shows me that it's 7:37 a.m. Dammit.

I grab my dirty cutlery (I don't want to encourage pests

into my locker – especially not if I'm falling asleep down there) and lock up the locker, balancing the armloads of stuff with the skill of a juggler. Then I race to the elevator.

When I get upstairs to our unit, my heart is pounding in my chest. 'Mom, I'm so sorry – I lost track of time.'

But when I enter the kitchen, it's not Mom I see, but Zora. She's perched on a stool in the kitchen. 'Oh, hey! I was just about to come down and get you,' she says, slurping down a bowl of cereal. 'How's Linus?'

'He's all good! Back to normal, I think.'

'Yay!' she squeals. I place Linus down on the counter and he scurries over to Zora. She lays down her palm and he leaps on to it, rushing up her arm to the leash on her ear, making delighted squeaking sounds. 'I missed you too!' says Zora.

I bite down on my bottom lip. It's strange to see Zora so ... giddy and emotional. The connection she's developed with Linus – even though she's only had him for a couple of days – seems so deep. I always knew that people developed attachments to their bakus, but I didn't think it would happen that instantly. I feel guilty for leaving mine packaged up in his box.

'Oh, here's your phone back,' says Zora.

'Thanks!' I say. I instantly relax when my phone hits my palm, tension I didn't realize I was holding in my shoulders releasing. It's crazy to have such a visceral reaction to a phone, but there you go. Maybe it's not so different with a baku after all.

'What's your beetle's unique ID and I'll store it with Linus in my Favourite contacts,' says Zora.

'Oh, I haven't leashed him yet,' I say. My fingers fly across the cracked screen of my phone, checking updates from social media across different platforms.

'You still haven't leashed your baku? La-*cey* . . .' I know that tone of voice from Mom. Sometimes she acts as if I'm an alien creature who's landed in her living room, as opposed to her own flesh and blood. She just doesn't get what that baku represents to me: failure.

I keep on scrolling.

My breath catches in my throat.

There's an email from the Board of Education. It has the same heading as the one a couple of days before. LACEY CHU: PROFECTUS APPLICATION STATUS. There's probably a bug in their system, emailing me for a double hit of rejection. Great. Like I need that.

Even though it makes my nose twitch to see the 'unread' notification, I don't open the email. Instead, I scroll through the Flashes from the people I follow. Pretty much all my St Agnes classmates are getting their new bakus in time for the new school year, and even people with the boring level 1 insects seem excited. Suddenly, it's like my phone is an old, dead object in my palm. Looking up at Zora, who is stroking Linus's nose as he projects updates on to her palm, or Mom creating a new recipe with Petal describing every step, I realize how silly I'm being. My phone is just a lump of metal, broken glass and plastic.

I need a baku.

'I left my beetle downstairs. I better go and grab it,' I say.

'Okay, but you come straight back up here, promise me? You've already spent too much time down there. You need more sunshine,' says Mom.

'You got it,' I reply.

'I'll come with you,' says Zora, shovelling the last spoonful into her mouth. 'If you let me borrow your new baku for a bit, I can upgrade some of your apps as a thank you for saving Linus.'

I shoot her a grateful smile. I want to fill her in on what happened last night – and get her take on the Moncha guard. I can always count on her logical brain to tell me whether I should be more worried about something than not.

Then there's the mysterious cat baku . . . but I don't know whether I'm ready to tell Zora about that discovery yet.

We walk over to the elevator as I tell her about my adventures in the ravine.

Her jaw drops. 'I'd heard they'd stepped up security in Monchaville, but didn't realize it was *that* bad. And I still can't believe you found him! The probability of that happening was very low,' Zora says. 'When I work on your beetle I'll load him up with some custom apps. I've got a few that I've coded . . . you'll love it, I promise. Have you decided on a name yet?'

I shake my head. 'Not yet, but . . .' My phone buzzes in my hand and I glance down at the splintered screen.

MESSAGE FOR LACEY CHU FROM BOARD
OF EDUCATION

I roll my eyes.

'What is it?' asks Zora.

I turn the screen to show her. She kisses her teeth. 'What do they want?'

'I guess it's time to find out.'

My finger hovers over the email app on the screen. Zora reaches out and squeezes my shoulder.

LACEY CHU: PROFECTUS APPLICATION STATUS

Dear Lacey,

We are delighted to offer you a place at Profectus Academy next year. We have registered your level 3 baku on our system.

Congratulations, and we look forward to seeing you in September.

Dr Grant

PRINCIPAL OF PROFECTUS ACADEMY

'WHAT?' I actually scream out loud after I've read the email.

I close it, then scroll back to find the original – but it's gone. Deleted. It's not in my Trash either. It's as if I never received it. I open the new email again and stare, wondering if the letters are going to rearrange in front of my eyes. But they don't. I'm in, for real.

'What is it? What's happened?' Zora asks.

I try to speak but can't. Zora grabs the phone from my hand.

'Holy baku,' she says as she reads the email, her hand flying to her mouth. 'But I thought—'

'Two days ago—'

We both start at the same time.

The rejection must have been a mistake all along. I can hardly believe it.

For a moment, there are no words I can find to describe how I'm feeling. Then . . .

'I'm in, Z. I'm in.' Tears shine in my eyes.

She steps forward, and gives me a hug.

But then her logical brain takes over and she steps back, holding me by the shoulders. 'Wait. I thought you hadn't leashed your baku yet? And it says here they have you registered with a level 3?'

My heart sinks. She knows as well as I do that I bought a level 1 beetle. Nothing like a level 3. And she's right, I haven't leashed it yet. Zora scrunches up her nose, as if she's trying to hold up the weight of her glasses while she stares down at my phone. She's realizing – as I am – that *this* email is actually the mistake. A practical joke. It's just the kind of thing Carter would do – probably in retaliation for yesterday.

Then, her eyes open wide. 'Oh my gosh – maybe they mean they're sending you a level 3 baku because you need financial aid! It's a good thing you didn't leash that beetle after all!'

Now she hugs me properly.

I squeeze her back, but my stomach churns with confusion.

I *know* that's not how it works at Profectus. They would never just send over a random baku. They would have given me grant money to go out and buy my own.

'Look, there's an attachment,' she says. Before I can stop her, she opens it up.

> APPLICANT NAME: LACEY JANE CHU
> APPLICANT NUMBER: 651
> BAKU: level 3 cat baku 'JINX' (unique ID J1NX89)
> STATUS: INCOMING PROFECTUS STUDENT 2067

Everything about the form looks perfectly legitimate – and hard to fake. The applicant number in particular – I remember it from when I sent in my application. There is no way that Carter would have been able to guess the correct one.

The level 3 cat baku statement is what has me chewing my lower lip, however. So many questions buzz into my brain at once, I feel like I'm being attacked by hornets. Yet one thought dominates over all the rest: Could it be referring to the broken baku I found yesterday?

It seems impossible, and yet … if it's true … I can't let anyone know the baku isn't really mine.

Not the Profectus Board. Not my mom. And not Zora.

'You're in.' A grin blossoms on Zora's face. 'You're in, Lacey! I knew the rejection was a mistake!' She grabs my arm and we spin around, bouncing up and down like maniacs.

For a moment I let the confusion fade. I'm going to Profectus. *I'M ACTUALLY GOING.*

Finally I collapse against the wall, my cheeks stinging from how wide my grin is.

'I can't wait to see your new baku, by the way. I love the name – Jinx. I really want to meet him! Come on, let's go back in and tell your mom.' She extends her hand. And reality begins to sink in.

Including one very big question.

Who on earth is Jinx?

CHAPTER NINE

NEWS SPREADS FAST IN OUR BUILDING. Mom had heard our happy screams and rushed out of the condo to find out what happened. She danced with joy alongside us, but then her face fell.

'Oh honey, I had everything prepared for a proper celebration but then when your rejection came through I cancelled the order because I didn't want to make you feel even worse,' Mom said, after processing the news.

'Oh ... I don't need any celebrations!' I'd replied, shifting on my feet. My stomach was still swirling with confusion, and I needed to get down to the basement to make sure my suspicion about the broken baku was true.

'Don't be silly, you've wanted this your whole life. I'm so happy for you.'

'Even with ... what happened to Dad?' I'd cringed then. I rarely brought it up. But if there was any moment it felt needed, it was right after getting my acceptance to Profectus. It's one step away from working at Moncha HQ, just like he did.

Mom shushed me, but she also turned her face away so I

couldn't see her get emotional. 'It doesn't matter what I think, and it definitely doesn't matter what your father would have thought. Your life is your own, and so are your dreams. I will always support you, no matter what.' She'd then kissed me on the forehead and ordered me to change out of the clothes I had slept in in my locker. Mom leapt into super hostess mode, Petal darting back and forth between the cupboards, projecting a recipe for a quick celebration cake she could whip up.

Less than an hour later, our unit is filled with Zora's family, neighbours from our floor, even Darwin, our porter – all celebrating my achievement. I receive more hugs and kisses than I can process. Paul shows up and he gives me a gruff hug. 'Knew you could do it! That probably means I won't be seeing you in the basement much.'

'I don't know about that ... there might be one last big project over this summer.'

He raises an eyebrow. 'Anything you need, you know who to ask.'

'Thanks, Paul.'

'I'm proud of you, little tinker.'

My cheeks burn with a mixture of pride and embarrassment at the same time.

After way too much cake, I slip out of the front door and edge along the hallway to the stairwell. If I take the elevator, I'm bound to bump into someone I know. Even though everyone is there for me, the noise and the people and the attention is all a bit too much.

Especially as I'm desperate to get down to my cave and

figure out if that broken hunk of metal could possibly be turned into a fully functioning level 3 baku – or else my career at Profectus might be short-lived after all.

Zora spots me escaping. 'Want me to run interference?' she asks, and I'm grateful she doesn't push to come with me.

I smile at her. 'That would be great.'

'Hey – when do you think they'll send the new baku – Jinx, isn't it?'

I play Zora off, even though I hate lying to her. 'Oh, they just emailed to say they'd send me the baku right before the start of term – something about not wanting me to get too attached.'

She frowns. 'That's odd.' Then, she shrugs. 'I guess you know more about Profectus than I do! But does that mean you won't have a baku all summer long? How am I going to get in touch with you?'

'You live in my building,' I say, with a grin. 'We'll just have to visit each other's units.'

'I suppose so,' she says. Linus wrinkles his nose in a gesture of solidarity with Zora's scepticism. 'I'd better get back to the party and make sure no one asks too many questions about where the guest of honour has gone,' she says with a wink.

'Thanks, Zora. I owe you one.'

When I get down to the locker, it's quiet. Eerily so. I fumble with the lock – it takes me two or three attempts to open – and once I'm inside, I take several deep breaths to calm myself down. When I feel more settled, I slide the box out from underneath the desk and there is the baku: still just as broken and messed up as I left it.

You can't just name a baku by saying a word aloud, I remind myself. *That isn't how baku registering works. You have to go through the leashing process and input the name, check that it hasn't been registered to a similar baku within a certain radius . . . all the things I was going to do with my beetle.*

Another, louder voice says: *But this has to be Jinx.*

There's no way that Profectus would send me a level 3 baku. Which means if I don't manage to get 'Jinx' before the start of term, I won't be starting school in September, acceptance or not.

I have no money to buy a new one. You can't buy second-hand bakus. So my only option is to fix the one that has somehow fallen into my hands.

I stare down at the cat baku, that looks nothing like a cat baku – yet – with those lifeless eyes and the gaping hole in its side, the tangle of wires and the broken paws.

The longer I stare, the more certain I am this is a crazy idea. I'm overwhelmed by how much work needs to be done. Finally, I blink, slumping against the back of my chair.

And the baku's one, unbroken eye lazily blinks back.

It's enough to jolt me out of my seat. But I'm *sure* I didn't imagine it this time.

If there's a spark of life, there's a spark of hope. It's all I need. That, and every second of summer vacation I can spare.

Three months to turn this scrap metal into a fully functional baku.

If I can pull this off, it will be a tinkering miracle.

CHAPTER TEN

I T DOES TAKE THE ENTIRE SUMMER, DOWN to the final hours. For the first time, I'm grateful that Zora has gone off to coding camp and that Mom works full time – it means I get away with working almost non-stop without facing too many awkward questions.

The month of June I'd spent tackling the basics. That one blinking eye kept me motivated, even though it took me another week of dedicated tinkering before I made any more progress: a twitching paw.

I'd been so excited about that, I took Mom out for ice cream in the park (she was getting critically worried about my levels of vitamin D at that point; I was spending so much time in the basement).

From the first paw, it was another few weeks (and most of July) before I got him standing on his own, then a matter of days until he was walking, the progress snowballing as I fixed the fundamental issues. I smoothed out all the dents and replaced the scorched parts with new. Whoever had made him had obviously spent a lot of time perfecting, scrutinizing, analyzing every component, because there were modifications in the tech that I had never come across before. Screws that were microscopic in size, wires so intricately knotted together they were like the plaits in Zora's hair.

Thankfully, Paul had gifted me an old 3D printer of his a year ago, so once I'd managed (carefully, so carefully) to extract one of the screws, I was able to map and print a copy of it. Gradually, as my confidence grew, I printed other parts. They weren't as beautiful as the rest of him, but if I wanted him to walk, run and jump again, I'd have to deal.

That meant in August, scavenging became my new pastime.

Outside Monchaville, not everyone treats their bakus the same. For the most part, people are careful and respectful – but others treat them roughly, pushing the limits of the machines until they burn out or break down. Some people – *rich* people – act as if they're disposable. Replaceable. And when they get bored, some of the people don't even take advantage of the recycling program Moncha offered, but put their old bakus in the trash and head to the Moncha Store to buy a new one.

That's where I came in. I salvaged the broken or forgotten bakus and I used them for Jinx's parts. I was mercenary about it. Nothing was sacred.

And, with every piece of Jinx I took apart to clean or replace, I searched for the signature of the companioneer who created him.

'Who made you?' I whispered to him.

I hadn't got around to fixing his speakers yet, so he couldn't respond to me.

But the signature had to be there somewhere, and I was desperate to find it. Using Jinx's browser, I searched the Moncha forums for some of the new tech I had seen, in an attempt to trace it back to the original owner. All I needed was a name, a symbol, a scrawl, something.

But Jinx was like nothing I'd ever seen before. And his creator remained an enigma. A mystery.

But as for who was fixing him, who was bringing him back to life – that was not.

That was all me.

It takes me right up until the night before I'm due to start at Profectus. I'm so close to having a fully functioning level 3 baku, but I know they're not going to allow me through the doors unless I get the final element of Jinx's operating system working: communication.

When I get downstairs, Jinx struts around the locker, leaping up on to the desk, the shelving, then skirting the very top of the cage, agile as a real cat. A surge of affection rushes through me as I watch his perfect movement. I've done well.

'Jinx, to me!' I say, alongside a crooked-arm gesture for him to return. If Jinx had been a *normal* baku, that would have worked. Instead, he stares at me from his perch on the highest shelf and blinks, once.

I frown. It's so late, it's early – only hours before I'm supposed to be in my uniform and heading to the school gates – and my eyes are burning with the desire to sleep. But I have to fix this one last thing or else I'll be showing up at Profectus with a baku that doesn't follow commands and an entire summer's worth of work wasted.

I take a sip of highly caffeinated soda, ready for one last burst of energy. Clambering up on to the desk, I reach out with one arm towards Jinx, the other hand tightly clutching the wire mesh for support. Just as my fingers are about to grab him, he leaps down off the shelf and on to the desk, where he sits down and licks at his paw.

I groan. 'Seriously?'

I get down off the desk *much* less gracefully than Jinx, then sit down at the desk, folding my arms across my chest. For a moment we stare at each other, girl and machine, unblinking.

I spot that there's a loose wire running from his front paw to the motherboard. It's a minor fix, but fixing something small might help me feel a sense of accomplishment that will lead to a bigger breakthrough. (That's the idea, anyway.) My mind is on how to fix his speakers so he can communicate with me, so I'm a little burly with my technique, forcing one of the metal wires back into place and holding it down with a piece of duct tape as I solder. Crude, but it works. I leash him up to my ear to give him a bit of extra charge.

And then in my ear, I hear a voice:

>>Jeez, could you be a bit more gentle next time? That hurt.

He sounds ... like an annoyed kid whose foot I'd just stepped on.

I almost jump out of my skin. 'What the hell?' I say, pawing at the leashing around my ear.

>>You can disconnect us, but that won't change anything.

Jinx? I say his name in my thoughts, and I hear his laughter in my ear.

>>That's me.

And you . . . and you can understand me? If I tell you to jump up there, you'll—

He jumps up on to the shelf, exactly as I ordered.

I dance around the locker with glee. I'm giddy with success. There's still something not quite right. I've made some kind of error – the fact that I'm not reading text from a projection or hearing his voice out loud but in my head is unsettling. But at this point, it doesn't matter.

There's a cough from behind me, and I spin around. Illuminated in a pool of light outside my locker is Zora. 'Hey, stranger,' she says.

'Z!' I run to the locker door and pull it open. 'How was coding camp?'

'Incredible. I've got so much to tell you. But first, I've come to meet the infamous Jinx!' Her eyes scan my locker, before settling on the shelf. Her jaw drops. 'Oh my God, Lace – is that him? He's gorgeous.'

>>Your friend has excellent taste, Jinx says.

It's still a shock hearing his voice in my head, enough to make me jump in my skin, and Zora gives me a funny look.

'Sorry, might be going a bit stir crazy.'

73

'Your mom sent me down here to tell you you have to come upstairs now and get some sleep or else she'll get Paul to change the padlock and lock you out of your cave for ever.'

I grin – not only because I know Mom would never do that to me, but because I actually *can* go upstairs now. I have an offer letter from Profectus, a school uniform and a level 3 baku that at least *appears* to follow orders.

I raise my hands to Zora to show her I'm not protesting. 'Come on then, Jinx. Let's go upstairs.'

>>Finally, we're getting outta here.

The baku leaps down to my feet, his movement smooth as silk, and he sashays out of my locker and into the real world.

Looks like things might be turning out all right, after all.

PART TWO

PROFECTUS

CHAPTER ELEVEN

J INX SLITHERS BETWEEN MY LEGS IN A
figure of eight, his impatience wearing at my already
plenty-frayed nerves. The dark navy woollen trousers
of the uniform are itchy enough in the lingering September
heat, but the pleated kilt – my other uniform option – is
definitely not my style. I rub my sweaty palms against
my trousers.

>>Just go in already. I'm tired of waiting.

Be quiet, you.

Jinx flicks my calf with his tail, and I grimace. But he's
right. I need to just go in.

Profectus Academy occupies an old university building, one
of those huge, imposing follies – complete with fake turrets –
designed to look like something more comfortable in Oxford
or Cambridge or some other old, academic British town.
Behind it, modern additions – steel and glass extensions –
spread out like wings, designed by a disciple of the same
architect who built the addition on the Royal Ontario
Museum. Monica Chan had loved it so much, the explosion

of crystal from old brick, that she commissioned him to transform an old building into the school of her dreams.

I've walked past this building a hundred times, counted the windows and wondered which classroom would one day be mine, stared up at the huge two-storey-high doors and pictured walking through them . . . and now I get to enter as a student. Someone who belongs. I'm going to become part of its history. Or rather, I'm going to be part of the future we are all trying to create by being here. The thought swells my chest, my chin lifting high.

I can't explain how I got in, but I feel like I belong, like rejection was the fluke – not the acceptance.

Streams of students pass by me with their bakus. There are dogs, cats, a few monkeys and birds. It's funny, walking around the streets of Toronto, you almost never see bakus higher than level 3. They're so expensive to buy and difficult to maintain. Maybe on Bloor Street, amongst the fancy designer shops and celebrity chef restaurants, you'll see custom designed level 4 bakus and rare breeds. But most people are content with their simple cat, dog or small furry mammal baku – they don't need anything fancier. Thankfully I don't catch sight of Carter's boar. Holed up in my cave fixing Jinx, I've managed to avoid him all summer (I've managed to avoid almost everyone – some, like Zora, not on purpose), and I'm not keen for a new confrontation – even if the circumstances have changed since then.

My plan is to get through today drama-free and experience this dream to the full.

'Just beat it! Beat it!' Michael Jackson blares at top volume from my feet. Looks like Jinx's speakers aren't broken after all. The student closest to me leaps a mile in the air and all eyes nearby turn in my direction. Crap. So much for getting through the first day – hell, even the first *minute* – of school without drawing attention myself. I drop to my heels and scoop Jinx up off the floor.

'Turn off, dammit!' I say, fumbling along his back for the right place which, if I touch it should, in theory, turn off his speakers.

But the music only seems to get louder. 'Jinx, please, please don't do this to me,' I whisper.

Maybe I finally find the right button or the desperation in my voice hits a nerve but the sound shuts off with a click. Thank God. I duck my head and race up the stairs two at a time and through the enormous doors. No hesitation now: I want to get away from the crowd of staring, questioning eyes.

Even the entrance feels different from any other high school that I've been in before. There's no ugly green and orange plastic floor (why are colour schemes in high schools so ugly?) – instead, there's rich mahogany hardwood that must be a nightmare to keep clean during the winters, when we'll be tracking in snow and salt from the sidewalks. But there's no expense spared here. The wood panelling continues up the walls, giving the atrium the feel of an old country club.

Written in gold script on a wooden beam across my head is the school's motto: *WE BUILD THE FUTURE.*

My fingertips tingle and heat rises in my cheeks. 'We've done it, Jinx,' I whisper to him. He wriggles out of my arms in response and jumps to the floor, arching his back and flicking his tail at me. 'Fine, don't care.' I stick my tongue out at him. He responds by choosing a direction and shooting off at lightning speed.

I jog to catch up with him, the orientation information from Profectus displayed on his back. When even a function this ordinary works on Jinx, a spike of pride shoots up my spine – to know that I fixed him up from next to nothing. He gives me the number and location of my locker, which is in one of the more modern wings. Now it's starting to feel more like an ordinary school. There are clusters of students in their uniforms, some lounging on the floor or leaning casually against their lockers.

I'm struck by how old some of students look, but then people graduate from Profectus when they're twenty – heading straight into a proper job at Moncha. Monica's dream – in the face of skyrocketing tuition fees and resultant student debt – was for Profectus to be a fully paid-up bridging academy for only the brightest and best who knew they wanted to work in science and technology. And there was no form of indenture – no debt to be repaid to Moncha, no obligation to work there. If another company – a rival firm like BRIGHTSPRK or Apple – wanted to offer a student a job, there was no clause that would prevent a graduate from going. But with the high starting salary, provided accommodation and excellent standard of living offered in

Monchaville, hardly anyone jumps ship, so it's a win-win for Moncha.

And a pretty great deal for those of us lucky enough to get in, too.

Jinx stops in front of a locker and, with a couple of bounding leaps, settles on a small shelf that is especially designed for bakus to hang out. To stop the bakus (big and small) from crowding the hallways, there are alcoves above each locker for bakus to leash up and charge between classes.

I stop and stare at Jinx, who appears to be 'grooming' himself, but which is really a way for him to run through his systems and check everything is working okay by brushing up against all his sensors. Then he crawls deep into the alcove, curling himself up so that only the two tiny LEDs in his pupils are visible. I run through the plan for the day, taking deep breaths to prepare myself. Most of the morning is blocked out for a giant orientation session. I'd looked it up online to see what that might entail, if there was anything I could do to prep. But there was surprisingly little information available.

'Lacey? What are you doing here?'

The slimy voice sends drippings of ice down my spine, which turn to shivers as I hear the snuffling and snorting of the boar. My body tenses, flashing back to the memory of the forest and the ravine.

I wait a beat, willing my voice to sound utterly normal. 'I'm getting ready for orientation.' I spin the combination of my locker, thankful that Jinx projects the code for the lock from his tail to a place on the locker just above my fingertips. I dump my bag, not taking out any of the postcards and pictures I brought along to stick to the inside of my locker door. There's no way I'm decorating it in front of Carter.

'Isn't your school a bit further down the street?'

I bite my lip and take a beat. *He doesn't have any advantage over you now,* I tell myself. *You belong here as much as he does.* I spin around to face him. 'Isn't it obvious?' I say, trying to sound as nonchalant as possible. 'I've got a locker, I'm in the uniform – I'm a Profectus student too, Carter. Just like you.'

His jaw drops. He attempts to rearrange his expression back to normal – but I've glimpsed the truth. He's worried about me being here.

I don't see why. It's not as if this is a competition. It's school.

He folds his arms across his chest. 'You can't be here. You need a level 3 baku in order to come here. I saw you buying that scarab.' He storms over to my locker, sticking his face right up to the alcove. Jinx lunges out, hissing like a wild cat.

Carter yelps and leaps backwards, sneakers squeaking on the hardwood. He almost falls backwards over his boar baku, but catches himself just before, then takes off down the hallway.

I turn to Jinx, my cheeks flushed post-confrontation. 'Come on then. Let's go get oriented.'

CHAPTER TWELVE

JINX LEADS ME DOWN TO WHAT IS MARKED as the school gym. I could never get lost with Jinx by my side, but I needn't have worried about that – there's a steady stream of students and bakus all heading in the same direction. Some of the students look a lot older than me, strutting the hallways as if they own the place. I try and hold my head high too, and act as if I belong. But being around lots of people always makes me feel nervous – I'm far more comfortable in the darkness of my cave than in the crowded hallways of school.

I wait for Jinx to react, but he doesn't. Strange. Bakus are designed to help soothe their owners if they're feeling stressed or anxious. Maybe I need to look into Jinx's empathetic sensors . . .

But all thoughts melt away as I enter the gym.

At first I'm a bit disappointed that it looks like an ordinary school gymnasium – with its glossy wooden floor painted with lines for different sports. Two glass-backed basketball hoops hang from metal rafters painted in pale green that criss-cross above our heads, serving as hanging posts for brightly coloured celebration banners. Not that any of them are for sports achievements (Profectus students aren't exactly known for being jocks). Instead, they're emblazoned with the Moncha logo, that same stylized M, and carry the names of former students. I wonder what they did to deserve having their names up there.

Different from my old gym at St Agnes, though, is the massive stadium-style seating on either side of the gym, rows of benches that stretch up across two storeys. There'd be room for the entire school in here – and then some. I'm grateful to see Carter and his boar taking a seat on the far side – well away from me.

I file into a row of seats about halfway up, confronted by a cacophony of noisy students and the wildest collection of bakus I've ever seen in a single place.

Monkeys. Dogs. Cats. A small version of a bear.

All of them level 3 and above.

And hovering above a guy sitting right in the front row: an eagle.

I recognize that eagle.

His wings are outstretched so I can't see the face that's behind them, but I know it all too well. I purse my lips. The eagle doesn't seem to have suffered any long-term damage from my pine cone throwing. He flaps his wings and soars up even higher. I wonder if the eagle senses me looking, because he spins his head so his dark mirrored eyes take me in, his gold-edged beak opening in a squawk. I quickly take a seat and stare at the back of the student in front of me.

Jinx crawls up on to my shoulder to get a better view of the action.

He licks his paw. >>Four hundred students entering, and counting.

'Hey, nice baku. Is that a new model? I've never seen one like it before.'

The guy sitting next to me reaches out to touch Jinx, but Jinx darts away, clambering up my arm to sit on my shoulder away from the would-be petter. *Do you have to be so unfriendly?* I think to Jinx. To my relief, the guy laughs, revealing a neat row of shiny teeth.

'A shy model, huh?' He extends his hand to me. 'I'm Jake. Jake Saunders. Third year Profectus.'

I take his hand. 'Lacey Chu. Um ... first year. And this is Jinx. Sorry he's a bit ... sensitive.'

'No problem! This is my baku, Vegas.' A calm-looking retriever model sits at his feet. 'Vegas, send friend request.'

A notification pops up on Jinx's paw, flashing it white.

>>JAKE SAUNDERS wants to be friends.

I click accept, and his profile spills out on to Jinx's back. He's a popular guy, with thousands of friends. 'Vegas?' I ask, raising an eyebrow.

'Yep, you can pet him if you like! He won't mind.'

I reach out and stroke the baku's smooth metal body – he doesn't have the individual strands of fur that Jinx does – and Vegas closes his eyes in a simulation of pleasure. He's a lovely baku.

'The name comes because I love a bit of in-school gambling.' Jake winks at me.

'Gambling? Is that legal?'

'You'll see,' he says, before pressing his lips tightly together.

Before I can press him any further, the peripheral lights around the gymnasium dim, and the noise from the other students quietens in anticipation. It's as if everyone is holding their breath.

>>Such drama, says Jinx, sarcasm dripping in his tone. I raise an eyebrow. I still can't get used to the baku having such a . . . personality. Nothing I'd read about having a baku had prepared me for that.

Shh, I don't want to miss anything.

There's a hum of electric life and a hole opens up in the centre of the gymnasium floor. A beautiful snow-white owl baku flies up out of it, circling over the students' heads, swiftly followed by a stern-looking woman in a sharp powersuit, who's lifted up on a rising podium until she's level with the middle row of seats.

Jinx buzzes with information.

>>Dr Sarah Grant, principal of Profectus, he informs me.

The principal leans her hands against the podium as her owl baku lands next to her, projecting her speech down in front of her. 'Welcome, students, to another year at Profectus! And welcome especially to our incoming students. We're delighted you'll be joining our thriving community.

'First things first, some legal business. If you look at your bakus, you will see I am sending you a link now, which you will use to receive your class schedule, hand in your school assignments, and report in for attendance.

'By accepting the link please be aware that you are agreeing to the strict legal document you will have been sent over the summer. Those of you who bothered to read it will remember that part of this includes a watertight non-disclosure clause when it comes to some of the activities that you will participate in here at Profectus Academy. To be absolutely clear, this means you cannot talk about the activities you will participate in here, outside of the Academy. This is mandatory, so if you want to opt out then you have the option to leave now. Any leavers?'

She pauses to see if anyone will leave. But of course, no one does. There's no way any of us would have come this far only to leave because of confidentiality clauses. We *want* to know what's behind the curtain.

'Good. Now that's out of the way ... No doubt many of you have been doing your research on the school online.'

There's some nervous tittering of laughter from the other freshmen, including me – of course, I tried to find out absolutely everything that I could. There was not much to go on. Only report after report that Profectus was the toughest – and most rewarding – school around, and that it produced the absolute best scientists and engineers in the country.

'Excellent. Now I know most of you will be itching to find out more about what makes life at Profectus so unique – and worth hiding behind such strict secrecy. But I'm not here to introduce that to you. Instead ... we have a very special guest, straight from Moncha headquarters.'

Oh my God. My hands squeeze around Jinx's body. *What if it's Monica Chan? What if it's her in the flesh?*

Jinx's whole body shivers with anticipation, the metal strands of his fur standing up on end. I wonder if he is emulating my own excitement levels, which are sky-rocketing.

A spotlight swivels around to the main entrance of the gym. And there, half-hidden by light streaming in from behind him, is Eric Smith, Monica's partner and second-in-command. Jinx deflates in my hands and I share some of his disappointment: I wanted it to be Monica herself. But having Eric Smith here is pretty cool too, even forgetting for a moment that he somehow raised someone as vile as Carter. It's impossible not to feel a thrill at the sight of him – and his incredible baku. It's a red panda, solemn and gorgeous, metal fur the colour of rust, wrapped around his shoulders almost like a scarf. There's thunderous applause as he enters, his arms spread open wide.

He looks as if he is drinking it in. And I can't help myself – I'm clapping as hard as everyone else.

Between Eric Smith and Monica Chan, life as we know it was *revolutionized*. They gave us bakus. Their names, their faces, are ingrained as part of our history – a history that I want to contribute to one day.

I might only be capable of adding a single word – maybe even just a letter – to the story. But I want to give something.

'Ah, thank you, thank you,' he says. He speaks softly, but his voice is amplified by his baku so we have no trouble hearing him. 'I'm sorry you have me – and not Monica herself – she hates not being here – but she is away on overseas business at the moment. So for your orientation, you've got to settle for me.' The crowd gives him an energetic round of applause, to show their appreciation for his visit.

Eric drinks in the applause, then holds up his hands. 'You all are the best of the best – if not, you wouldn't be sitting here today. If you would indulge me – especially returning students, who would have seen this before, I have a short presentation for you – and then, I promise, we will get on to the good stuff.'

The lights dim again and screens lower from the rafters in the ceiling. The image on the screens flicker, as if the movie were being played from an old-fashioned reel.

A voiceover talks us through the history of robotics as we know it – from the very first automatons in the medieval ages through to the bakus of today. Images play of those initial designs: purely mechanical objects of cogs, bolts and springs, designed to instil wonder – and sometimes, fear.

I swallow, thinking of Jinx. Fear and robotics have often walked hand in hand – and for good reason. Fear of robots taking human jobs, of an intelligence explosion where robots become smarter than humans, of passing the Turing Test and reaching the point where they are able to harm us of their own free will. Asimov's Three Laws becoming overturned, obsolete.

But it took Monica Chan to really think about robots in a different way.

She didn't understand why robots needed to look like humans. The 'uncanny valley' – the phrase that describes the unsettled feeling people have around a machine that looks human but isn't – was something she understood all too well. She couldn't imagine wanting to live with something that appeared human in every way, except with only electronic life behind their eyes. Not only that, but from an engineering point of view, building a robot that could walk smoothly on two legs was incredibly challenging and inefficient. That's when the baku idea was born.

An *animal* design offered what people wanted – companionship, convenience, assistance, easy maintenance – and yet it wasn't so creepy. Quickly after their launch, the baku became an integral part of everyday modern life. Another Moncha slogan – *Accompanying you to your happiest life ever* – became reality.

The movie flies on. Despite the fact that I am already a Moncha-fan through and through, I find myself swept away in the emotion of Monica's rise and rise. Watching the film puts a grin on my face. Monica's journey is a tale I've heard so many times it is practically a bedtime story for me. A fairytale, but not of princes and frogs, ballgowns and pumpkins, but of makers and metal, of wire and ingenuity and inspiration and creativity and invention.

The video is immersive, spinning us over the city of Toronto. There are images of bakus scaling the CN Tower, showing off how seamlessly they have been incorporated into all aspects of life – from the city traders using their pigeon bakus to trade messages, joggers running along the waterfront with their dog bakus projecting their route and updating them on speed, people on restaurant patios, talking to each other rather than looking at their phones, while never missing a beat with their social media updates thanks to their bakus.

Then it focuses in on one of Monica's main aims for the bakus. On a young woman who is about to go up for a presentation in front of a huge audience, her heart beating wildly, her eyes closed but her breaths sharp and shallow. Her fists clench and unclench. She wants to leave, to throw up, to be finished, to be anywhere else. Then her baku leaps into her arms, and within a few moments of stroking his metallic fur, she feels calm. She feels ready. And she takes the stage and smashes it out of the park.

The woman? Monica Chan herself, the baku managing to relieve her not only of her smartphone addiction, but of some of her anxieties.

I think of the other bakus I've known in my life, and what an impact they've had on the people closest to me. The truth is, Petal makes Mom smile – knows what videos she wanted to watch when she was down, what music to listen to to calm her down, what podcasts to play so that she could feel smart and be better at her job.

A line from the voiceover snaps me out of my daydream: 'And simply, the final goal of Moncha Corp: to make life better. And to make people happier.'

The screens fade to black and the lights come up. Eric Smith has moved so that he is now on the podium with Dr Grant. 'And now, today, I'm here to ask you what you see for the future of Moncha Corp. Are you ready to join the next generation of companioneers, mechanics, programmers, designers and coders who are going to take bakus to the next level? Now that we are reaching a point in time where almost every adult has chosen their baku, their companion, we need to keep asking ourselves the question – how can we keep on *accompanying people to their happiest lives ever*? We want to make sure that everyone is achieving their peak happiness.'

Eric Smith is the epitome of comfortable. Relaxed. His hands drop into his pockets and he smiles down at all of us as if we were part of his family. 'Yes, I know. Can simple engineering make people happy? We have a team of psychologists and philosophers looking into this, but really it's people like you – the makers of the future – who are going to transform the ways we live our lives in ways we never knew. Ways we could never have imagined. I'm excited by what you have to offer. By how you will inspire us.

'I'm sure you've heard plenty of stories about Profectus, and the incredible technology that you will have access to while you are here. But forget everything you've ever heard. Because Moncha is in the business of staying one step ahead. And I bet you're wondering how we move innovation forward at Profectus?'

Shivers of anticipation dance down my spine as he talks. There's a rumble from the older students and it feels as if the crowd leans forward as one entity, sweeping me forward with it. I catch sight of Tobias in the front row. He's leaning back, his arms folded across his chest, the ghost of a smile playing on his lips. Four other seniors next to him are the same – an island of calm in an ocean of anticipation.

I wonder what they know that we don't.

I don't have to wait long to find out.

'I'm delighted to open this season of Baku Battles.'

The roar that shakes the gymnasium is almost deafening.

CHAPTER THIRTEEN

ERIC SMITH SPREADS HIS ARMS AND THE gym transforms before my very eyes.

The shiny, laminated oak flooring flickers once, twice, then turns bright white. The older students are hooting and hollering, stamping their feet, adding earthquake-like vibrations.

>>Where are they going?

Jinx flicks his tail in the direction of Tobias and four other seniors who file out of the gym. But I don't have much time to wonder about that. I'm too busy being dazzled by the tech on display. The floor begins to ... split open, is the only way that I can describe it, around the podium where Dr Grant and Eric Smith are standing. It shifts, moves, unfurls, panels I didn't realize were panels folding on top of each other, revealing a deep doughnut-shaped arena, with the podium at the very centre of it. The column-like podium is wallpapered in screens, and at clock-like intervals on the floor are five silver rings. Along with everyone else in my class, I lean forward, craning my neck to see into the pit. The rings flash and spin, opening like manhole covers. The five senior students I saw leaving are lifted up into the arena, their bakus appearing in front of them.

Tobias is lifted up almost directly beneath me. I can see the curly tips of his short black hair and the golden head of his eagle baku.

I can't see his face, so I look to the screen, which is showcasing the different students' faces one by one. Tobias still has that easy grin on his face, as if he is totally confident in what is about to happen.

The next face to flash up is captioned 'Gemma'. In contrast to Tobias's calm appearance, she looks fierce, her copper-bright hair tied back in a long plait, an impressive tiger baku pacing at her feet. The others are introduced: Dorian, Pearce and Elektra. All the seniors have the same aura of barely contained excitement, a mix of confidence and aggression simmering under the surface.

Eric Smith speaks again. 'Let me first say a special thanks to our team captains – for putting their bakus on the line for this demonstration. The outcomes here will have no bearing on the battles themselves – they will officially start at the end of this month, as per usual. But, as always, my advice is the same – battle to win.'

Tobias rolls his shoulders back, cricking his neck from side to side in an attempt to loosen up the tension. I feel tense as well, my knuckles white as I grip the bench by my side to lean forward and get as close to the action as possible. A Baku Battle. I never thought it would be possible. It shouldn't be: bakus are programmed not to fight.

>>Look at his wing, Jinx says. And her paw.

I try to see what Jinx is referring to. And then I catch it: a little gold circle attached to all the bakus. Maybe that's what overrides the code that prevents one baku from attacking another in the real world.

'Players, play to win. You have thirty minutes. And so ... begin.'

Dr Grant's owl baku releases a piercing screech and the teams are off.

The preamble is so short – there's no ready, steady, go. Tobias immediately makes a hit on Dorian's snarling wolf baku, his eagle stretching his talons out, wings spread wide to keep him hovering – and to enable a quick getaway from the wolf's surprisingly high jump.

The eagle makes short work of the wolf, one of his talons snaring a key wire from behind its neck and rendering it useless in less than thirty seconds.

I clutch Jinx tightly to my chest. The bakus in front of my eyes are being torn apart, their wires shredded, bodies mangled by metal claws and teeth and talons. There are no yelps of pain but there are electronic whines and the agonized cries of the fighting students. When their baku is pronounced 'dead', the student's face goes grey on the screen.

Within a matter of minutes, the only faces that are illuminated are those of Gemma and Tobias. They look utterly serious now, all trace of previous bravado and play gone. All they can focus on is winning. The eagle flaps his wings, the tiger prowls on the arena floor, their eyes lifted and locked in each other's gaze. There's highwire excitement all around the gymnasium as we wait to see who is going to be the final winner. My heart is thumping inside my chest. If this is what it means to baku battle, I am equal parts thrilled and appalled.

The lights turn up, flooding the stage in a bright white glow, and I recoil, throwing my arm in front of my eyes. I'm not the only one. Almost everyone groans, so caught up in the action that the bright light is like being forced awake from a riveting dream. Tobias and Gemma freeze, their bakus turning their attention to the centre of the room. *This would be the moment to strike*, I think. *If someone wanted to win.*

Tobias and Gemma have almost the exact same thought at the exact same time. There's a flurry of movement on both sides, but a buzzer sounds – and a clock on the jumbotron reaches 0:00. I hadn't even noticed the countdown, I've been so engrossed in the battle.

Eric Smith's voice rings out above the thunderous applause. 'Congratulations, Tobias Washington and Gemma Morris. You are the joint winners of this Baku Battle demonstration. You can stand down your bakus.'

There's hesitation on both sides, but the gold tags drop off their bakus and so they have no choice but to retreat. My eyes leave Tobias and Gemma, however, and turn to the losing students, cradling the mess of their ruined bakus. None of them – even the eagle and the tiger – has escaped totally unscathed. Everyone is going to need some sort of repair.

The floor closes back over the arena, and I blink – it's hard to believe I'm not actually dreaming.

'What do you think?' asks Jake.

'I think ... I think that was the coolest thing I think I have *ever* seen.'

'Pretty awesome, right? But I could never be on a team,' he says, running his hand over his dog baku's back.

'These are the Baku Battles,' says Dr Grant, silencing us all once again with her voice. 'Making it on to the team is a position of honour for any student – and first years ... you'll have your opportunity to prove yourself very shortly. But if you don't make it on to a team, don't worry. There will still be plenty to keep you busy. The team captains will be watching you during your class orientations and making their selection by the end of the day. To end off orientation, I'd like to thank Eric Smith for visiting us and helping to usher in this new Profectus school year.'

'It's my pleasure. Good luck, everyone. I'm sure I'll be seeing some of you before too long.'

I glance around at all the students and I can see how everyone is looking at the team captains. With admiration and respect. They're really a part of something. And the determination I can see in Tobias and Gemma's eyes is something that I recognize.

This could really be where I shine.

Life at Profectus is shaping up to be more exciting than I could have possibly imagined.

CHAPTER FOURTEEN

'Y OU SHOULD ALL HAVE YOUR CLASS schedules now. Older students, you may head off – but freshmen, would you please stay behind,' says Dr Grant. The podium descends and all around me, students are standing and preparing to head off to their first classes of the day.

I look down at Jinx's back and, sure enough, my schedule for the week is displayed. Next up is a class called 'Gathering' – and it's repeated every morning for the rest of the week. That must be the Profectus-equivalent of 'Homeroom'. Apart from that, I can see some of the standard classes I would have taken at St Agnes: Maths and English, French, Phys-Ed (ugh) . . . but also in the mix are some *much* more interesting options: Coding, Design and the one I've been waiting for, Companioneering. We have fifteen minutes in each classroom today, meeting the teachers and finding out what's expected of us.

'Now you know what kind of gambling can go on at this school,' says Jake.

'You bet on the Baku Battles?'

'You bet we do!' Jake laughs. 'You going to try for a team?'

'Do you think I should? It looks so exciting but . . .' I cling tightly to Jinx. I can't imagine wanting to see him torn apart after all the hard work I've done putting him back together.

'Well remember – first years don't get to battle – they're just alternates in the case of player sickness or baku malfunction.'

'Oh well, in that case – maybe it would be cool to be on a team,' I say, with genuine excitement. I've never been great at teamwork, preferring to work on my own most of the time at St Agnes. But at Profectus, it feels like anything could happen. 'Any tips on who the best team captain is?'

'Well, it should be Tobias hands down,' says Jake. 'His brother, Nathan, won it last year. But I wouldn't count Gemma out. And they say this year might be a *wild card* year, so there might be some surprises. Anyway, I'd better go. Catch you later,' he says.

'Bye,' I reply. He reaches out to touch Jinx again, but Jinx hisses in response. I attempt to laugh it off but I can see confusion warring on Jake's face.

Please behave . . . I try to make my tone sound like a warning, but I can hear Jinx's scoff in my head. He knows my threats are empty. We might have *communication* down, but *commands*? I don't think I have any control over the baku at all. I might have to do some deeper digging into the code.

I head down to the gym floor where the other first years are mingling before Jake can ask me any questions. There's a mix of nationalities and bakus, and almost everyone has a level 3. The notable exception is Carter, and I skirt the edge of the crowd to avoid him.

Jinx suddenly buzzes at my feet, strands of his fur lighting up in an undulating pattern.

What's going on? I ask.

>>Someone is trying to access our data to find out more about you. Happened so quickly they almost bypassed . . .

'Miss Chu, is it?'

I look up and freeze in place. Eric Smith is standing within touching distance of me, his red panda baku staring down at me with onyx-dark eyes. 'Looking forward to starting at Profectus?'

'Uh … yes, sir,' I say, my cheeks burning with the attention.

He smiles at me, but it seems to falter as he reads data from his baku. 'Lacey Chu …' he says, and a small wrinkle appears in his forehead.

Dread fills my stomach, and I turn the ring on my thumb anxiously.

He shakes his head. 'Must be a coincidence,' he mutters, mostly to himself. 'Are you going to make one of the Baku Battle teams?'

'I hope so, sir,' I stutter out.

'You have better odds than my son here,' he gestures to Carter, who's appeared behind me. 'He's not the most natural athlete, even with the help of a level 4 baku. How you convinced your mother to buy you that thing . . . what a waste of a darn good baku, if you ask me.'

I can almost feel the heat radiating from Carter next to me, and he's huffing like his boar. If it was anyone else, the surge of pity I feel for him in this moment would be an avalanche. So not everything is great and easy in the life of Carter Smith.

'Where's your baku, Miss Chu?' Eric asks me.

I look down at my feet – Jinx is nowhere to be seen. 'Uhh . . .'

'Mr Smith! Can I introduce myself . . .' a bubbly student bounds in between us, preventing me from having to answer. I take a few steps back and almost step into Carter. Traces of beetroot-red shame linger at his temples, but he tries to keep up the cocky attitude. I almost admire him for it. *Almost*.

'You shouldn't be here,' he hisses. 'You should be at St Agnes with your loser friend. I wouldn't even try to get on to a team if I were you, I'd only have to destroy you.' Suddenly he yelps, and he looks down at his hand – which has a tiny scratch mark that beads with blood. 'What the hell?' he asks. He looks at me accusingly, but I haven't done anything.

Jinx rubs up against my legs.

I swallow, emboldened by Jinx's appearance. 'Look, this is a new school year – can we just forget about St Agnes?'

'You don't get it, do you? Your dad might be a loser who couldn't handle life at Moncha, but my dad *runs* the place. You're lucky I didn't tell my dad exactly who you are. He'd have you kicked out of the school for sure.'

I step back as if I'd been slapped. 'Lay off my family, Carter.'

'Oh, now you're defending him?'

'I'm not doing anything. I just want to start my school year in peace. If you don't want to be civil then leave me alone.'

'Suit yourself. Stay out of my way and I'll stay out of yours.'

'Fine by me.'

Thankfully Carter and I are separated into different groups, and we head off on our classroom tour separately. If there's anything that could take my mind off Carter and his comments about my dad, it's discovering all the wonders of Profectus.

Even the normal classrooms, the ones for subjects like Maths, English, French and History, are equipped with state-of-the-art e-ink desks and leashes that the bakus plug into during classtime – so that they're under control, but can still help with assignments.

Another cool thing I find out is that each one of our professors is an actual employee of Moncha Corp. It gives them a little break from the high intensity work environment of their regular jobs, while enabling them to keep an eye out on the next generation and help to foster new talent. Our advanced coding teacher, Ms Watson, normally works on emotional AIs and gamification within the software engineering sector. After seeing the facilities that Profectus offers, I'm not surprised that employees don't mind taking some time off to teach. The coding classroom has floor-to-ceiling screens, and Ms Watson seems to delight in showing off all the customizations she can make to the walls and ceilings – while teaching us at the same time.

I'm equally blown away by the materials testing lab, which includes a gigantic universal testing machine (it looks like an old-fashioned guillotine, except it's used to test the strength of different materials), the huge wind tunnel, for students studying aeronautical engineering, and the drafting classroom, with extra-wide desks and skylights that allow in lots of clear bright light.

Everything is even better than I could possibly have imagined. The vision board did not do it justice.

But there's one class I've been waiting for even more than all the others.

Companioneering.

The classroom is almost disappointingly normal-looking, with a blackboard in front and several neat rows of desks. I take a seat at one of the desks near the middle and attempt to get Jinx to leash up. He doesn't.

The door opens and I look up in anticipation. But it's the team captains who enter, filing in one by one with their bakus. I'm glad this is the one that they've come to observe us in – I know that I can prove myself here, and Carter isn't in this class to distract me.

Jinx stalks around the classroom as if he were lion-shaped rather than a house cat. Most bakus don't roam as far from their owners as he does to me, and I keep willing him back, tugging at the leash on my ear to call him. But he ignores me. I'm learning that nothing I do will make him stay where I want him to, so I resort to begging.

Please come back.

He doesn't reply.

The classroom door opens again and a man in a plain white T-shirt and jeans (and maybe an oil-stain on his shirt too?) hurries into the room, an owl baku – the standard, I've learned, for teaching staff – flapping behind him. The owl lands on the desk and projects his name on to the wall behind him: DEREK BAIRD. *This* is our teacher? He looks more dishevelled than any of the students, but then again we're all forced to wear a uniform.

He must have some sort of authority though, as the other students quieten down and settle into their seats. Jinx still hasn't returned to my side, which makes me uneasy. He's supposed to help register me for class. I don't want to mess everything up in front of the team captains.

Mr Baird claps his hands together and then rubs them fiercely as if he's trying to start a fire. 'Right, guys, right! Welcome back to day one of the rest of your lives! And here in the best class of all – companioneering!' He has a lilting Scottish accent that somehow makes me want to sit up even straighter in my chair.

There's a rumble of laughter around the room, but my stomach clenches. This man's casual attitude to something that I've wanted my entire life is freaking me out.

No one else seems to care though. There's a girl next to me, her auburn hair cropped short on her head, leaning forward on her hands, as if she's trying desperately to soak in everything that she can. Her posture is almost the mirror image of mine. I'm leaning so far forward, my belly is pressed up against the edge of the desk and digging in. I sit back a bit and try to relax.

I look down at her feet and see a tabby cat baku at her feet, leashed up to the desk and streaming information about companioneering on to her desk. A *helpful* cat baku.

>>Instead you're stuck with me.

Oh, so now you'll talk with me. Come back here and behave like that baku and maybe I'd be happy. Will you?

>>Not a chance. Her name is Nalini, by the way, and her baku is Ginger.

I roll my eyes, but then catch Nalini looking at me, a frown on her face. *Oh no,* I hope she doesn't think I'm rolling my eyes at her. I smile weakly and try to say hi, but Mr Baird starts talking.

'So, hands up, who's interested in companioneering?' Mr Baird looks expectantly around the classroom.

Nalini shoots her hand straight up and mine follows, more slowly. I take a quick glance over my shoulder and see that there are only about five hands out of the twenty-something first years in the classroom. The team captains look at us appraisingly, taking notes, and as I glance around, I catch the eye of Tobias – who is now staring straight at me. My throat feels like it's swelling up and I find it hard to swallow – caught in the light streaming into the classroom, his dark green eyes look light, the colour of moss in early spring. I look away. He almost caused Zora to lose Linus. I cannot like him, no matter what the light does to the colour of his eyes.

'Well, we only have a few minutes together today and I'm

sure you're all feeling completely overwhelmed by everything you've seen so far. If you're not, you're not normal.' There's a titter of nervous laughter from the classroom. 'You'll notice we've got visitors,' – he gestures to the team captains standing by the wall – 'but don't worry about impressing them; they've made their selections already. Remember all that hard work you did trying to get *in* to Profectus in the first place? Well, that's all been sent straight to the team captains' bakus. Your fates are sealed, young ones. But if you don't get picked – don't worry. You'll have the chance to prove yourselves before next year's selections, when the real fun begins.'

I frown, disappointed at Mr Baird's news. That's my shot at being selected over with. I barely scraped an acceptance into Profectus.

'Now, if you could all please ask your bakus to bring up the first—' But Mr Baird doesn't get to finish his sentence. There's a loud crash as books, files and an old globe are sent tumbling from a high shelf above the heads of the team captains. Everyone watches as the team captains shield their bakus from the falling objects. But I look up to the shelf, a sick feeling turning my stomach. My heart lurches. Yep, standing stock still as a statue, staring at me as if I didn't know *exactly* who was the culprit, is Jinx.

>>What, me? I can almost hear him say. The wide eyes and uplifted tail say it all.

He flicks his tail now, nonchalant about the chaos he's just caused, and leaps down off the shelf.

'Stop that baku!' Mr Baird shouts.

The other students kick out their legs or reach down to grab at Jinx as he passes, but he nimbly jumps and dodges them all, until he reaches me and jumps up into my lap.

Crap.

CHAPTER FIFTEEN

'T HAT THING IS YOURS?' MR BAIRD ASKS, his eyes blazing.

'Probably defective,' says one of the other students, and everyone starts laughing – the tension broken.

'I ... I'm really sorry ...' I begin to say, but Mr Baird's owl flaps his wings past me, dropping a small token into my lap. It's a black disc, not much bigger than a coin. I pick it up and turn it over in my palm.

'That's not for you, it's for your baku,' Mr Baird snaps. 'It's a black mark. A one hour enforced power down. You won't be able to use your baku for the next hour. And you'll see me after class for detention for the disruption you've caused.'

As if by magic – but more likely, by magnet – the black disc jumps out of my palm and locks itself to Jinx's tail. Instantly, Jinx slumps in my arms, his power sapped. He's almost back to the way he was when I first found him – just a misshapen hunk of metal. I'm in shock for a moment, but then panic sets in. 'What? You can't do that!' I tug the metal disc but it won't budge.

'One hour, Miss ...' he looks down at his baku, 'Chu. You didn't think you could come to Profectus Academy, *the* official training programme for Moncha Corp, and not end up finding out about some new, proprietary technology, do you? And let this be a lesson to all of you newbies,' he says, lifting his stern gaze away from me and addressing the rest of the class. 'Any sign of misbehaviour by the bakus, or by yourselves, and we have ways of shutting you down. Black marks are real. While you are on these school grounds, you are under Moncha's rules. The older students know that all too well. Don't you?'

The team captains nod, staring at me with a mixture of disbelief and bemusement that makes my cheeks burn. I've never been one to get in trouble with my teachers, and I hate that I might have made a bad impression already in front of the captains. Anger tenses up all my muscles. My fingers worry at the black mark, trying to pry it off, but it's no good.

'Well, I'd say it's almost time for the team selections,' says Mr Baird. 'And considering this is the *best* class, it won't shock you that this is where you'll be finding out just who's made the team.'

There's some commotion as the doors open and other freshmen years file in. I take the opportunity to look at the captains – *other* than Tobias, who is glaring at me and sheltering his eagle protectively. *What's his problem?* I wonder. I avoid his gaze and instead study Gemma, with her fierce tiger baku. She seems amazing – strong, and in sync with her

110

baku. It's for the chance to get to meet people like her that I wanted to come to Profectus.

To be around *my* kind of people.

'Everyone here?' asks Mr Baird, to his baku. The owl nods and hoots once. 'Let's find out who's made the team then.'

In the classroom all around us, bakus buzz and light up with notifications. There's an immediate scramble as everyone rushes to see if they've been selected for a team. I'm the only one who can't check her baku – because he's lying motionless in my arms. That black mark might have ruined all my chances.

The girl next to me squeals with excitement. She looks up at Elektra. 'I've made your team!'

'Welcome, Nalini!' says the captain with bright blue hair.

I cross my arms, miserable, waiting to see who else has been chosen. Of course, I hear the snuffling of Carter's boar as he saunters up to the front. But there's something unsure about the way he's walking, and he frowns down at his baku. He stops in front of Tobias, but then hesitates. Tobias and Gemma turn to each other – Gemma folding her arms across her chest. 'Did you do this on purpose?' she asks. She looks angry.

'No, did you?' he snaps back.

I frown, looking between the two team captains. I feel like I've missed something.

I'm not the only one. 'Problem, guys?' Mr Baird raises an eyebrow.

'It's nothing,' snaps Gemma. 'Welcome to my team,

Carter.' Carter and his boar take up their position next to Gemma, but I can see him looking over at Tobias.

There are four first years standing at the front now – but no one in front of Tobias.

'Well? Aren't you coming?' Tobias asks. To my surprise, he's looking right at me.

I look down at Jinx – but of course, he's still black-marked. Dead to the world.

'Your selection is Miss Chu?' asks Mr Baird.

Tobias nods. He looks down at his baku as if to check that's right – as if he thinks he might have made a mistake.

'Well, Miss Chu?'

I scramble to my feet, rushing down the row towards the front of the classroom. I feel the eyes of the other students on my back as I pass. I reach Tobias and I'm flustered, my hair coming out of its hasty ponytail, strands of it sticking to the back of my neck. I dare a glance at Carter, and he's shooting daggers at me with his eyes. So much for staying out of each other's way. We're going to be pitted against each other.

'Come on then,' Tobias says. There's no *Welcome to the team, Lacey*, I notice. 'Let's go and meet the others.'

PART THREE

TEAM TOBIAS

CHAPTER SIXTEEN

I FOLLOW TOBIAS OUT OF THE CLASSROOM, Jinx in my arms. Strangely, Tobias is also cradling his eagle baku – not allowing it to fly, like I've seen before.

He grunts at me. 'Not plotting any more harm to Aero are you?'

'*Excuse* me?'

'First the pine cones. Now you try to drop a ton of books on his head.'

I stop in my tracks. 'The pine cones?' So he *does* remember what happened at the beginning of the summer ... but not the same way that I recall the incident happening at all. 'Hang on a second, you sent your eagle to scare my friend! She almost lost her brand new baku because of you.'

He stops too, pivoting on the heels of his sneakers. 'Aero wasn't scaring your friend. He was catching a baku ball. Carter threw it at her head and it would have hit her if it wasn't for me. He was being an idiot.'

I open my mouth to protest, but then I realize he could be telling the truth. 'Oh,' is all I say.

Tobias's eyes search my face, then he starts walking again – and I have no choice but to follow. He leads me to an empty classroom, where the rest of the team is waiting. I trail a little bit behind, still wary of his story – and regardless, it doesn't change the fact he's friends with Carter. Unfortunately, it's harder to remember the grudge when he looks at me with his deep green eyes. I grit my teeth and tamp down on those feelings as much as possible.

He swings open the classroom door, and I'm greeted by three expectant faces – two guys and a girl. One of the guy's faces turns sour immediately, giving me a dark scowl.

'Guys, this is our first year teammate, Lacey Chu. Her baku is . . .'

'Jinx,' I reply. I give the group a nervous wave, confused by the wave of hostility coming from the guy – who has the tallest spiked hair I've ever seen. He has a beautiful large husky-type baku at his feet. Tobias gestures to him first. 'This is Kai, and his baku Oka. He's my second-in-command, a third year like me, and the team's main companioneer.'

'What's up with your baku?' Kai asks, folding his arms across his chest.

I swallow, but Tobias answers for me. 'He got black-marked in Mr Baird's class.'

Kai looks aghast. 'Toby, man . . . What the hell? This isn't what we agreed.'

Something passes between the two teammates that I don't understand. It seems like they're talking in code, similar to what passed between Tobias and Gemma in Mr Baird's classroom. I hug my arms around my waist, uncomfortable with the feeling that this is all to do with me – even though I've done nothing wrong except, apparently, having been chosen.

'I'll tell you later,' says Tobias. Before I have chance to question it, he moves on. He points to the second guy – a tall, lanky red-haired guy with a face covered in freckles. His baku is – unusually – an oversized frog, but still a level 3. 'This is River. He's also a third year – and a mad talented designer. His baku is Lizard.'

I frown, looking at his baku – which is clearly a frog. 'But that's a . . .'

'I know. Don't ask. He'll be the one responsible for any mods we want to make.'

'All right, Lacey?' River asks, but his head is down and he's sketching in a notebook – so I don't get the impression he really wants to know the answer.

'Hi,' I say anyway.

'And then this is Ashley – our second year, and electronics geek. Her baku is Jupiter.'

'Welcome to Team Tobias!' she says, giving me the first warm welcome from the new team, along with a Hollywood-style, mega-watt grin that's impossible not to return. Her long blonde hair is tied back in a casual messy bun – the sort that every teenage girl is supposed to be able to pull off effortlessly, but I can't achieve no matter how hard I try. I look down at her feet and feel a stab of jealous at the beautiful spaniel baku at her feet. He's the closest thing so far to what I would have chosen if I'd had the opportunity. 'Hey, come sit over here,' she says, standing up on her chair and jumping up on to the desk next to it.

'Thanks,' I say, bumping awkwardly into the back of the chair before finally managing to sit down. I close my eyes for a second, trying to calm my nerves. I wish more than anything that Jinx was awake – he might not be able to ease my anxiety, but he's at least good at distracting me.

Tobias takes point in the middle of his team. 'Right. This is my third year of Baku Battles, so I'm not going to let anything – or any*one* – mess this up for me.' Tobias's eyes flick to me. My cheeks burn for what feels like the millionth time today – it's so unfair, because he must have chosen me and seen *some* potential, but because of the black mark I've somehow been judged as inadequate.

I stare down at Jinx's inert form in my arms. I miss having his banter in my ear. No doubt he would be commenting in my ear about my teammates, or offering insights into the Baku Battles. I miss it, even though it's been less than twenty-four hours since he first spoke.

Tobias continues: 'I'm deadly serious about winning this year, so the hard work is going to start today. No one has any plans, right?' As if anyone would dare to disagree with the ferocity on Tobias's face. He turns to Kai sitting next to me. 'What do you think of following a similar strategy to Nathan's last year?'

I jump in before I can stop myself. 'But what exactly *is* the Baku Battle competition?'

Tobias stares at me and Kai rolls his eyes, but I see Ashley nodding and smiling at me encouragingly.

When I turn back to Tobias, his chest swells out and his chin lifts. He's enjoying this. He's in his element – a leader – and as if by divine intervention, a perverse sunbeam slices through a slat in the blinds to cast a band of gold on his dark brown skin.

He looks positively regal.

He takes a deep breath before beginning. Even my fingertips are tingling with anticipation at what he is about to say. 'Baku Battles,' he pauses for dramatic effect, 'are a long-standing tradition at Profectus. Pitting baku against baku teaches us how to innovate – to create, to imagine – in the most extreme environment, with stakes that actually matter to us. You've heard the old saying that war drives technological advancement? Well, we don't want to have *actual* war, so we've got to simulate it. Of course, you can't fight bakus in the real world but here, under strict rules, in a controlled environment … we get to go *nuts*.' His eyes flash as he talks, and my heart twists inside my chest. This is amazing. It's even better than I could have hoped. I knew Profectus would be competitive, but this is on another level.

This is competing, but the results for us could mean inventing technology that could help society. Advance it. Monica Chan's vision truly come to life. These are the types of secrets I dreamed about knowing.

And now I get a front row seat to the action.

'So we are going to train, and train hard. Preparation is

119

absolutely key. The competition is made up of three different battles. You earn points by defeating all the other bakus in the arena or lasting the thirty minutes – but you can also earn a share of the points by repairing bakus that have been broken during battle before school begins the next day. The team with the most points wins the competition. And every single winning teammate gets a guaranteed summer internship in the Moncha division of their choice and one-on-one time with Monica Chan herself.'

My jaw drops. It's an incredible opportunity: and a guaranteed opportunity for me to meet my idol.

'Although maybe it will be Eric Smith this year,' says Tobias, with a shrug, which snaps me from my daydream.

'Why do you say that?' I ask.

'Because Monica is normally the one to give the orientation speech. Maybe she's taking some time off this year. But working for Eric Smith will be just as good,' says Tobias.

'Maybe better,' says Kai. 'My folks say she's taken a real step back. I want to work for someone who's still at the top of their game.'

No one could be better than Monica Chan. I don't say the words out loud though, because I don't want to antagonize my teammates any further.

Tobias continues. 'The final battle takes place inside Moncha headquarters, which is always a trip. The arena in there is *insane*. I missed out on a win in my first two years,' he says, clenching his fingers into a fist, as if the losses happened yesterday – not years ago. 'But my brother was the captain last year, and we kicked ass. And I'll be damned if we don't win again this year. That means no shenanigans from my team. This is our future we're talking about.

'And absolutely no black marks.' He isn't looking at me when he says it, but my fingers instinctively tighten around Jinx's inactive body.

The bell for the end of school rings, the mark pops off Jinx and he springs back to life. I can't help the grin that appears on my face. Part of me had been worried that the stasis might be permanent – with Jinx, I'm starting to learn that things don't always work the way they are supposed to. I stare down at the black mark and wonder if I should return it to Mr Baird.

>>Keep that thing away from me.

I'm not planning on using it on you. Although, if you're bad . . .

>>I will pee on your bed sheets.

You don't pee.

>>That doesn't mean I don't have my ways.

I laugh, but then I cringe at the thought of anyone finding out just how *un*official Jinx really is. He's a chimera, composed of so many spare parts and garbled together connections, I don't know what anyone would think of him if they took a closer look.

'All right, team, I'm sending your bakus the coordinates for the training session this afternoon. I want to see you all there in half an hour, no exceptions.'

I raise my hand tentatively.

'Dude, we're not in class. Just ask your frickin' question,' says Kai, rolling his eyes.

Tobias looks at me expectantly.

'I . . . uh, have detention this afternoon.'

Tobias's lips purse together. 'I forgot about that. Well, you'll have to miss this one then. But that's the only one you're going to miss, got it?' He snaps his fingers at his baku, Aero, and storms out of the classroom.

'He's a bit intense,' says Ashley, leaning over. 'But he's a good guy. It's kind of hard living in his brother's shadow.'

'His brother?'

'Nathan. He won last year. Pressure's on for Tobias to step up too.'

My eyes widen. I know a lot about pressure – asking me not to put pressure on myself is like asking water not to boil when it's placed over a heat source.

'He said if he doesn't win, his parents might send him to work at BRIGHTSPRK,' says River, jumping in on our conversation.

Ashley and my expression are almost mirrors of each other: the same instant grimace at the name BRIGHTSPRK. They're Moncha's biggest rivals, and they started their own school following the Moncha model. They're based out of San Francisco, but mini BRIGHTCities are popping up all over the world.

But they don't have bakus, so as fast as BRIGHTCities are popping up, Monchavilles are taking over. And I can't

122

imagine Tobias being happy about giving up Aero. Another incentive for him to win.

The simultaneous grimace bonds Ashley and me. 'Good luck at detention,' she says. 'Hope Mr Baird's not too hard on you. See you around, teammate!'

'See you,' I reply. I'm left all alone in the classroom, in no hurry to find out what sort of detention Mr Baird has in store for me. I want Jinx to send Zora a message about the Baku Battles and what's happened, but then I remember the Profectus rules – plus, to prevent secrets (and distractions), external communication coverage is disabled within these walls. In an emergency, there are codes that can be used to override the signal blackout, but if they are used in vain then there are even worse punishments that can be doled out than just a black mark.

I finally can't put it off any longer.

Time to find out what detention is like at Profectus.

CHAPTER SEVENTEEN

I STAND UP JUST AS THE DOOR TO THE classroom opens. Mr Baird's head pops around the door. 'Miss Chu? You're late.'

Crap. I've already got on his bad side once today; I can't afford to again. Jinx's hackles rise as the teacher's owl flies overhead and Mr Baird looks down at him, frowning. I beg Jinx to stop behaving so weirdly, fidgeting with the leash at my ear, and kind of to my surprise he stops and jumps up into my arms. Instinctively my arms close around his surprisingly soft metallic body, and I brush down his back with my fingers, feeling my heart rate and breath return to normal as he softly purrs.

'What version of a cat baku is that? I'm not sure I've seen . . .' he reaches out to touch Jinx's fur, but Jinx leaps back out of my arms and darts away down the hallway.

I shrug and laugh it off. 'No, he's not a new version. Totally standard level 3 house cat baku,' I say.

I'm not sure he believes me, if the quivering frownline between his eyebrows is anything to go by. 'Well, a place on the team *and* detention on your first day. You're gaining yourself quite a reputation at the school already.'

My throat feels like it's constricting.

'Detention is going to be a bit different today. I have a task for you.'

Obediently, I follow – breathing a small sigh of relief as we turn round the corner and Jinx is there, waiting in a doorway, his eyes bright and alert. Mr Baird doesn't pay him any particular attention once he trots at my heel, behaving for all the world like an ordinary baku. *Please stay that way*, I think.

>>Not a chance.

I grimace.

Just as Jinx trots at my heel, I trot at Mr Baird's, following him three levels down a wide staircase at the very back of the school. I'm glad that Jinx's inbuilt GPS will be keeping tabs on all these routes, mapping the labyrinth of hallways. There's absolutely no way that I would be able to remember where to go without him. My brain might be perfect for solving engineering puzzles, but when it comes to a sense of direction? Yeah, not my forte. Reading books that involved kids heading out into the wilderness with only an analogue compass and a paper map used to bring me out in hives.

The owl baku goes ahead of us, opening each door as we pass through. 'You won't be able to get through here without a teacher or senior student,' says Mr Baird. 'So there's no point in trying. The security is inbuilt into our bakus, state-of-the-art. You won't be able to practise in secret,' he says, his eyes shining. 'But what you can do is clean this up.'

With a brush of his wing (likely embedded with some sort of code), the owl opens the last door – and I realize that I've been led straight down into the arena beneath the gymnasium. It looks different down here in the dark. Smaller. Creepier. It's also an absolute mess: there are bits of metal and plastic everywhere, bolts and wires pulled from the battling bakus strewn across the surface. There are marks from the rubber soles of the bakus, as they ran around during the battle. I can almost trace the choreography of the fights, based solely on the wreckage. Jinx paces over to where the wolf was brought down, sniffing tentatively at a piece of scrap metal on the ground.

Mr Baird coughs, and I look up. 'Well, can you help?' he asks.

'What do you want me to do?'

'Get all of this tidied up. There's a recycling bin for all the spare materials just outside here, and you'll find cleaning supplies in this closet. When you're done, leave the room and it will lock automatically behind you.'

'Profectus detention is intense,' I say.

His eyes sparkle with amusement – I'm glad I'm able to make him laugh rather than grimace this time. 'If you can get this done in time, you might just be able to make the end of your meeting.' He pauses in the doorway. His eyes flick from me to Jinx, and I can see he wants to say something more.

'I got it, Mr Baird. You can count on me.' I show my

eagerness by grabbing a broom from the closet, and start sweeping up the arena. I hear the soft swoosh of the doors, and I'm left in peace.

>>Thank Moncha he's gone! Now we can have some real fun.

'Jinx, seriously – I don't even clean up my room. You think cleaning this up is going to be fun?'

>>We can find all sorts of goodies in here I bet. Like, look at this. His paw brushes up against a smashed-up printed circuit board – if one of the bakus is missing that, they're going to be seriously screwed.

I lean down to pick it up. Jinx is right – this *is* interesting, and I could definitely put it to use in my lab at home. I drop it into my backpack. Once we get on a roll, sweeping up and examining the wreckage for useful things, it becomes much more fun. A bit like panning for gold. Besides, I'm able to get a much better sense of the arena. The floor seems to be made of a smooth substance that doesn't scratch despite the metallic claws and talons of the creatures. Then there are the five rings set out at intervals around the arena – where Tobias, Gemma and the others were standing. I guess in order to make it fair – and safe – they keep the players in one place.

Finally, once everything is about as tidy as I can stand to make it, I put away the brooms, mops and cleaning supplies and let my curiosity take over. I take a stand in one of the circles, planting my feet on top of two tiny silver dots, which I presume are place markers. I just want to feel what it's like to be one of the battlers – if just for a moment.

But, as I'm quickly learning, nothing at Profectus is there by accident.

Immediately the silver pads beneath my feet heat up, and I become encased in a projection that shows me the different areas of the battlefield – including the side of the doughnut that is invisible to me. My view automatically swerves so that I can see from Jinx's point of view – and above him, like a bird's eye, if I turn my head slightly.

>>We're connected!

'Oh my gosh, you can feel this too?'

>>Absolutely. It must be how you would send me commands. You know. If I listened to that sort of thing.

I roll my eyes. 'You would have to listen to me in a Baku Battle. What if something was coming behind you?'

>>Trust me, I would have much better instincts on that front than you.

As if to prove his point, he ripples his back, arching it so his tail flicks. At the same time, he lights up every one of his sensors, so it looks like moonlight sparkling off waves on an ink-black ocean. 'Show off,' I say, sticking my tongue out.

I play around a bit with the hologram, moving the field of vision this way and that, and watching as Jinx's stats light up on the screen. It's an impressive bit of kit – and the fact that you can't tell it exists until you are inside the circle is even more impressive. The silver disks must not only be pressure points, but must form part of the leash connection.

I wish I could toy around with it all night, but I can see

in the corner that the time is already flashing five p.m. School's been out for an hour and a half – I'm sure most of the training sessions have finished already. Mom will be wondering where I've got to.

With reluctance, I step off the silver pads, and the hologram drops. I pick my backpack off the floor with a grunt, weighed down by the bits and pieces I've collected from the arena. Lots to sort out in the cave tonight.

I wave my hand in front of the door and it opens. I step through. But Jinx doesn't follow. I spin around on my heels as the door slides shut on me. 'Jinx!!' I cry out, slamming my fists on to the door. 'Dammit, Jinx, why didn't you come?' I push on the door, then press my hand on the keypad, but it flashes up a series of red lights at me: CODE INVALID.

I groan. I stand on my tiptoes, looking through the small window into the room. I see Jinx's tail dash across the floor – he's not at all worried about being separated from me. Instead, I see him look back over his shoulder, catch my eye, and then disappear through a different sliding door on the opposite side.

I slam my fist one more time, shouting his name. But it's no use. He's gone. Now I have to find him in a maze of hallways, laboratories and classrooms, some blocked off by security that I have no idea how to navigate. So much for being able to make a quick getaway home.

My last glance through the window confirms that Jinx is no longer there – the arena is now dark and, thanks to me, clean. I take a mental note of which door he went through, so that I can make my way round in that direction. He can't go far – I'm certain that he wouldn't run away from me for good. Bakus don't do that. *But maybe this one does*, says an uncomfortable voice in the back of my mind. I can't risk it. I have to find him.

I dig around for a pen inside my bag (Mom insisted I bring one, though I haven't written anything down in ages) and jot down a rough map of the arena on my palm: the door where I am, and where Jinx has gone. It's lame, but the best idea I can think of in the moment. Then I dash back along the hallway, to the stairs that I walked down with Mr Baird. There's a couple of other doors leading from the stairwell, and – confusingly – both lead in the direction that I want to go. There's nothing – no signage or even door numbers – to indicate which would be my best option, so I go for the closest. I yank at it, but it won't budge. There's no lock pad or even keyhole that I can see – maybe it only opens one way?

I run around to the other door, which pushes open easily. 'Jinx?' I call out tentatively. Nothing. I need to keep following the hallways around to the left in order to make sure that I'm following the circle around – and not heading further out into one of the numerous wings.

I keep moving, occasionally coming up against locked doors or dead-ends. I try every handle in desperation, pushing against every window in case there's an alternative way through. I've moved beyond the surgically white hallways of the science wing, into a part of the Academy that has a more relaxed vibe – with beanbag chairs for resting in, and did I spot a ping-pong table? It looks like one of the visions of perfect corporate life that I've seen in old movies and television shows. Mentally I try and bring up a picture of what I know the school to be like – maybe this is where the kids who board stay? It would be a pretty cool place to live. But there's no one around.

I come across a huge lounge-type room, with oversized armchairs, two elaborate fireplaces and inspirational messages printed on to the walls in foiled type that catches the low light. The lights turn on as I enter, and I brace for some sort of alarm – but nothing happens.

I catch a glimpse of Jinx in the far corner of the room. Just the end of his slinky tail, but it's enough. 'Wait for me!' I cry out. I sprint across the hall, jumping over a low-lying coffee table and trying not to slip on the brightly coloured rugs.

Jinx is halfway through an open door when I take a flying leap and finally manage to grab him, by sliding into him on the knees of my woollen uniform. I'm thankful I didn't decide to wear the kilt after all – I would have serious rubber burns on my legs otherwise. 'Gotcha!' I laugh, grabbing him tightly around the stomach. Thankfully, he doesn't struggle.

But that's when I realize I'm not alone in the darkened room. A pair of heavy boots enters my sightline, their wearer breathing heavily.

'Get. Out. Now.'

CHAPTER EIGHTEEN

'WHAT ARE YOU DOING HERE?' TOBIAS stands over me, his hands on his hips, his voice dripping with icy-cold anger – and an undercurrent of something else. Fear? But that can't be right – I'm no threat to him.

At any rate, I'm taken aback by his tone. I scramble backwards towards the door, accidentally loosening my grip, and Jinx takes advantage to shoot out of my arms.

I close my eyes for a second, cursing him. My back hits against the door frame in my haste to put as much space between me and Tobias as possible. 'I . . . I'm sorry,' I say. 'I was just following Jinx trying to find a way out of here . . .' I don't want him to know that I don't have control of what my baku does.

He presses his fingers against the bridge of his nose. 'Finished detention?'

I nod.

'You're new here – you wouldn't know – but these rooms are supposed to be totally private, that's all.' Tobias shifts his body to try and intercept Jinx. As he moves, I catch sight of his eagle baku on the ground, inert. My curiosity piques, and Tobias – realizing his mistake – rushes to block my view again. He's breathing heavily and colour is rising in his cheeks.

He wants me out of there.

But I can see Jinx's eyes glowing in the darkness of the far corner, and he doesn't seem to be in a hurry to go anywhere.

'Come on, Jinx,' I whisper to him, but Jinx grooms his tail, ignoring me. Inwardly, I groan. I'm going to have to walk across the room to collect him.

I swallow then take a step in, keeping as close to the edge of the room as possible. 'I'll get my baku and then I'll leave you alone,' I force myself to say. Maybe boys are like animals. If you talk softly, they won't get so spooked.

To my frustration, Jinx leaps out of the way.

'God, what's that thing's problem?' Tobias says. 'You need to get it looked at by one of the vets.'

'He's fine,' I snap back. 'Yours is the one with the problem.' As the words fall out of my mouth, I can see straight away that I'm right – it really *does* have a problem. Even though it didn't look as if the eagle had received much damage during the Baku Battle, there are some serious dents and broken wires.

His jaw tightens. 'Yeah, don't you think I know that?'

I can't help it: now I'm really curious. I leave the comfort of the edge of the room and creep towards the broken eagle. He's lying on the ground, as if powered down and nothing is wrong, but every so often he twitches his neck, almost like an involuntary spasm. There's been an obvious attempt at a repair: some pretty shoddy soldering work is visible, at odds with the rest of the creature's beautifully crafted engineering. I wrinkle my nose, unable to hide my disgust at the workmanship. 'Who did this?'

'Kai,' Tobias says. He folds one arm over his chest and rubs at his eyes with his other hand. He walks over so that he's standing on the opposite side of the eagle to me. 'During our team session today. I picked him for the team because he's supposed to be the best companioneer in his class, but he's never fixed anything as complicated as my eagle.'

'Why not take it to a Moncha vet?' I ask.

He scoffs. 'You don't get it yet, do you? With Profectus, with the Baku Battles, the whole *point* is that we have to do everything ourselves. Or, as a team, anyway. I could maybe take it to one of the teachers, but we'll be handicapped in the battle. They have punishments that they can dole out – like the black marks – or they have bonuses they can give for good behaviour too – like revive chips that will give a baku an extra boost if it's injured. We get points deducted from our total if we pay for professional help. It's *meant* to be challenging. The idea is to get to the very end without asking for help – just applying the knowledge that we've learned at the Academy. Kai was supposed to be good, but I think Nathan was the one who was really good at the hardware stuff. He probably set me up to fail.'

'Nathan sounds like an ass,' I say.

Tobias laughs, but the sound is laced with bitterness that makes me cringe a little inside. 'That ass is not only my brother, but an ass with a great job interning for Monica Chan.'

I raise an eyebrow. 'Well. Now I'm jealous of an ass – never thought I'd say that.' Thankfully, I get a chuckle from Tobias, breaking some of the thick tension that's been building in the room ever since I interrupted him. I take the moment to look around the room. It's not *quite* as well equipped as my cave back home, but it has a few supplies. I don't think the damage to Tobias's eagle is terminal, at any rate. I can already see one major connection that I *know* is wrong.

'Hey, what are you doing?' Tobias sounds alarmed.

'Oh!' I snap my hand away from the eagle. I'd moved in to start fixing it without even asking. 'I'm so sorry . . . I just think if we moved this connection over, and wound it back underneath this part, he would have a lot more freedom of movement again and wouldn't be so twitchy?'

Tobias frowns, then walks over to where I am standing. I move aside to show him what I mean and – since he doesn't seem to protest any more, I reach over to the eagle and show him exactly what I want to do. The eagle's metallic feathers are soft under my touch, and the brutal work that Kai did is a travesty to the craft.

'You think?' he asks, scepticism lacing his tone – but I'm not sure it's my words that are giving him pause, or the fact that they are coming from a puny first year.

'Oh, for sure.'

He raises an eyebrow at my confidence, and I feel a blush rising in my cheeks. I focus back on the eagle's twisted metal, trying not to think about Tobias's moss-green eyes staring at me. Or the fact that he's so close, I can feel his breath on my neck. Heat radiates off his body like an engine, and if I'm not careful, that blush is going to cover more than just my cheeks. I have a tendency to go full-blown tomato-red right from my hairline down my neck and across my chest – not a good look, and it tends to give everything away about how I'm feeling.

'The best thing for me to do is just show you,' I say, trying to inject more confidence in my voice than I feel.

I sense he's about to protest again, so I change my tack. 'Look, how long have you been working on this?'

'Since school let out,' he says, with a conceding shrug. 'The team left about fifteen minutes ago. And if my eagle's not fixed by tomorrow ... I might have to withdraw. I can't believe it's all gone so wrong, and school has barely begun.'

Now that he's not looking at me, I take a moment to look at him. He is so serious, a deep frownline criss-crossing his otherwise perfectly smooth forehead. Neither of us have turned on any lights, and his skin is so dark in the half-light, it reflects almost blue. 'So you were just going to stand here all night staring at it?'

'Look, I've had two years of training and studying to do exactly this, okay? I just don't want to get it wrong.'

'But you've tried everything you can think of.'

His jaw tightens. 'Yes.'

'So what's the harm in letting me have a go? Give me half an hour. I promise I won't do anything that you can't reverse.'

He throws his hands up in the air. 'Okay, Miss Confident. You try and do what we couldn't.'

I bite my lower lip and nod. Jinx rubs up against my leg – typical that when I don't feel like leaving, he comes to me of his own accord. He crawls up my leg, coming to rest on my shoulder.

>>Woah. He's beat up pretty bad.

'That's for sure,' I mutter.

'What was that?' asks Tobias.

I cringe. I've already become so used to Jinx's voice in my head that I forget it's a bug in his code that I have to fix. 'Sorry, just talking to myself.'

'Oh great, I've got a potential psychopath on my team,' he says, but I notice that he doesn't actually ask me to stop what I'm doing. Instead, he watches my hands intently, as if he's interested in seeing what happens next. The thought of Tobias watching me sends a shiver down my spine. 'Any chance we can turn the lights on?' I ask. The lights might mean he can see my blush – but I'm hoping the more clinical, less – ahem – romantic, atmosphere might help me to concentrate. Plus I can hardly see what I'm working with.

Tobias shakes his head. 'We're not exactly supposed to be in here this late. And besides, the lights are on a timer. Energy saving or something.'

'Hmm,' I say, followed by a short, sharp exhale as I take stock. 'Jinx, turn on your light.' He rolls his tail over and turns on his flashlight. At least that helps me. 'This okay?' I ask Tobias, who nods.

I use Jinx's camera to take pictures of the damage, and set him to scan the internet for the original schematics for the eagle baku. He finds them within seconds, and he projects the blueprint on to the eagle's back. I take my safety glasses from out of my jacket pocket (I'm such a nerd that I carry them around with me), and crouch down closer to the eagle. Kai has botched one of the main connections between the motherboard and the circuit that controls the eagle's head and neck movements. I wrinkle my nose. 'I hope he didn't damage the electronics with what he did,' I say. 'Why didn't he use the correct schematic to fix it?'

Now it's Tobias's turn to look confused. 'What do you mean? My eagle is a level 5 baku – unique and customized to me. There aren't any typical schematics for this.'

'Then what . . .' I stop talking before yet another one of Jinx's secrets is revealed.

>>Told you I have my ways.

Shut it, you.

Out loud, I say: 'Oh, right. I mean – I'm just looking at a schema for one of the other bird bakus, and you can see that he's soldered this wire to the wrong connection. You're never going to get proper movement that way. Not only that but it looks like he's used old solder here.' Instead of the connection being shiny and smooth, it was dull grey. 'That won't conduct electricity well. If I clean it off and replace it, it will be a lot more conductive. Let's move him up on to the table.' I get Jinx to switch to layer a level 3 bird baku's schema over the top of the eagle's connections, to disguise how clever he'd been. From that point, it's easy to show Tobias exactly what I mean.

'Um, hang on a second. That's so cool – how did you get your baku to do that? Cat bakus don't have projectors on their tails.'

'Well, that bit's easy. I just added in the projector from an old rodent baku that I found.'

Tobias scans my face, but the open admiration on his is what makes me blush again. 'You're telling me *you* customized this baku?' he says.

'Well, yeah . . .'

'Maybe Kai isn't the best companioneer on the team after all . . .'

For the next hour, Tobias and I work together, stripping wires and melting solder, and I end up using a little compressed air to clean up the dirty work surface that Kai has left me. Thankfully he didn't heat up the PCB too much, so it isn't damaged. I also use a good old-fashioned hammer to help sort out some of the dents and welts in the eagle's casing – it seems such a shame for such a beautiful creature to look anything less than perfect. The whole time, Jinx projects different measurements at me – from the perfect pressure to apply to a dent, to whether the connections are working properly – so that I can test my theories even before Tobias leashes him up to full power. Once the neck twitch is sorted, I give the rest of the baku a quick look over – mostly so that I can admire the beautiful tech. It's truly a masterpiece. To make a baku that can fly as smoothly as this eagle, each component is feather-light, dusted with solar nanoparticles that draw power from the sunlight.

>>Pfft, he's nowhere near as cool as I am.

Whatever, Jinx. Can you fly?

>>I could if I wanted to. If you built me some wings.

You'd be a Pegasus cat then.

'Okay, I think he's ready to be leashed up,' I say. I pull the glasses down off my nose and rub my eyes, the familiar prickle of dryness entering my awareness now the focus is gone.

Tobias leashes Aero and it takes only a few seconds before he is fully booted up. He runs a diagnostic check. 'Well, holy crap. You did it. Diagnostics say that he's back up to full functionality.'

I shrug, trying to control the giant smile that wants to plaster itself on my face. Instead, I concentrate on stretching out my fingers, which are stiff from gripping the soldering iron so tightly. 'It wasn't too hard.'

My eyes flick up and catch his – and to my surprise, the expression on his face is one of pure and simple admiration. 'You're just full of surprises.'

He seems genuine, and it's the first time that I realize my skills might end up being more valuable than I thought. I'm touched.

'Good job, teammate.'

'You're welcome.' In my awkwardness, I put out my hand. Inwardly, I'm cringing.

Jinx echoes my thoughts. >>A handshake? That's really what you're going for in this situation?

Shh, I hiss. It's too late for me to back out now. Thankfully, Tobias takes it in his stride. He clasps my hand.

I don't know if he feels it too. A spark. A moment where electricity leaps from my hand to his, where all the neurons in my palm seem to light up. It takes my breath away. It feels like our hands are clasped for a lifetime.

And then the moment is over. His hand slips from mine. 'I'll see you around then, Lacey,' he says.

I swear there is a tiny smile playing on his lips.

Whatever it is, he leaves the room, taking his newly fixed eagle with him. And I have to catch myself on the desk or else risk melting into a puddle on the floor.

CHAPTER NINETEEN

LECTURES, NOT CLASSES.

Professionals, not teachers.

Gathering, not homeroom.

And Baku Battles – not homework.

This is my first month at Profectus. Baku Battles seep into every aspect of my life, to the point that I wake up in the middle of the night, drenched in sweat, as I fend off razor-sharp eagle talons and shiny metallic tiger baku teeth. Jinx is never the one in the arena, it is always me. But then, Jinx isn't allowed in the arena anyway.

I spend every spare moment not in school with the team in the Profectus team practice grounds, running drills, watching videos of old battles and preparing strategies.

Mom's pretty worried about my late hours. This is exactly what she was afraid of – that I would first disappear into my hobby, then into the school, then into a job – and then maybe for good. But I'm doing this for the two of us. To get us a better life. If that means working harder now so that I can relax later, then so be it.

Plus, I'm sure things will die down once the first battles are over.

And I've promised to see Zora this weekend to stream the latest season of our favourite sci-fi TV series, OUTERLANDS, which is launching Saturday at eight p.m. – prime time. She's been pretty understanding that I had to concentrate during that first month of school, even though I can't fill her in on exactly *why* I've been so busy.

But before I can think about the weekend there's the first battle to get through. Ashley and Jupiter are going to be up first. According to Tobias, the first battles are always for low level students and bakus. It's a chance for teams to test their mettle before the bigger events and to save their strongest players until later in the competition.

'Any insider tips?' asks Jake, seeking me out by my locker. He's running the school's gambling ring with aplomb, reworking old code so that the betting app makes suggestions based on heart rate spikes and pupil dilation. He calls it 'tapping into instinct'.

I call it a load of crap. Which it is, but it doesn't stop the entire student body (and most of the teachers) from downloading and using it.

'No – and even if I did, you know I couldn't tell you!'

'Fair enough. Have to ask these things! Good luck, little Lacey.'

'Thanks, Jake.'

The atmosphere for the first official battle is tense, and the entire school comes out to watch. My heart goes out to

Ashley. She has to last thirty minutes to guarantee a share of the full one hundred points. If Jupiter goes down, we'll have until the following morning to repair any damage back up to minimum 90% functionality.

'Ready, Ashley?' asks Mr Baird. As the companioneering teacher, he runs the battles.

She nods, her pale face tinged grey. She follows Mr Baird down into the competitors' preparation room, where she'll be loaded into one of the lifts to be brought up into the arena.

'She's going to get murdered,' mutters Kai, as we file into the team box to watch. Front row seats to the action.

'Come on now,' says Tobias, but his expression is dark too.

'You know she's too soft about that baku of hers.'

'Well, that's why we're sending her in first. She'll have to toughen up. And you know she's the best electronical engineer in the second year, so we had to have her on our team.'

'At least she's up against other level 3 bakus,' says River.

'I'm not so sure about that.'

All the eyes of the team flick to me. Because while Tobias, Kai and River have been focused on the strategies laid out on the backs of their bakus, I've been watching the other teams: in particular, Gemma's team. And Gemma's second year is walking into the team box.

'Noooo,' says Kai, as the reality sinks in.

It's *Carter* and his level 4 boar who have been entered into the arena in the first round.

Jinx arches his back and hisses. I know exactly how he feels.

144

'I thought you said first years *couldn't* fight in the battles,' I say to Tobias.

'They can't,' he says. 'Well, they can't unless one of the other team members volunteers to step down, which basically never happens . . .'

'Or they were forced to back down,' I say, raising one of my eyebrows.

'Or that,' Tobias concedes.

I feel my throat tighten at the thought of Jupiter going up against Hunter. Carter's not exactly the type of guy to go easy in competition. I know that all too well.

River stares at me with wide eyes, then clasps me on the shoulder. 'I'm glad we've got you on our team instead. I would *not* have stepped down.'

'Instead?' I ask, frowning. River shrugs, and before I can question him, a fanfare of music begins.

'She really is going to get murdered,' mutters Kai.

Tobias doesn't respond, but a sheen of sweat on his brow speaks volumes.

I don't have any more time to process. After the music, the competitors are lifted up into the arena. Swept up in the action, I cry out, 'Go Ashley! Go Jupiter!'

She turns to the team box and gives us a thumbs up. But even from here, I can see that she's shaking, her knees unsteady, her feet shuffling on the silver pads. Carter, by contrast, looks way too confident. Having a baku that's a full level higher than the others on the playing field will do that.

'You just have to last thirty minutes,' I mutter to Ashley, even though I know she can't hear me. But I bet thirty minutes feels like a lifetime in that arena.

And the battle begins.

It's a fast-paced, frenzied start. Like Ashley, Team Dorian's player – a second year called Wayne, with a bulldog baku – is also on the defensive, trying to protect as much of his baku's functionality as possible to last out the thirty minutes.

Others, like Carter from Team Gemma, go in hardcore, attempting to inflict as much damage as possible on the other opponents to try and make them as difficult to repair as possible. Those silver tusks look extra dangerous in that arena, as if he had sharpened them specifically for the purpose of inflicting maximum damage and pain. Jupiter, by contrast, looks so small, so domestic and tame, in the arena.

Tobias switches for a more aggressive strategy as the battlefield narrows. He pushes Ashley to in turn push her baku to the very limit, not allowing her to let up until the thirty minutes are up and there is only one other baku left.

Carter's.

I clutch Jinx's little paws, even as he attempts to crawl out from beneath my fierce grip.

>>She's a goner.

But we'll fix her.

>>You think that's a good idea?

Why wouldn't it be?

Jinx says something but I don't hear it – my eyes are transfixed by the sight of Hunter rocketing towards Jupiter at lightning speed. Ashley just isn't quick enough. The two bakus connect and the crunching sound is excruciating. Jupiter is thrown almost the full length of the arena, smashing into the curved wall underneath us, ricocheting around the outside wall like a pinball. Carter pumps his fist, triumphant.

'Giving up, Ashley? Your poor doggie is almost out,' he says, his tone full of swagger. He's right – Jupiter's stats are now at 15%. She could forfeit now. 'Go on, put her out of her misery.'

Ashley stares from Hunter to Jupiter. Her baku is attempting to stand up even though one of her legs is twisted so it's pointing backwards, and part of her wiring is trailing on the floor. Even though everyone knows that she feels no pain, has no awareness, it is gut-wrenching to watch. Maybe it's Ashley's face that makes it worse. She's even paler than she was before – I didn't think that was possible – her face ashen, with a sickly sheen from sweat, worry and adrenaline. She looks as if she wants to forfeit the battle. Her eyes flick to Tobias in the team box, who is speaking furiously to Aero. The eagle is presumably transmitting the message to Ashley, for only her to hear. And I can see in Tobias's eyes that he wants her to continue. There's only a few minutes left on the clock. If Ashley can hold out then she will have won us a share of the remaining points.

I bite my nails, chewing down the quick. I can't believe Tobias is making her continue – he should pull her now and give us a better chance of fixing her for tomorrow morning. I try to catch his eye, but his focus is laser-like on Ashley.

Ashley closes her eyes for a beat, and when she opens them again, she is filled with determination. 'You can do this,' I whisper to her. My fists are balled into tight fists at my side, as I will her every ounce of luck I can spare.

Carter rolls his eyes. 'Seriously? Come on, Hunter, let's finish this baku off.'

The roar in the room rises to a frenzied level, students shouting and jeering both competitors equally. There's dismay that Ashley is continuing, and a loud chorus of people telling her to give up.

Hunter stalks around the circle, surprisingly graceful for a machine that looks like a boar. My mind drifts off as I imagine what sort of person would voluntarily choose a baku shaped like that, and I almost miss the key moment when he goes in for the kill.

Because when it happens, it's rapid and brutal. Hunter still has full freedom of movement, his head swaying with the weight of his tusks, his legs nimble, whereas every command Ashley sends to Jupiter takes a few seconds too long to reach him – a vital receiver must be damaged, and so she can't respond quick enough. When the blow comes, it ravishes Jupiter. The boar's tusks rip through the already exposed electrics of the dog baku's central core, ripping through the 'brain', which – just like in Jinx's schematics – is located in her stomach.

'Good luck fixing *this* piece of junk,' Carter shouts. And, as if to make his point even stronger, Hunter shakes his head and – with a second to spare – sends the two halves of the robotic spaniel spinning across the arena and colliding with opposite sides of the wall.

Down in her circle, Ashley cries out. I feel every ounce of her pain. The thought of something like that happening to Jinx . . .

I take him up in my arms and squeeze him against my chest. He's not a robot to me. He's my companion.

The whistle sounds, signalling the end of the battle. Mr Baird stands up in the centre of the arena. 'The winner of the first round of Baku Battles is Carter and his baku, Hunter. Gemma's team are awarded one hundred points.'

He turns to the team box. 'Other teams, you have until the first assembly bell tomorrow to attempt to fix your eliminated bakus, in order to split the winning round total of one hundred points with Team Gemma. If the baku isn't at least 90% functional, however, your loss this round will be confirmed.' Even he sounds dubious at the prospect of any of the bakus rising to fight again.

Ashley's face looks distraught, clutching the remains of Jupiter.

Tobias looks sick, seeing his strategy fail and the points slip away.

It's not the end yet. If we can fix Ashley's baku, we can get the team back on track. But even with Profectus's state-of-the-art facilities, I know there's one place that will give us a better shot – and we can work there all through the night.

I just have to convince the team to trust me.

CHAPTER TWENTY

'THIS IS PERFECT,' SAYS KAI, AND I SMILE. I wonder if he's finally warming to me – even though I have no idea what I did to get on his bad side to begin with. But then he sneers at the entrance to my building. 'No one is going to spy on us in this crappy place. People actually *live* here?'

'I do,' I say through gritted teeth. I bristle. It's not that bad. It might be a bit boring and functional – an uninspired condo block of concrete and tinted glass, but it's not dirty or falling down.

'Kai, that's enough,' says Tobias.

'What?' He shrugs. 'I was trying to say it's a good thing for our team. You can bet Team Gemma aren't working somewhere so . . .'

The elevator doors ping, and he doesn't finish his sentence.

Ashley shivers. Since Jupiter's battle, she's seemed like a shell of her former, bubbly self.

Watching the four of them step into the elevator to the

basement, I can't believe I've brought them here. To my sanctuary. My companioneering haven.

Mom is delighted I'm bringing back friends from school. I haven't the heart to tell her that this isn't exactly the start of a busy social life for me.

It's an emergency.

Jupiter is in pieces. Ashley carries the remains in her arms, her cheeks damp with tears. The absolute annihilation she experienced in her Baku Battle would have been enough to scar me for life – I have no idea how she's even standing upright.

And what makes it even worse is that Carter is the cause. He and that awful boar of his, that snuffling, snarling beast. I've never wanted a baku to be put in its place before, but I'd like to see that thing put down. I am willing to do anything to make sure that *Carter* isn't a reason that his team ends up on top. He hasn't won yet.

>>Yeah right, as if it isn't the physiological changes in your body I witness when in close proximity to Tobias Washington that aren't the real reason you keep allowing him to use your skills — and your private lab.

I cringe. Jinx knows too much for his own good. And he seems to be getting smarter. Just last night, I was working on my French homework when I started hearing his voice in my head, translating for me. I had to tell him to stop – if the Academy found out, I'd be expelled for cheating for sure. Bakus aren't supposed to do anything like that unless

151

specifically commanded. I add it to the list of things I need to check in Jinx's code – if my other work ever lets up and I have a spare moment to squeeze it in.

I worry every day about slipping up and revealing that Jinx is no ordinary baku. But so far, the team haven't seemed to notice that Jinx is any different. And that's how I want it to stay.

With five people and five bakus crammed into the tiny storage locker, space is tight. River leaps up on to the desk with his oversized frog baku mimicking him by sitting with his knees up. He's like a contortionist, able to squeeze himself into the most unlikely places – as if he's more comfortable being uncomfortable. I don't know what that says about him.

Tobias leads Ashley in, and sits her down on my chair.

'So, what are we doing here?' Kai asks, his hands on his hips. Oka, his husky baku, paces underfoot. Kai tries to take up the biggest amount of space in the room, his chest puffed out like a frigatebird from the Galapagos.

'We need a share of the points if we're going to have any chance of winning the Baku Battles,' says Tobias. 'And that means, we have to fix Jupiter. I think Lacey here can do it.'

'Uh, have you seen that baku? It's scrap metal!' cries Kai, picking up a piece of Jupiter that has dropped out of Ashley's arms and on to the floor, wielding it as a prime example of what he means. 'Not even the best Moncha companioneer could fix this pile of garbage. Look, Tobias, my man, we shouldn't be worrying about how to fix this,' he gestures to the mess in Ashley's arms, and she whimpers, 'but planning our next round attack strategy. Like how that freaky dude,' he points at River, 'and I are going to stand a chance in the next round. Especially as Gemma is going to have *three* bakus to our two, so we'll still have that boar to contend with. That is *not* the kind of baku you expect a first year to have.'

That's right. I'd forgotten that since Carter survived this round of Baku Battles, that means Gemma's team will have an additional advantage next time around. No wonder Tobias is desperate. I can see how the first win for Gemma could snowball until catching her up becomes an impossibility.

'You and I should go in there together,' says Kai to Tobias. 'It could be a good strategy.' His husky growls in hungry anticipation. 'Oka will eat up that pig in one bite. Everyone else will be entering their next lowest level baku. We can knock them out, then send in the frog-man to take on the last level. With any luck, Oka and Aero will survive all the way to the end. Then ...' He flares out his hand like he's dropping a bomb. 'BOOM. Winners.'

'Hell yeah!' echoes River.

Tobias looks as if he's about to reply, when a small voice makes everyone shut up.

'You might be able to fix her?' Ashley looks up at me, her blue eyes – made even paler by the sheen of tears – boring into mine. 'Is that why we're here?' She stares around at all the mechanical paraphernalia on my walls, the machinery tucked away into corners, the broken bits of other bakus that I've found stuffed into boxes.

I shrug, not wanting to promise too much, but also itching to have a go.

Tobias answers for me. 'Yes. That's why we're all here. Lacey is one of the most accomplished companioneers I've ever met – she was the one who brought Aero back from the brink. It wasn't me.' Bright spots of colour appear on the tops of his cheeks – it's obviously something that is a struggle for him to admit. 'If anyone can do this, Lacey can.'

Kai stares at me, confusion warring on his face. 'Whatever,' he mutters. He folds his arms across his chest, then leans against the mesh of the locker, standing back. I forget about him, letting him and his doubt fade into the background. My focus is on Jupiter.

'Let's lay her out on the floor,' I say. Ashley gently places the main part of the baku's body on the ground, then we position what's left of her pieces around in the rough position that they should be. There are two immediate problems: one that she is split in half, and the other is that her front right leg is totally mangled. 'This can't be repaired,' I say, matter-of-factly, pointing at the leg.

'See?' says Kai, as Tobias groans and Ashley lets out a whimper. Only River is still looking at me.

'You don't seem to be fazed by that,' he says.

'Well, no,' I reply. That shuts the others up. 'We can print another one pretty easily.'

'From where?' asks Kai.

'From where River is.' Everyone's heads turn to River who just so happens to be perched next to my 3D printer.

'Oh, that's awesome that you have one of these,' says Tobias. 'They're super limited access at school. Where did you get this?'

I think about how I would even begin to describe Paul and the underground network of tinkers that collect, swap and bargain for exactly this sort of thing – and then I give up. 'Oh, you know. I came across it in a junkyard and then I've been slowly repairing it over the years.'

'And where do you get the material to feed into the machine? That gets expensive,' says Kai, still sceptical.

'That's the easy part,' I say. 'Look next to you.' There's a big drum next to him, and he lifts off the top (I can see that I've piqued his curiosity, no matter how aloof he is trying to appear). Inside are rolls of filament – from different plastics like PVA and nylon, to more sophisticated and fiddly metal spools – plus all the scrap bits of baku that I've found over the past few months, including the parts I found in the arena. 'I can make my own filament using the scrap material if I need to make a more exact match to Ashley's baku.'

'Wow, this is so cool!' says River.

'I don't have an oven here hot enough to melt it down,' I continue. 'But my friend Paul does. We'll just figure out how much we need, then I'll go get the material ready while you guys program the printer.'

'You're insane,' says River, a huge grin on his face.

'Thanks, I think?' I say, returning the smile.

Ashley, who has been silent throughout this whole conversation, suddenly throws her arms around me and plants a big kiss on my cheek. That I was *not* expecting. 'Thank you, thank you, thank you!' she says, over and over.

'Just wait a bit,' I say. 'I haven't done anything yet.' Then, I frown, and Jinx – reading my thoughts as always – projects the time on to the wall in front of us. It's going to be an all-nighter if we're going to have any chance of getting this done on time.

'Tell me what you need us to do,' says Tobias. 'Everyone on the team is yours for the night. The *whole* night – right, guys?' He glares at the rest of his team members, and they all nod – even Kai – and then River claps his hands together and fists pumps the air. 'All right!' he exclaims. 'I love an underdog story. Or a *broken* dog story, in this case.'

His enthusiasm makes me laugh. I think I like the guy. 'Okay,' I say, uncomfortable with my new leadership position but also knowing it has to be all hands on deck if we have a robot's chance in hell at getting this done on time. 'First things first. No one's getting hurt in my locker.' I take my safety glasses out of my pocket and slip them on, then I point the others to where I keep my spares – along with gloves, aprons and any other safety paraphernalia we might end up needing. 'I'm going to get the metal for this leg melted and spun out, then we can print it. Tobias and Kai – do you think you can handle the basic resoldering of the wires on her motherboard? I can leave the schematic . . .'

'I've got a basic level 3 spaniel schematic,' Kai says, rolling his eyes but coming forward to kneel down by the broken machine – at least he's showing *some* willingness to work on this with me. 'But some of these wires are totally shredded and unusable.' He lifts up a handful of mangled red and yellow wire, splintered and fried at the ends. He's right – they won't work at all. Luckily, I have just the thing. I spin around, opening and closing drawers in the giant shelving unit behind me. I've been meaning to do a proper categorization of everything, but fixing Jinx took up so much of my summer that I totally forgot.

'Aha – here we go.' I pull out a roll of brand new wiring. There'd been an online sale and I'd bought a whole bunch in one go. You can never have too much wire. I toss it down on to the floor. 'There should be whatever tools you need, including strippers, solder, the soldering iron, and whatever else over by the workbench. River, do you know how to use a hammer?'

'Do I!' He bounces up and down on the desk, and I'm worried he's going to bash his head on the shelves above him.

'I'll take that as a yes. Can you examine all of Jupiter's casings and bash out any dents – or if anything is too damaged, bring it to me so that I can print out new ones?'

'You got it, boss lady.'

'Right. Okay, I'll go and get this . . .'

'And what about me? I can help too.' Ashley jumps up to her feet. 'I don't have much experience with companioneering but I can check the electrics once her wiring is fixed.'

'Perfect. You can hook up to the monitor on my desk when Tobias and Kai are done. In the meantime . . .' I don't know how to ask without sounding like a totally crappy person, but thankfully Ashley is eminently sensible – and senses what I'm going to ask without me needing to spell it out.

'Coffee. Snacks. I'm on it. How does everyone take it?'

As I give her my order for my coffee of preference (black – no sugar or milk, nice and simple), I whisper to her: 'You are a lifesaver.'

She shakes her head and grips me by my shoulders. 'No, Lacey. You are.'

CHAPTER TWENTY-ONE

W HEN I'M OUT OF EARSHOT OF MY locker and striding down towards Paul's, I finally feel like I'm able to catch my breath. The lights come on one at a time as I pass underneath the motion sensors. I wish Zora could be here. I'm annoyed with myself that I haven't found the time to see her recently.

Then I realize something else is different. *I'm* the one setting off the motion sensors. That means I'm walking in front. I haven't walked in front of Jinx ... since I first fixed his ability to walk. He's always racing ahead of me – totally *not* normal baku behaviour – but at the moment he's a few paces behind. If anyone were around to watch, they would find that pretty unusual too. Most of the time bakus walk directly at their owner's side.

Everything okay? I ask.

Jinx is silent. I sneak a look over my shoulder and see that his head is hanging down low, his pace languorous.

Jinx?

>>Is that what I'm like? Inside?

I frown. *What do you mean?*

Rather than replying with words, he projects a short video he took of Jupiter laid out on the floor of my locker, her wires and electronics all exposed and broken.

Well . . . yes. You know that. You've seen the inside of a baku before. Like Aero.

>>I know. It's just — if you put Jupiter back together, does that mean you created her?

No — I just repaired her. I'm not her creator. I'm . . . I'm more like her doctor. Ashley is her owner. And Moncha Corp is her creator. Moncha Corp created all the bakus. Even you.

>>Are you sure about that?

My heart quickens. *Why? Who do you think made you?*

Before Jinx can answer, Paul's voice pops up out of the darkness. 'Lacey, is that you?'

We'll continue this conversation later, I think to Jinx.

When I see Paul, I feel overcome with the urge to spill everything to him about what it's like at Profectus – about the Baku Battles and how they push the students and bakus to the very limit, how there's a chance for me to really make a name for myself, how all his help teaching me over the years, learning how to tinker with bakus, is finally going to pay off. But the looming Profectus NDA hangs over my head and I can't risk another black mark – or worse, getting expelled.

'Hey, Paul,' I say, instead.

'What can I do you for?' he asks.

'I was wondering if I could use your super melter? I have a part to print tonight ASAP.'

'A rush job, huh? Something for your new school?'

'Something like that.'

George swings from the rafters, before jumping down and grabbing the bucket of metal scraps from my arm. 'Thanks, George,' I say to the lemur baku.

There's a burst of laughter from where Tobias is working with his team. Paul raises an eyebrow. 'You got people in your locker?'

'Yeah, some people from school . . .'

'Well, look at you. Making friends and everything. Never thought I'd see the day.'

I stick my tongue out at him, but then fold my arms over my chest. 'They're not really friends. They're my teammates.'

'Hmm.'

'Anyway, I don't have time for friends. I have to focus on my studies and . . .'

'Lacey, my dear. You should *always* make time for your friends. When was the last time you saw Zora?'

'Um . . . I'm going to see her this weekend,' I say, but all of a sudden it doesn't feel enough. My list of excuses is a mile long but none of them are adequate. Sure, I've been busy – but I haven't thought about what she might be up to. And suddenly I know what I want to do. 'Will you let me know when this is ready?'

Paul nods, flicking switches to start up the oven. Supermelters, just like 3D printers, used to take forever to work, but now he's able to melt down the material for me in only a few minutes.

I instruct Jinx to call Zora. It takes her a few seconds to

pick up, and I feel anxious. But eventually her face appears on Jinx's chest. I smile, breathing a sigh of relief. 'Zora, is that you? Guess where I am?'

'Your storage locker?' Zora replies, but she doesn't make eye contact.

'Oookay, maybe that wasn't so hard to guess,' I say, trying to laugh it off and pretend that everything is normal. 'There's a whole group of people from Profectus here . . .'

Now Zora's eyes snap to mine. 'Wait up. You mean to tell me you let a bunch of kids from your school into your locker after only a month. It took me years of friendship before you would let me in?'

'Well . . . it was an emergency.'

'Yeah, okay.' Zora purses her lips. The last thing I wanted to do was annoy her, so I think of the one thing I know will always cheer her up.

'Anyway, I'm calling especially to ask you if you want to come around and take a look at a level 3 spaniel baku code? I bet you'd find it really interesting and you can help debug it for us before tomorrow . . . it will be like old times!'

'Um, I think I'm going to pass,' she says. 'I want to get an early night before school tomorrow. I have a *big* day.'

Now, it's my turn to frown. 'Wait, what's your big day?'

Zora rolls her eyes. 'Oh, so now you're interested? I've got to go . . .' Her face is illuminated on Jinx's chest, and I can see from her eyes that she isn't looking at me again, her gaze drifting up above the height of Linus's camera. I know I've lost her for the night. I can't blame her.

'See you Saturday?' I ask.

'Bye,' Zora says sharply, and when she hangs up I'm plunged into almost total darkness.

Paul gives his locker door a small shake. 'Your metal is all ready to go.'

'Thanks, Paul,' I say with a sigh. I look up at him. 'Is it normal for things to ... not be exactly what you expected them to be?'

He chuckles. 'Normal? Honey, that's just life.'

'Right.' Disappointment settles on my shoulders.

Jinx rubs up against my legs, and I reach down to pick him up.

>>Come on, he says. You've got a job to do.

I nod and give myself a small shake. *That's right.*

I'm part of a team now. They need me.

CHAPTER TWENTY-TWO

DESPITE THE FACT THAT I HAVEN'T SLEPT a wink, I arrive at school extra early. I don't want to miss a moment of what's about to happen.

I'm not the only one. It feels like the entire school has turned up to see if any of the teams will steal some of Gemma's team points. Carter is there with Hunter, sitting in the front row with the rest of his teammates – except for Gemma. He doesn't look at me as I walk past him to take my seat – I'm beneath his gaze, not worth even looking at – but I take in every inch of the smug grin on his face, because I want to compare it exactly to what it looks like when it gets wiped off.

Mr Baird is in the centre of the gymnasium floor, dressed in a lab coat that falls to his knees, next to Gemma. On a jumbotron screen at the far end of the gymnasium are the point totals. At the moment, Team Gemma are the only ones with anything on the board.

One by one, the other team captains shuffle in with their team's 'repaired' baku to be assessed. Mr Baird's owl baku flies forwards and connects to the repaired baku's leash. Then he projects their functionality. No one even gets close to 90%. I think Team Dorian actually made their baku *worse* off with their repairs.

The clock ticks past 8:15, 8:20, 8:25 ... only five minutes until the bell sounds and time is up.

'Looks like Ashley might not even show – what a coward,' says Carter, *just* loud enough for most of the school to hear and titter away. I've bitten my fingernails down to the nailbed, and I have to sit on my hands before I destroy them any more.

What if something's happened to Jupiter since we left them?

>>Only idiots could have broken what you fixed. I mean I wouldn't put it past them to be idiots but . . .

Jinx doesn't need to continue, because just then the doors open and Aero flies through. The baku takes my breath away every time. Almost as much as the guy who struts in behind, his head held high. I flick back to Carter, and see him shifting uncomfortably in his seat. His façade of bravado is wavering.

Tobias walks over and stands in front of Mr Baird.

Carter lets out an audible sigh of relief, and foolishly he stands up. I almost want to shout at him to sit down and stay with his team – and it seems like Gemma feels the same way. She's hissing something furiously at him, but he waves her off. I relax back into my seat. I want to watch this spectacle play out, because I know what's coming. 'Come to forfeit in person, Toby? No hard feelings right, my man?' Carter

165

walks forward as he talks, cutting Tobias off before he can reach the stage, sticking out his fist to bump him. I frown, wondering what the story is between them.

Tobias stops abruptly, looks Carter up and down, then dismisses the outstretched fist to go and stand next to Mr Baird. Internally, I cheer. Carter frowns, then tries to style it out. 'Whatever. Sore loser.' He turns to walk back to his team, just in time to see all their eyes open wide.

'We haven't lost yet, Carter,' says Ashley, who's just come through the doors. There are audible gasps as Jupiter trots up to her heel, looking *brand spanking new*. It's enough to make even my tired eyes bulge from my head. She didn't look this good when she left the locker – Ashley must have spent the rest of the morning polishing her to perfection.

The impact is immediate. The whole school explodes with the sound of students talking all at once, and even the teachers exchange glances and hushed whispers of amazement. Mr Baird's face is white with shock.

'What? How?' splutters Carter. 'That's not possible.'

'Mr Baird, I'd like to submit Jupiter for review,' says Tobias, his voice loud, clear and firm. 'We believe she is back to well above 90% capacity – maybe even *full* strength – and that we should be able to split the first battle points with Gemma's team.'

'Certainly – I'll run the diagnostic tests.' Mr Baird's voice tries to remain steady and impassive, but I can tell that he's impressed.

It's a tense few minutes as Mr Baird's baku leashes up to

Jupiter. Even that doesn't seem to be enough. The owl sends various commands to Jupiter – from asking her to walk, then trot, then run to making sure that she can perform advanced functions, such as 360° video capture, facial recognition and multi-way phone calls. Jupiter passes all of the tests with flying colours – and ends with a spectacular demonstration of running through a baku obstacle course, which is set up on the walls around the gym. Ashley is beaming from ear to ear, her pride naked on her face. She catches my eye at one point and gives me a small thumbs up. I grin back, and hoot loudly while clapping with all my might after Jupiter performs a final jump through a small hoop. What a star baku that is.

There's a huge cheer as Jupiter's percentage is displayed: 98%. 'Well, not *quite* 100, but it looks to me that everything is in order with your baku, Ashley. I don't know how your team did it, but you appear to have pulled off a miracle. I don't think I've ever seen a comeback quite like it.' He turns so that he is facing the school. 'After the first round of Baku Battles, the top two teams – Gemma and Tobias – split the round points, giving them fifty each. The next battle will take place the first week of November. Be ready, everyone. Now, get to class.'

As if timed to perfection, the bell rings, signalling the official start of the day. Jinx threads through the crowd in front of me, so I have no choice but to follow. As I approach, I catch the tail end of Mr Baird's conversation with Tobias. 'Maybe when all this is over, you can give us a masterclass of just how you did it, Tobias? I'm very intrigued how you managed to fix that baku. In all honesty, I'm not sure that I could have done it myself – not in a single night – and not with the resources you have access to.'

Tobias catches sight of me just over Mr Baird's shoulder, and – to the delight of the butterflies in my stomach – he winks at me. 'I might just have found a secret weapon, sir.' I feel like I might burst into flames on the spot – at any rate, I feel my face burning bright red. I duck my head so that my fringe falls over my face, hiding it. Then I think to myself: no. I don't need to hide. We just spent all night working together. This is an inside joke. I have nothing to be ashamed off. I raise my chin, shaking my fringe out of my eyes . . . and I wink back. Tobias flashes me a white-toothed grin, then turns back to Mr Baird. 'But you won't mind if I keep it to myself until the end of term?'

Mr Baird chuckles. 'Not at all.'

Behind them, I catch sight of Carter. He's staring at me intently, his boar's ears pricked forward – exactly in the direction of where Tobias and Mr Baird had been talking. I turn away immediately. Did he catch my wink to Tobias? Did he understand what it meant? Surely not. If I keep on walking, maybe nothing will have changed . . .

The team gathers around Ashley and Jupiter. Tobias looks visibly relieved, and it's nice to see a genuine smile on his face instead of the normal frown. Instantly he seems more relaxed. Happier.

'We should do something to celebrate, don't you think?' he says. 'How about BakuBeats tomorrow night?'

'Yes!' says Kai. 'I kicked your ass at that last year.'

'I'm in!' says River.

'Me too,' says Ashley.

My heart leaps with excitement. I've always wanted to go to BakuBeats. It's a new Moncha-owned attraction that's opened up – you bring your baku to a giant converted warehouse with dozens of soundproof, clear-plastic bubbles filled with different instruments. It's a blend of karaoke and pretending to be your own rock band while your baku helps you not to sound terrible, and bright lights sync along with the music. It sounds ace – and expensive – and the bubbles have been booked up for months so I never thought I'd get a chance to go.

I hesitate. 'My treat,' Tobias says, bumping me on the shoulder.

'I'll be there!' I say, with a relieved grin.

'Let's meet there at seven.'

'I'd better be getting to class,' says Ashley. 'Don't want to risk a detention.'

'Me too – I have been falling *way* behind in History class,' I say.

Tobias's serious face returns. 'Good plan. Let's all go. See you guys tomorrow.'

As I leave the gym, Jinx's paw lights up.

>>Got an incoming message from Tobias Washington. Want to read it now?

My throat instantly goes dry as I wonder what I've done wrong. *Um . . . yes!*

I stand outside the classroom door as I wait for the message to appear on Jinx's back. When it does, my jaw drops.

TOBIAS: Hey Lacey, meant to say – I have something for you to thank you for letting us use your place yesterday. Can you meet me at my house tomorrow before BakuBeats? I'll ping you the address.

My heartbeat hammering in my ears, I compose a quick reply.

LACEY: Yeah should work.

TOBIAS: Great, see you there at five?

LACEY: Sure

The address comes through. I can't believe it. Tobias lives on Companioneers Crescent. I'm about to see what my dream life looks like, up close and personal.

>>And maybe get up close and personal with a certain resident?

'Jinx!' I say out loud, a blush rising in my cheeks. I grimace at him. I forgot he's constantly monitoring me – not just my heart rate but the quickness of my breathing, my internal body temperature – so he can see *exactly* what looking at Tobias does to me.

>>I've composed a message to Zora Layeni to send when we are outside the restricted communication zone. Want to read it?

I frown. *A message to Zora . . . why?*

But then I gasp. I don't need him to answer that question. It's just hit me. Tomorrow is Saturday: the day I was supposed to be hanging out with Zora. I'm going to have to disappoint her all over again.

I am officially the worst friend in the world.

CHAPTER TWENTY-THREE

T HANKFULLY, AFTER FINDING OUT THAT
the reason I was ditching out on our *Outerlands*
streaming session was because of an invite from
Tobias Washington, Zora is excited for me, not mad. She
definitely approves of Tobias, especially after I explained to
her about the mix-up on the bridge. It's much easier to hold
a grudge against Carter than Tobias (whose outrageous good
looks probably helped to change Zora's mind).

'You do know this is a date, right?' she says. She's lying
on her stomach on my bed, her legs kicked up in the air,
her chin propped up in her hands. Linus plays us a 'Getting
Ready' dance mix – his speakers surprisingly loud and clear
for such a little baku.

'It's not a date, it's a team outing.' I run a brush through my
unruly dark hair, trying to shape it into something remotely
resembling a cool hairstyle. This is where having a beetle
baku might have come in handy – I could've downloaded a
tutorial from the internet and run a program for the beetle
to do my hair for me. Jinx is too big for that – but besides,

he wouldn't deign to do something as mundane as my hair in the first place.

'But you're going to his house first.'

'Well, yes. But that's because he wants to give me something.'

Zora waggles her eyebrows and I throw my hairbrush at her.

'Honestly, he doesn't have any interest in me that way.'

'And how do you know that?'

I shrug. I pull down a denim shirt from a hanger inside my closet and throw it on over a white vest.

'A super cool level 3 baku, a place at the fancy Academy, a date with a hot guy, an evening at BakuBeats . . . you really are living the dream, aren't you, Lace?' Her voice sounds wistful, but she smiles at me. 'I'm really happy for you.'

I shuffle awkwardly in my socks. It all feels too good to be true.

'Oh, you might not want this any more but I've been meaning to give it back to you . . . we just haven't seen each other.' Zora puts my old beetle baku on the desk in my room. I'd forgotten that I'd given it to her. 'I just added a couple of custom apps and tweaked some things as a thank you for Linus. No big deal. Maybe you can sell it to earn some extra cash?'

'Thanks,' I say.

'Don't wear that shirt,' Zora says. 'Wear the other one – with the little cats on it. And roll up the sleeves. Much more on brand.' Then she grins. 'Don't worry. You're going to be great.'

I take her advice, switching my shirts and taking one last look in the mirror, before letting out a deep breath. 'I hope so.'

* * *

I can't believe I'm about to visit the home of Tobias Washington.

Just stepping on to Companioneers Crescent is as incredible as I imagined it. As someone who's grown up living the vertical condo life, seeing the oversized mansions lined up in a row makes me feel overawed.

This is a part of Toronto that hasn't changed in fifty years – whereas most of the city has grown *up*, a concrete and glass jungle maze of high rise condominiums and office blocks – this is a preserved pocket of old-fashioned suburbia – big detached homes, with grand design features like Romanesque columns and perfectly manicured hedges, with driverless cars parked on paved, circular, heated driveways. There are even real garages here, like the ones from my tech history books. I'm envious.

Tobias's home is one of the biggest on the block. The Moncha logo is embossed above the front door, but it's slightly modified – with a cluster of stars in the corner. I stare at it as I wait for the entry camera to approve Jinx for entry.

The door clicks open, and Tobias is standing in the hallway. My breath catches, and my feet feel frozen on the step.

I must have faltered for a second longer than is normal,

because a small frown creeps on to Tobias's face. 'Are you coming in?'

Jinx gives me a tiny electric shock that makes me jump – and gets me moving.

Yet stepping into the house itself does nothing to alleviate my anxiety. It's the grandest home I've ever been in, palatial in size compared to my condo. In fact, I'm pretty sure our 'open plan' kitchen and living room would fit inside their entrance hall. Or when it's this big, does it get called an atrium, like at the Academy?

There's a wide staircase that spirals up to the second floor and a blown-glass chandelier hangs down from the ceiling. I can barely fathom living in a home with a second floor and I'm dying with curiosity to see what the upstairs is like, but Tobias leads me past that and into their kitchen. The hallway is wallpapered with photographs and videos of Tobias's family: his parents, his brother, Nathan, and him. I can't help myself – I stop in front of one of the videos. I see a different Tobias to the one that I've come to know. He's standing in the background of the shot, while his brother – equally handsome, if not slightly *more* so in a conventional sense, takes centre-stage shooting hoops. Yet there's something harder about his brother, a glint in his eye, an air of arrogance that comes across even in the way he celebrates with an exaggerated fist pump, and throws the ball back to his brother just a little *too* hard.

Tobias comes up and stands next to me, staring at the video. 'You know how some families get kind of crazy about sports? They push their kids to train harder, yell at coaches to make sure they get a spot on the first team, line up scouts and judge performance by the number of trophies on the shelf? Well, that's my family, but with science. Oh, and basketball.'

'Woah,' I say.

'We actually have an inter-family leaderboard, if you can believe it,' he says, with a grin that seems half-grimace.

'What's that like?'

He shrugs. 'Just means I have to work extra hard to take over the number one spot.'

I can't imagine what it must be like to grow up with that kind of family pressure. I've only ever placed it on myself – I know that Mom would never force me to achieve, or reach any kind of goals that weren't my own.

'Come on, I'd better give this thing to you and then we can get going to BakuBeats.'

I follow Tobias through to the kitchen, which almost takes my breath away. The counters are a polished white granite, which sparkles as it catches the light streaming in from the floor-to-ceiling bifold doors that lead to the enormous backyard. It would be my mom's dream come true to have a kitchen like this.

'Here you go,' he says. On the counter is a circle of silver. It looks like a bracelet of some sort.

I don't want to sound ungrateful, especially as he's looking at me so expectantly. I pick it up and hold it delicately between my fingers. 'It's beautiful but ... uh ... what is it?' I ask.

Tobias laughs. 'It's a boost collar. Top of the line, straight from Moncha Corp. Your baku wears it around its neck and it enhances some of its functions – like speed and accuracy on the battlefield. I was going to give it to Ashley if she won the battle, but seeing as you were the one responsible for fixing up Jupiter . . . it's for you.'

'Wow, this is . . . amazing.'

'Put it on your baku!'

For a second, I falter. I don't know how Jinx will respond to having an . . . accessory.

Jinx, do you want to wear this? I ask.

He saunters over to it and sniffs. >>I guess.

If you hate it, we can take it off . . . but not until we get home.

I hook the collar around his neck. The lights on the edge of his fur light up, and he buzzes twice.

>>I like it! he says, and he sounds genuinely pleased.

I look up at Tobias and beam.

'He says he likes it.' Immediately I realize my mistake.

Tobias falters for a second, then laughs. 'You seem to really understand each other!'

I laugh too, slightly overloud, as if I'd made a really funny joke instead of almost letting slip about Jinx's *unusual* communication style.

'Hang on, let me get my coat and then we can get the car down to BakuBeats,' he says, shaking his head at me and chuckling.

I'm sad to leave his amazing house, but it makes me all the more determined to move Mom and me into one of our own one day. The dream is so close, I can almost taste it.

We settle into the self-driving car, which Tobias programs to take us to BakuBeats. The interior is the softest leather I've ever sat on, and I barely feel a thing as the engine starts.

There's even a special basket in front for bakus to sit in, and Jinx immediately curls up inside.

>>Oh this is nice. Very nice.

What is it? I ask.

>>They've made this basket out of microfibres that if I just . . . he wriggles around in the basket. He's *rubbing* himself up against it, as if it's giving him pleasure.

>>Ah, That's it. I'll sparkle like new by the time I get out of this.

I grin. Moncha knows how to keep the bakus happy even while travelling in a moving vehicle.

Our destination is not far from Moncha HQ. 'I can't wait to visit the headquarters for the final battle!' I say.

He grins. 'You'll love it. Although I'm pretty excited to be the team captain this year.'

'What do you mean?'

'Well, the captains get a tour of the headquarters before the battle – probably to give us added incentive by reminding us of the summer internship – as if we needed reminding!'

'So teammates don't get to come on the tour?'

''fraid not. Captains only. But you'll get your chance – I have no doubt you'll be a team captain one day.'

His praise makes me blush.

There's something else I've been dying to ask him. I speak

the words before I lose my nerve. 'So . . . what's the deal with you and Carter?' I ask.

He cocks an eyebrow. 'I could ask you the same thing.'

'You first.' I grin.

Tobias flashes me a quick smile, before turning serious. 'Carter Smith . . .' he gestures over to the Moncha logo embossed into the leather – the same symbol I saw on their front door – with the added stars. 'My father is one of the top coders in Eric Smith's personal department at Moncha: Team Happiness is what they call themselves. Dad said specifically for me to "take Carter Smith under your wing, son".' Tobias deepens his voice and puffs out his chest, emulating his father. Then he deflates, and catches my eye. His eyes search my face, and he looks almost – guilty. 'It's a favour to his boss or something. I mean, I've known Carter for years – he's always been annoying as hell but I used to pity him. I wouldn't want Eric Smith as a father. But I should tell you something. And before I say this – you have to know, I'm really glad about the way things have worked out.'

'What do you mean?'

'Well . . . you weren't supposed to be on my team.'

I frown. 'Huh?'

'I didn't pick you. Gemma did. We think something was switched in the announcements. I mean . . . she made a good choice. Your stats were off the charts – your grades from your old school were top notch – you clearly know your way around a lab, your connection with your baku is super strong. Like, *really* strong. But my father had made it clear to me that having Carter on my team was the only option. Kai also thought it was a done deal – he thought we'd be guaranteed winners because we'd have another high level baku on the team. That's why he was a bit ... hard on you in the beginning.'

'A bit?'

Tobias barks a laugh. 'Well, okay, a lot. And, with your grades and your stats, you're a bit intimidating, you know?'

'Me?' Emotions swirl in my stomach. Just like my Profectus acceptance, getting on to Tobias's team is just another thing that was sort of ... a fluke.

>>Who cares if it was a fluke, as long as it happened?

Not helpful. I frown at Jinx.

'Hey, I'm glad you're on my team now.' His hand brushes the bare skin on my arm, where I've rolled my shirt sleeves up. Once again I feel the electricity of being with him, near him, but I'm sure he doesn't feel the same way about me.

We inhabit totally different worlds. He's seen the basement where I do my work – it's nothing compared to the opulence he's used to.

'So, what's *your* deal with Carter?' he asks.

I shrug. 'We've been academic rivals since sixth grade. I beat him in a couple of regional science competitions ...'

'Not a surprise.'

'And then I got a higher mark than him in some exams. He didn't like it. But I thought it was a bit of healthy competition ... until the Profectus thing.'

180

Now it's Tobias's turn to look sceptical. 'Feels like a bit more than academic competition to me.'

'Well, my dad might have something to do with it too.'

'Huh? What do you mean?'

I can't look at him any longer, so I turn my attention to Jinx, who is crawling out of the basket and leaning his paws against the door frame, so he can stare out of the window. 'My dad was one of Monica's original companioneers.'

'Wait – your dad was Albert Chu?'

I nod. 'Yeah.'

Tobias's jaw drops. 'Damn. I didn't know.'

'No one does. Heck, I barely knew.'

'But what . . .'

'What happened to him? I have no clue. My mom says he had a nervous breakdown and left us when I was five. It's something I try not to think about.' The car comes to a halt, and I breathe a sigh of relief that we've arrived and I won't have to talk about Dad any more. The door opens automatically. Jinx darts out while I'm still fumbling with my seatbelt. 'Wait – hey! Jinx!'

Jinx, what are you doing? I shout in my head.

'Lacey? What's going on?' I hear Tobias say, but my vision is tunnelled towards following where Jinx is going.

'I'll catch you up inside – just gotta do one thing!' I call out behind me, running off after Jinx.

I curse the stupid baku all the way down the street – convinced that he's even faster now that he has that collar on. I don't know this part of the city so well – but as I catch sight of his tail darting down an alleyway between two high rise buildings, my heart drops. I know that there are parts of the city where you're not supposed to wander around alone.

'Jinx, where are you going?' I shout out.

He doesn't answer. Instead, he shoots away, disappearing even further down the alley.

'What the hell!' I run after him, my feet slipping inside my shoes. I take the corner too sharply, my shoulder bashing up against the brick wall. The alleyway is stuffed with garbage bags, the walls covered in graffiti, but I just about catch sight of Jinx's metal tail disappearing around yet another corner.

'Stop right now!' I yell at him, even though I know he's not going to listen.

I follow him deeper into the city, into the labyrinth of high rise buildings. He finally seems to leave the tight alleyways, and I breathe a sigh of relief as I see him sitting, staring at a small patch of green space – an inner city park. I catch up with him, scooping him up into my arms.

Then I see what he was running towards. The park is filled with cats. Real ones. Crawling all over the benches, rolling around in the fallen leaves, scrapping over food. I've heard of these places, where some of the city's former pets have been turned loose – and now they congregate here, together. Jinx is transfixed. 'Come on, Jinx, let's go,' I say, keeping my voice gentle. As I slowly turn around to walk back, his head swivels, following the cats.

>>But what do they do all day? he asks.

'I suppose they just get to be real cats.'

>>Just real cats.

'That's right.'

>>And what do real cats do?

I shrug, attempting to trace back my steps through the narrow alleys. 'They eat. Hunt. Explore. Play. Sleep. Lots of sleep.'

>>It's quicker if you turn left here, he says. I follow his instructions, and they bring me back out to the main road.

>>Sleep, huh? What . . . all day?

I chuckle. 'Sometimes. Depends if they've had a big meal or not.'

>>Sounds . . .

I wait for him to finish, but he doesn't say any more. I hug him close.

>>We're here, he says.

Sure enough, I look up and we're outside the BakuBeats hall. 'Is everything okay? Are you going to run away again?'

>>I just had to see. But . . . no. I won't run away again.

'Okay then.' I gingerly set him down on the floor. Then I grin. 'Let's go move to some beats.'

'YOU MADE IT!' SAYS ASHLEY, AS I WALK up the stairs and into the giant converted warehouse that houses Moncha Corp's BakuBeats. Heavy bass thumps in my ears, and it takes my eyes some time to adjust to the brightly coloured flashing lights.

Yet I can't wipe the grin off my face. The reception area is on a mezzanine level high above the main BakuBeats floor. I gaze down at the myriad of soundproof bubbles, most of them filled with other teenage groups like ours. I spot some of my old classmates from St Agnes singing their hearts out in one of the pods. Even though I can't hear what they're saying, they look like they're having a blast, their arms wrapped around each other's shoulders, swaying in time to some music.

'Good call on us not walking in together,' says Tobias quietly to me – even though that wasn't why I'd bolted from the car. 'Would have looked a bit weird to our teammates.'

'Oh right, no problem,' I say.

He's rolled his shirt sleeves up now too, showing off his

tightly muscled forearms. He has a constellation of marks on his right arm, slightly darker than his naturally dark skin tone, almost like a tattoo. It takes a lot of self-control for me to not want to lean in to look closer.

'Tobias Washington.' He gives his name to the attendant with the retriever baku.

The baku lights up and the attendant's eyes seem to light up with it. 'My baku tells me that you're all students at Profectus?' We all nod. 'Well, because of that I can give you some extra perks and upgrade you to the premium bubble. It's the full package: unlimited song choices, whatever food you want, and you get to be in our best bubble: the suspended one.'

'Seriously?' Ashley squeaks. 'It's always been fully booked when I've been here before,' she says to me.

'I've never been here,' I reply.

'You're going to *love* it.'

The suspended bubble hangs in mid-air in the centre of the space – and from the promotional videos I've watched, it's normally reserved for visiting celebrities ... or, apparently, Profectus students. I look down through the clear plastic see-through floor of the bubble and see my old St Agnes classmates pointing at us and wondering who is being led up into there.

It's even better than we could have imagined. The bubble is divided into a 'stage' area, filled with instruments, and an 'audience' section, with oversized beanbag chairs and low-lying tables (which soon fill up with the pizza, nachos and drinks that we order). Ashley picks up an electric guitar and syncs it to Jupiter, and immediately the transparent plastic of the bubble transforms into a screen depicting a roaring crowd, as if she's a proper rock star performing a concert.

It's hilarious to watch Ashley, Kai, River and Tobias take it in turns to rock out on the big stage. River takes on a nineties rap song and nails every lyric. Since the others have been here before, they're quick to draw up a playlist of their favourite tunes.

'Come on, Lacey,' Tobias drops down on to a beanbag chair next to me. 'Aren't you going to pick a song?'

I grin. 'I'm happy just watching you guys! You're all awesome.'

'Oh no, that's not how it works.' He stands up and extends his hand out to me. Tentatively, I take it, and he pulls me up to my feet. He grabs a microphone from the ground and thrusts it into my hands. 'Your turn now!'

'But . . . I don't know what song . . .'

I don't get a moment to decide. Because just at that moment, the beat shifts, picking up into a song I know *all* too well. It's the theme tune to *Outerlands*, performed by my favourite boy band. I look over at Jinx, who has synced to the BakuBeats screen, and all of a sudden the bubble's screen shifts so it's almost as if we're *inside* the television programme, on board the alien ship that travels to different worlds.

It's like I'm playing a rock concert in space. And I could sing these lyrics in my sleep. I can't help myself. I get swept away, and it's not long before I'm dancing and singing alongside my teammates, having the time of my life.

We spend the next couple of hours belting our hearts out to our favourite songs, discovering each other's hidden talents along the way. It turns out River has a surprisingly sharp memory for lots of different rap lyrics, and Kai's voice can reach high octaves like that of an angel. I have no musical talent whatsoever, but with Jinx at my side I bash away at the drums with lots of enthusiasm and he translates my horrible syncopated playing into something that actually sounds halfway decent. The bakus light up in time with the music, and we dance until sweat drips from our foreheads and our pulses are racing and we're closer as a team than ever before.

After the musical interlude is over, we all collapse down on to the plush velvety cushions and order more pizza up to the bubble. I don't think I've thought about Profectus or my career once since being here. I always knew Profectus would help me achieve my goals but I had no idea it could be so FUN. It's . . . refreshing. It's like a dream state.

Jinx vibrates on my lap, a familiar hum of an incoming text. I look down at his back, reading the message as it appears.

ZORA: TELL ME EVERYTHING. I am so jealous right now. >:(

LACEY: OMG IT'S AMAZING. I don't want to be a companioneer any more, I want to be a rock star.

ZORA: Haha yeah right!

187

LACEY: OK, you got me! But it is awesome.

ZORA: Glad you're having an ace time. Text me
back when you're home.

All too soon, it's time for us to leave the Beats pod. When we get back out into the lobby, Tobias clears his throat gently. 'Okay, guys – this has been so much fun but Monday it's back to the hard work and the training sessions.'

Ashley rolls her eyes. 'This basically *was* as intense as a training session.'

'True. But now that we know what we're up against ... surely you want to be extra prepared?'

Ashley shivers – the memory of Jupiter's defeat still fresh in her mind. 'Okay, you're right.'

'Good. Normal place then?'

The others nod.

'Normal place?' I ask.

'We meet at an old hockey rink near my house I've commandeered as a makeshift arena.'

Jinx's tail swishes. There's another vibration from him, and I wonder if Zora has messaged. 'I'll send you the coordinates – but it's just behind my house.'

'I'll be there.'

Then, in a move that almost stops my heart completely, he grabs my hand. 'Today was really fun. I'm glad I got to share this with you. You seem to really get it.'

My palm doesn't stop tingling for the rest of the weekend.

CHAPTER TWENTY-FIVE

A T HOME ON SUNDAY, AFTER THE exhilaration of BakuBeats, I see things through different eyes. Mom is at the stove cooking. I notice that it's the exact same meal as last weekend – a big pot roast that we can eat the leftovers of throughout the week. Her old cookbooks are abandoned on the shelf above her, grease-and flour-stained. They used to fuel Mom's explosions of flavours, but now they lie dormant. She could have so much more. A huge kitchen. The money to buy whatever ingredients or appliances she needs. I could give that to her.

I'd planned on popping down to the locker to pick up some supplies, but the elevators are down for maintenance. 'Doesn't it bother you that the lifts are broken again? It's so annoying!'

Mom shrugs. 'They have to fix them sometime. At least it's on a Sunday and not during the week when I need to get to work. Petal informs me they should be finished very soon.'

I lift my eyes to watch Mom, pottering around the kitchen,

throwing salt into the pan with a chunk of beef. She stirs the pot with one hand, the other tracing the recipe with her fingers. I have memories of them trying out different recipes, her hands flour-covered or spice-dusted, the apartment scented with their success (or sometimes with the caramel-dark burn of their disasters). I try to cast my mind back to the last time I'd seen her cook something that wasn't on Petal's list of recommended eats.

Perfectly nutritious, calorie-controlled and generally tasty – celebrity-chef endorsed, to boot. There is nothing wrong with the recipes Petal provides. As I have to consistently remind myself, being fed at all is a privilege, having decent food to warm my belly and a roof over my head, and a baku by my side to keep me connected and never lonely. There are so many people in the world who aren't that lucky.

And I have a guaranteed job at Moncha HQ once I graduate from Profectus. But my problem – and it gnaws at me that I even consider this a problem – is that I'm so arrogant as to think I deserve it. I don't want a boring baku marketing role like my mom. I want a career that sets my soul on fire, that fans the flames of passion that smoulder deep in my belly – that I guard with my hardness and intellect. I want a place to unleash that which burns inside me.

And I know exactly where that is.

In the companioneering department of Moncha Corp.

I take a deep breath. 'Mom, can I ask you something about Dad?' I don't want to upset her, but I have to know more.

Mom's face drops.

'I didn't tell you but ... one of my teammates recognized Dad's name. They knew about him. And I don't know anything at all. Can you tell me what really happened?'

She sighs, and I cringe at the look of pain on her face. She never looks angry. Only sad, and I hate reminding her of that time. 'That's your father's story to tell. I wish I had the answers for you, Lacey. I don't know where he is, or I would tell you how to find him. But if you're asking me what I think ...'

I feel a sharp pang in my chest, a wound I'd long closed over ripping open. Every fibre of my being wishes I had known my dad. He would have been interested in what I was learning at Profectus. He would've known and understood what it meant to me. The ring on my finger proves that.

'Why did he leave Moncha Corp?'

I nod.

She sighs. 'I think he burned out. All I know is that one day he packed up and left – his dream job, us ... That's why I worry about you and this school. I don't want you to face that same pressure.'

I pause. 'There really was nothing else? Did he work with Eric Smith?'

'What makes you say that?' says Mom, sharply. There's a tiny flicker of doubt on Mom's face, but she smooths it out again. 'I don't know the story. Your dad didn't even give me a chance to ask. But I don't think badly of him – he gave me you! You remind me too much of him for that. But whatever you end up doing, I know we'll be okay.'

I grimace, despite myself, but immediately regret it as a stricken look appears on my mom's face. I know I need to drop the subject.

'Do you mind if I go and see Zora?'

Mom smiles, glad for the change of subject. 'Not at all. But be back for dinner at seven. It feels like an age since we've had dinner together.'

'Will do.'

Zora greets me at the door of her apartment and we hole up in her room. When we're firmly ensconced with the door shut, we both start to talk at once.

I start: 'I wish you'd been able to come to BakuBeats, you would have loved it.'

She starts: 'You never texted me back last night . . .'

We face off then – me with a big smile on my face, that drops – and her with a frown, that softens. Standing looking at her now, Linus swaying his thin, curly tail over her shoulder, her pint-sized body tense, I realize how much I've neglected her. We've only been at separate schools for a couple of months and it feels like a lifetime.

'I . . . I'm sorry,' I stammer out.

'Forget it,' she says. She places her hand on mine, and the familiar scent of coconut butter hits my nostrils. It's a tug of familiarity that brings me back down to earth.

'Why don't you tell me about St Agnes?'

Zora shrugs. 'Oh, it's boring. Same old, same old.' But still, she launches into tales of the drama in the cafeteria. Yet even as I listen to stories of the people that I used to know, I can sense my interest waning. I even side-eye Jinx, worry that he's going to give something away, but he sits docile at my feet. There's nothing like the Baku Battles back in my old school. No way for students to progress their skills outside the classroom. Heck, there's no way a student at St Agnes would want to stay for a second longer than they had to at that school.

I compare that to Profectus. To all the extra hours I've already put in with Team Tobias. How the teams work well into the night, devoting their spare time to the cause. And even the students who aren't on teams, they're working hard too. There's a sense of pride in industry, in achievement, and a genuine interest in what we're learning about that I had never sensed before. A community of learning. I'd always heard this was what university was like. But I was getting to experience it now.

I nod, smiling at the right intervals and exclaiming in appropriate places. But it's now clearer to me than ever. Profectus is the way for me to live the kind of life that I want, to give Mom the freedom to pursue her passions free from worry and stress.

And even though sitting in Zora's bedroom is comfortable ... normal, even, I'm itching for the weekend to be over.

Because all I know is ... I can't wait to get back to school.

CHAPTER TWENTY-SIX

AFTER DINNER, I HELP MOM WITH THE washing up, then head to my room. Jinx is curled up on my bed, right on top of the laundry-fresh clothes that I haven't put away. He lifts his head as I walk in, his eyes blinking lazily, as if he's just woken up from a dream. 'Everything okay, Jinx?' I ask. I try to gently coax him off the laundry, but he won't come, so I push him a little more forcefully. He gives me an unappreciative tail flick, but crawls further on to the bedclothes – at least just far enough for me to grab the laundry and start putting it away. 'Thanks,' I say, sarcasm dripping over my voice. But I still love him.

>>What would you do to find out more about your dad? Jinx asks.

'Anything,' I say, honestly. But Jinx knows better than anyone that I've exhausted all the avenues I can think of. He's seen my search history. There's nothing out there about him. He's been erased from the digital world.

'Why do you ask?'

>>No reason.

He moves so that his head rests against my neck. These are some of my favourite moments with Jinx. I rest my hand on his fur and he purrs softly, lulling me into a half-sleep.

>>You've had some messages through.

'Anything important?' I whisper. I've become used to Jinx's filtering of my messages, even though it's not something I've ever asked him to do and I haven't heard of anyone else's bakus doing it. But I like it. It's as if he knows when I want to stay focused so I'm not constantly interrupted.

>>There's a bunch here from Tobias Washington.

'What?' I shriek and sit up abruptly, Jinx tumbling on to the mattress beside me. 'What, do you mean Tobias Washington has been sending me messages? And you didn't tell me? What if it was something important? What if it was . . .'

Jinx yawns. >>Not important. Unless you consider 'Hey' and 'S'up' are important messages.

'I *do* consider that important!' I look at the timestamp on the messages. Almost two hours ago. Two whole hours have gone by, with Tobias thinking that I'm just ignoring him. I could kill Jinx.

>>There's a couple more.

'Jinx, you had better show me every single one of those messages right now or else you're going to the scrapyard where no one will have a chance to fix you.'

Jinx makes a series of beeping noises that I interpret as the baku equivalent of a scoff, but he projects all the messages on to the square of duvet in front of me. I read them so fast,

I feel like I'm a starving person who's been offered up a tasty meal. I don't even know what I'm looking for, so I force myself to stop, sit back, and read them more slowly.

'Hey.'

'S'up.'

'Just wondering if you had time tonight to go over some companioneering stuff? I want to know how you merged a rodent-link camera tail to your feline baku.'

Three unread messages, all from a couple of hours ago. He's going to think I've totally ignored him all evening. I don't know how to do this. Is there the possibility of anything more here? I painstakingly compose a message back, reworking it over in my head until I think it strikes the right tone.

Hey! Sorry, had a family dinner . . . no messages at the table and all that. I think there might be something wrong with my baku too, I wasn't getting any notifications.

>>There isn't anything wrong with me and you know it.

'Shut it, Jinx,' I say, still fuming that he hid these from me.

>>Well, look at that, says Jinx.

196

I look up. I hadn't even finished my message – I had planned on answering his question. But I can see a stream of dots that show that Tobias is in the middle of replying already. My heart seems to stop beating inside my chest.

'Jinx, did you send that before I even asked you to?'

>>What? I thought you were finished. Read fine to me.

'I wasn't finished! I hadn't even said if I was free or not . . .'

Then Tobias's reply pops up.

That's cool, no problem.

Now I reply to his question.

I can't do tonight – Mom will kill me if I leave *again*.
But I can talk you through it?

'Okay, Jinx – you can send that.'

>>You got it, boss.

Now is my turn to scoff. 'As if there's any way you'd let me be your boss.' Then I type something more to Tobias.

Do you have a strategy down yet for the battle?

He replies:

I might have something up my sleeve. We need to get through to the next round alive, and I'm worried what Carter might do now that we've really ticked him off.

Look forward to watching it! I reply. Then some words come up that I didn't write. P.S. I think you're really hot and can you please be my boyfriend?

I shriek and jump on the bed. 'JINX, DO NOT SEND THAT.'

Thankfully the words disappear without being sent and I collapse on to the mattress, my heart pounding in my chest. Jinx leaps up on to my stomach, his face looking down over mine.

>>Don't worry, it was just a joke!

For about a millisecond, I'm mad, but the anger bubbles over into laughter instead. I pull Jinx down towards my chest, and even though he squirms a little, he nestles into my neck and purrs.

He might be a pain in the butt, but I wouldn't change him for the world.

>>Lacey?

His voice sounds different than I'm used to. Smaller, somehow. Quieter.

Yes, Jinx?

>>Did you make me?

I take a deep breath. I knew this conversation was going to come up again. 'No ... Mocha Corp did.'

>>So I'm just the same as all the other bakus —
just an ordinary house cat model 2.0.

Now, I frown. *Well, no. You're not the same. There's
definitely something strange about you. You're unique. The way
that we communicate – like this – it's different. Your ability to
make your own decisions, outside of the commands I give you –
that's not like other bakus.*

>>Oh. So I'm not like other bakus.

*No. Not to me. Even mechanically you're different. You're –
so much better. But I haven't really looked into your code. It's
possible that this is all something someone wrote into you, and
if I was a better coder then I would be able to tell you what that
is. I don't speak that language very well.*

>>But you could look into it if you wanted to.
The person who created me — they might have left a
trace of themselves in my code.

*That would mean revealing that I didn't exactly come across
you in the 'traditional' way. I didn't buy you from the Moncha
Store. That's what everyone thinks. If I tell anyone . . . they
might take you away from me.*

A thought strikes me that's so painful, it's as if a searing
hot dagger has plunged its way into my heart. Maybe Jinx
doesn't *want* to be with me. What if he wants to be with his
original owner? I never even considered that possibility.

*I promise you, if you want to find out who made you, I will
help you in any way that I can.*

199

CHAPTER TWENTY-SEVEN

LIFE AT THE ACADEMY IS HECTIC, AND being so involved in Baku Battles takes its toll on my other classes. For the first time, I come close to flunking a test in History – I just haven't had any time to study.

It's almost a relief when classes are over on Monday, and I stroll to the end of Companioneers Crescent, following the directions sent to me by Tobias. Behind the beautiful houses, there's a large park, with a baseball diamond in one corner, basketball and tennis courts in the other, and in the centre, a large, floodlit hockey rink – surrounded by boards and red-painted wire caging that stretches up into the sky. I spot Kai's bright orange puffer jacket right in the centre of the rink, with the rest of Team Tobias hanging around the boards.

Ashley sees me first, and nudges Tobias's shoulder. I shrink down into my powder-blue winter coat, the cold air making the end of my nose tingle. There's no ice on the rink yet – there's still a couple more weeks until it will be cold enough for City to flood the rinks and start up the artificial cooling systems to maintain the ice – but I can see how it's the perfect place to practise in arena-like conditions. Tobias is a smart captain. Especially as we know that Gemma's team have access to the best conditions of all – thanks to Carter.

'Hi, Lacey!' Tobias waves me over.

I can't help the goofy grin that plasters itself on my face. When I get to the boards, I lean over the edge – not wanting to climb on to the rink while Kai and River are battling. I do hold up the yellow cardboard box of doughnut holes that I've brought over – and Ashley claps her mittened hands together in delight. Treats make everyone happy, and by now I know all their favourite flavours.

Oka is facing off against Lizard, the husky running circles around the oversized frog. They're not properly battling of course – neither one is causing any damage to the other – but I can see them running through drills that test how quickly they can respond and move.

'Kai, can you see if you can practise that crawl and strike move – we're going to need to confuse the boar if we have any chance of taking him down.'

'You got it, boss,' says Kai. He's standing within a spray-painted circle, so he's also getting practice sending distance commands. He has to be able to tell Oka exactly what he wants him to do, as he passes within range. He holds his hand up to the leash. Even though he doesn't *technically* need to be holding the leash in order to send commands, having that physical connection seems to help the battlers.

Kai's square jaw tightens and his eyebrows knit together

201

in concentration. It takes a couple of seconds – maybe a couple of seconds too long – but Oka springs into action, using his powerful legs to propel himself to the side of the arena. Then, in a move I haven't seen before – but which I could see would work extremely well on the slick-sided walls of the Profectus arena – Lizard leaps up on to the boards and crawls at ninety degrees to the floor in evasive action. Still, Oka picks up momentum as he races around the side, before – on Kai's command – he springs forward and lands on Lizard's back.

Or he would do – if we were in the arena. As it happens, Oka leaps over Lizard, leaving neither with any sort of damage.

Ashley, Tobias and I burst into applause. 'Great work, guys. I think we can take a break for a bit,' says Tobias.

'I brought snacks,' I say.

'I knew there was a reason I liked you!' says River, laughing and digging into the open box of doughnuts and grabbing all the chocolate ones.

Kai is a bit more reserved, holding back.

'No sugar for you?' I ask him.

'I don't eat that junk,' he says.

Tobias shoves his shoulder. 'Lighten up, protein dude.'

'Good luck lightening up eating *that* kind of thing.'

I shrug at Tobias, trying to show him it's no big deal. After all, it's Kai and River in the arena next – with Ashley as back-up. I think Kai is nervous.

I decide to change the subject. 'Hey, I was wondering . . . do any of you guys know much about coding?'

Tobias looks at Kai, who shrugs. 'I almost flunked that class.'

'I know a bit,' says River. 'But I'm more of a design geek.'

'Don't look at me,' says Ashley, throwing her hands up in the air. 'I'm into the electronics side of things.'

'There's a strong coding department at Profectus, but coders don't normally get selected for the Baku Battle teams,' explains Tobias. 'We're not allowed to mess with the code of our bakus during or before a battle, so what's the point? Other than what we get taught in class, I'm not that strong. Do you need help with something?'

I shake my head. 'Don't worry. I'll figure it out.'

Sorry, Jinx, I think to him. *I'll figure out another way to get a look at your code, don't worry.*

Aero outstretches his wings, and the rest of the team snaps to attention. I haven't been paying attention to what Tobias's baku has been doing, but when I look back at the rink, there are obstacles set up and markings in blue paint on the floor. The bakus all move into various positions around the outer edge of the rink. They all seem to run so in sync, even though they've only been doing these training sessions for the past couple of months. Watching them is awe-inspiring – and almost makes me forget how cold I am.

'Ashley, you're up,' Tobias says. Ashley nods, her lips pulled taut into a thin line, and she and Jupiter step on to the ice rink. There are blue lines painted on the concrete floor – markings, I realize, that are a specific choreography for a battle. It's like a drill, or an obstacle course. Ashley needs to run through it, proving that she and Jupiter have been practising their moves so they can perform them in battle as if they are second nature.

'I've added in a few different things this time, Ashley,' Tobias says. 'Make sure you're ready.' She nods, and a bead of sweat appears on her brow. Even though it's just a training run, I can tell she's traumatized by her last encounter in the arena. She needs to overcome that trauma if she's going to have any hope in the second round. She attempts it the first time, but struggles on the second move, her baku colliding with one of the high obstacles. She's clearly frustrated, banging her fist against the palm of her hand, but she goes back to the beginning with Jupiter.

The atmosphere is tense – until suddenly there's a blast of music. It's the theme song from the movie *Rocky*. It's coming from the loudspeakers set up all around the arena. I look around and see Jinx coming out of a small concrete building – that must be where the set-up for the speakers is kept.

Tobias follows my gaze and then turns to me, his jaw almost on the floor. 'What's going on? How are you doing that? We haven't been able to get those speakers to work in years,' Tobias asks me.

'Thought I'd try something …' I look around for the naughty baku, panic growing on my face. *Jinx, stop it – you're drawing attention to yourself.*

>>Are you kidding? It's working.

And it does seem to work. This time, Ashley and Jupiter

204

run through the course cleanly, her fist pumping the air at the end. 'Thanks, Lacey,' she says, giving me a high five as she bounds over to us in triumph.

'No . . . problem?'

'Or should I really be thanking Jinx,' she says, slyly.

'Oh . . . um . . . what?' I say with a nervous laugh. Does she suspect the truth: that it's Jinx all along, and I have nothing to do with it?

But she winks at me and grins. 'He's the one that managed to squeeze in to where the speakers are, right?'

'Right.' I breathe a sigh of relief.

As each baku steps up to run his paces, Jinx chooses a song and blasts it. All the bakus – including Aero – complete the task in record time. At the end, Jinx plays the latest pop tracks at top volume from the speakers, so we end up laughing and singing along and dancing under the floodlights.

Aero spreads his wings one more time, showing us all the time. It's late. When Aero closes his wings, Jinx shuts off the music.

'Catch you later, guys!' says Kai, swinging his backpack over his shoulder. Oka pants at his side.

'Lacey, can you hold up a sec?' Tobias asks me as I prepare to follow Kai, River and Ashley out towards the main road.

'Oh, sure.'

I hang around the edge of the rink while Tobias packs up the obstacle course. He seems to be taking his time, waiting for a gap to build up between us and the rest of the team. Finally, he walks over to me, carrying a duffel bag full of equipment. Aero takes it out of his hands and flies with it towards the road.

Tobias grins at me. 'Look, I'm glad you came today. I wanted to let you know that I'm going to ask Ashley to step down from the fighting team. Is that okay?'

'What?' I stare at Ashley's retreating back, the spring in her step – and Jupiter trotting at her side. 'You want to replace Ashley?'

'Ash and Jupiter are great, but you and Jinx are better – especially with that boost collar I gave you. And if Carter can fight, then so can you.'

I take an involuntary step backward, my back colliding with the boards. I put my arms out to steady myself, avoiding Tobias's gaze. 'No, you can't do that. I'll . . . I'm fine on the sidelines.'

Tobias takes a step forward, then reaches out and puts his hand on my arm. 'Hey, it's okay. Ash will get over it – I don't think she wants to risk Jupiter again anyway.'

'But it might stop her from being chosen on a team again . . .'

His hand travels down from my arm to my hand. He interlaces his fingers in mine, and pulls me close. 'You're the best companioneer I've ever met, Lacey. What you can do . . . it's incredible. You're so in control of your baku.' I almost laugh at that, but stop myself just in time. 'And I get to pick the team. I'm the captain.'

My heart pounds, my brain unable to compute that Tobias Washington is holding my hand. But also I hear a resounding *no* in my brain – I don't want to fight. I don't want to risk Jinx. I don't want . . .

>>Wait, you don't want this? I thought this was what we've been working towards? Jinx's voice whines in my head.

I can't risk you. What if you get ripped apart? All that hard work . . .

>>I won't lose. I want to fight.

'No!' I don't realize I shout the word out loud until I catch Tobias's shocked expression.

'Hey, I get it,' he says, and he takes a step back. 'I won't push it. I thought maybe it was what you wanted . . .'

I look up at him, our eyes locking. My mouth opens to speak, but I'm not sure that any words really come out. 'What do you mean?'

'I thought you wanted . . .' His moss-green eyes shine in the bright light of the floodlights. Without waiting for a second beat, he leans forward and kisses me, pressing his soft lips against mine. I melt back against the boards of the hockey rink, and for a moment it doesn't matter that my baku is having an existential crisis, that my mom doesn't understand me and things have changed.

Because Tobias Washington is kissing me. And in that moment, I am perfectly and completely happy.

PART FOUR

WILD CARD

CHAPTER TWENTY-EIGHT

THE ATMOSPHERE FOR THE SECOND Baku Battle has the entire school buzzing. In the hallways leading up to my locker, I pass by students making bets on their apps, trying to guess the strategies. Jake is the mastermind of the gambling ring – I even hear some of the teachers are getting involved. With at least two bakus in the arena (Team Tobias and Team Gemma have three) per team, it's going to be more hectic than ever – and there are two hundred points up for grabs this time.

'I'm going to put ten bucks on Team Tobias,' says one student in passing as I'm collecting my books from my locker. They stop a few feet away from me.

'Nah, Team Gemma all the way. Have you seen how that guy with the hog baku has been walking around the school? He's definitely got something up his sleeve.'

The guy looks up to see me staring. He's weedy and tall, with lanky brown hair, glasses and a face full of acne. But he gives me a big grin when he sees me. 'Hey, you're on Team

Tobias, right? Got any tips for us? Everyone on your team feeling all right?'

I press my lips firmly together.

Jinx, however, does a flying leap up into the alcove above my locker – something he shouldn't be able to do. The guy's smile widens even further. 'Dude – you are so going to regret betting on Team Gemma,' he says to his friend. He gives me a wink.

I glare at Jinx for showing off, but I can't keep a frown on my face for long. Since last night, I've been floating on air. My teachers give up on getting me to focus – they blame the Baku Battle, but it's not the real reason.

I can't stop thinking about Tobias.

Tobias and me.

It doesn't seem real.

I can't wait for the final bell, not only because it's battle time. It means that I will get to see him. Jinx makes a beeline for the team box. He weaves through the legs of the other students, dodging their bakus – he really is useful like that.

Thanks, J, I think.

>>You always seem so surprised when I'm useful.

That's because most of the time I don't expect it!

>>You wouldn't change me for the world.

And the problem is that you know it.

My knees won't stop shaking, my legs juddering up and down like I've had way too much caffeine. Jinx purrs, attempting to calm me. He's right, I need to relax before I see Tobias again.

It's just going to be the two of us in the team box, after all.

'Hey.'

My heart skips a beat as I hear his caramel-smooth voice. I spin around in my chair and match his wide grin. 'Hey back.'

'Excited?'

'Can't wait,' I say. I bite down on my lip as he sits next to me, his thigh bumping up against mine. He leans forward over the barrier, so he's looking down into the arena, and the fanfare begins.

Focus on the battle, Lacey, I tell myself.

The players lift up – and gasps are audible from around the stadium. Team Elektra have come in fighting. Elektra is there herself, with her level 4 captain's baku – a cloud leopard – to go up with her teammate Terence and his bulldog baku, against the teams of three. It's the only chance they'll have of lasting the thirty minutes.

But they're not the only ones using that strategy. Gemma and her tiger baku, Stripe, are in the arena too.

Team Tobias might be in big trouble.

The smugness on Carter's face is unsettling. But between his boar, Hunter, Gemma's tiger, Stripe, and Gemma's third, Frank, with his German Shepherd baku, Bones . . . they seem unbeatable.

Beside me, Tobias tenses, his fists clenching together. 'Dammit,' he mutters. The buzzer sounds and instead of thinking about how close Tobias is, I'm swept away in the rhythm of the battle, the energy of the crowd. Using Jinx's technology, I scan across the battlefield, able to pause and rewind key moments on impulse.

The action takes off as two cat bakus – a lithe Persian belonging to Team Dorian and the beautiful grey-white clouded leopard belonging to Elektra – go after each other in a whirl of claws and snarling teeth. Hunter is locked in battle with a Team Pearce baku, a lizard named Scythe, with Bones assisting. Scythe doesn't stand a chance. It's chaotic with twelve bakus in the arena, but bakus are going down like flies. After only five minutes, Team Pearce is out completely and Elektra and Dorian's teams are down to one baku each. Only Team Tobias and Team Gemma are at full strength.

Even Ashley is holding her own, Jupiter hanging back as Oka and Lizard take down the other teams. I think the other teams have decided she is a weak link; someone they can pick off easily once they've defeated the other stronger bakus. They don't want to waste any unnecessary energy on her. They want to use strength on strength, saving her for last.

'Come on, guys,' I mutter under my breath.

Jinx informs me that the status of the Persian, Lista, is now critical; the poor baku is on her last legs. I think she's going to be totally beyond repair, thereby leaving Team Dorian out of the points. Two levels down, and not a single point scored.

With Lista down, the clouded leopard, Frost, turns to Jupiter, flicking his tail menacingly and baring his teeth. I see that Elektra has made cosmetic alterations to Frost in order to make him look more intimidating – with extra sharp teeth and dark, pointed eyebrows. I never really understood it before – the bakus were battling each other, so they surely didn't care how menacing the other one looked? But now that I see it up on screen, I understand the importance of showmanship. He looks intimidating, powerful, and as the 'underdog' baku – the only one from a pointless team – he has the crowd on side. Poor Ashley is shaking with nerves now, even though I can tell she is really attempting to hold it together. Oka and River are engaged in a battle with Stripe and Bones, needing to use every ounce of concentration to take on the tiger. If they're going to have any hope, Jupiter is going to have to step up in the battle against Frost and inflict at least *some* damage.

Ashley takes a deep breath and tries to draw herself up to stand tall. She wants to project confidence. Her battling skills have definitely improved.

The clouded leopard is lightning fast, rounding on poor Jupiter with barely a delay. Ashley sends commands for Jupiter to move out of the way, but too late – Frost swipes out with a sharp paw and part of Jupiter's surface panelling is torn. Nothing too critical, but his damage level moves instantly to 75% on the jumbotron. Jinx winces as if he was the one hit, rather than Jupiter. I know the feeling. I pray that Ashley can get her head in the game and figure out how to counter Frost's speed.

Ashley seems to remember some of her drills, and gets Jupiter to take aim at Frost's tail. If she can dislodge the mechanisms there, the baku will be thrown off balance – making it much more difficult to move with speed and accuracy. No point moving quickly if you can't move in the right direction. It's an easier target than the body – we already noted in our opposition studies that Frost likes to show off by swinging his big bushy tail from side to side. All Jupiter needs to do is to get close enough to take a bite.

Ashley deploys a risky strategy, allowing Jupiter to be a bit more vulnerable, luring Frost into making another attack without thinking through the consequences. It works: the leopard leaps, taking aim at Jupiter's shoulder, but Jupiter darts around to take a bite out of the leopard's tail.

A cheer goes up from the crowd at the plucky move. Frost's damage rate sits at 65%, and Jupiter's drops to 50%. Not bad. This is exactly what Ashley needs to be doing.

'Come on, Jupiter!' shouts Tobias from beside me.

Jinx stands on my knees so his paws are propped up on the railing, peering intently into the arena and down at the battle between Frost and Jupiter. I shift my attention to the other raging battle between Oka, Lizard, Stripe and Bones. The boys from Team Tobias are making good progress and Bones' stats are dropping rapidly. Gemma is barking orders at Carter, telling him to hold Hunter back. Hunter is pacing as if he's itching to dive headfirst back into the action, and Carter looks equally frustrated at being left out of the action, his hands opening and closing into fists. But I can see Gemma's plan. She wants to weaken Oka and Lizard as much as possible before sending Hunter in for the kill.

There's a groan throughout the audience that snaps my attention back. Jinx hisses loudly, and I wince as his claws extend into the meat of my thighs. Jupiter has been hit badly by Frost – even with the tail damage, he's a lethal weapon – and Jupiter's stats drop to 29%. Almost critical level. I can see Ashley's eyes dart to Tobias, waiting to see when she can pull her baku out of the battle.

But Tobias doesn't look at Ashley. Instead, he signals something to Kai, who nods from his position in the arena. Oka suddenly switches tactics, leaving Lizard alone against Stripe and Bones as he goes after Hunter. Carter is taken totally by surprise, and the boar doesn't defend himself – his stats knocking down to below the 20% threshold with one hit. Hunter is down and out, just like that. I let out the loudest whoop that I can.

Kai sends Oka back to face-off against the tiger. Lizard is taken out by a direct hit by the Stripe's paw. In the meantime, Frost gets one final swipe at Jupiter – dropping the baku finally down to 20%.

'Get out of there!' I scream at Ashley, jumping up out of my seat. Jinx leaps from my lap to the floor. She turns her head up to look at me.

Because I can see now why Carter looked so smug at the beginning of the battle. He's been offered a revive chip by Dr Grant – he must have earned it doing some extra credit – and even though Hunter is out of action, with the revive chip he surges back up to 50%. With one target in sight: Jupiter.

Ashley isn't able to drag her baku out of the arena in time. Hunter slams into Jupiter, the spaniel baku crumpling in on itself, all our careful repairs being turned into dust. Hunter isn't content to just tear it apart. He stomps over the little spaniel, grinding parts between his teeth. It's an unfair power-up, something that shouldn't have been given to Carter, no matter what he'd done to earn it. The entire audience gasps at the impact, and I feel my heart lurch. Ashley releases a scream that is something primal: the second time she's had to watch as her companion is ripped into shreds. But this time, as I watch Jupiter's stats sink, I know if it continues this way, there won't be any way to repair her. Carter is making absolutely sure of that this time.

Hunter is annihilating the baku.

Carter looks triumphant. He fist pumps the sky, drinking in the attention from the crowd.

But there's more. Something is happening on the arena floor, something my eyes can't take in fast enough for me to understand. There's a flash of shadow, quick as a bullet, entering the damaged hole in Hunter's side. The boar falters, twitching and convulsing, as something is destroying him from the inside out.

Carter's face is a picture of confusion and horror, his jaw hanging open, watching as his baku's stats drop to 0% – utterly ruining any chance he would have of using his baku in the final round. 'What the hell is going on?' his voice is a high-pitched shriek. 'Gemma!' he yells to his captain. 'Attack whatever is doing that!'

I lean forward against the barrier to get a better view. Then a face emerges from the hole in Hunter's side. A face that stops my heart. Jinx.

The boar collapses to the ground as Jinx hops out, barely a scratch on him.

Gemma's tiger drops into a low pounce, her jaws snapping and snarling. But Jinx is impossibly nimble. With a few moves, he's darted around Stripe, sliding underneath her belly and gutting the baku so that her electronics are entrails on the arena floor, her stats plummeting to 11%. Gemma has no choice but to pull her baku from the battle.

'Lacey, what are you doing?' Tobias yells, grabbing my arm, but I can't look at him yet. I'm transfixed by the battlefield.

It's all happened so quickly, the other bakus left on the field – Oka and Lizard and Bones – are still locked in battle. Frank pulls Bones from battle at 22% – still within repairable range.

Everyone is confused, the crowd tittering, Mr Baird and Dr Grant gesturing frantically at each other, all wondering who the rogue baku on the arena floor belongs to – but the few people who recognize Jinx all have their eyes tuned on me. Including Tobias. I finally risk a glance at him. The look on his face turns my stomach. His expression is thunder and confusion and even a bit of fear. All his carefully laid strategies – everything we discussed – have fallen to pieces.

I've changed the game.

Or rather . . . Jinx has.

Jinx stands, hackles raised, staring at Oka. Jupiter is behind him, saved from total annihilation, still attempting to stand upright. I remind myself that these are robots, not real animals – even as it pains me to watch Jupiter attempting to fight until her very last percentage point. Ashley pulls Jupiter from the arena before any more damage can be done.

I turn my attention to Mr Baird. He can black-mark Jinx, put a stop to this right now. Tobias is looking over at him too. But Mr Baird is looking at Jinx, his brows knitted together in an expression of anger ... but also a hint of curiosity. Then he draws up the microphone and announces: 'There are still two bakus remaining in the arena. The battles continue.'

I swallow, hard. That means that Jinx and Oka are expected to fight. But how is that possible? We're on the same team. At least – I think we are. Tobias looks at me with disgust, pacing backwards until there's physical distance between us, and I wince.

'Jinx! Come back here!' I finally find my voice.

'Well, aren't you going to go in?'

I spin around to see Jake, who's standing behind the team box. He's looking at me with one eyebrow raised. 'I'm not impressed that you didn't tell me you were the wild card. You know that this is going to ruin all my bets today. You owe me one, Lacey Chu.'

'The wild card? But ...' I'm torn. I don't know what Jinx is playing at, I don't know what a wild card team is, but I do know that I need to somewhat pretend that I am in control of the situation if we're going to keep up any semblance of normality. I have to go along with it. I avoid admitting or denying anything with a shrug of my shoulders.

'Good luck, Lace. You're going to need it.' Jake smiles at me encouragingly – probably out of pity, to counteract the waves of animosity slamming towards me from Tobias's direction.

I take a deep breath, then vault up and over the barrier. I drop down into the arena, landing with a thud. I walk into one of the circles. As I pass Kai, he hisses in my ear: 'What do you think you're doing?'

'Nothing,' I murmur as I move inside a circle. 'This is all a big mistake, I promise you.'

'Yeah, I don't think your *promises* means very much right now. Shame I'm going to have to destroy your little baku. He was a cool one.'

I step into one of the silver circles. My face flickers up on to one of the screens, my fear and nerves writ large. Under my name are the words: WILD CARD.

It's as if this has all been planned.

And once again, I'm the one that's in the dark.

Jinx, what is going on?

>>I couldn't let Jupiter be destroyed.

Even though I know he entered the arena to protect Jupiter, I'm filled with fury. Especially as now he's going to have to take down Oka.

Let's get this over with, then.

Oka doesn't stand a chance against Jinx. Jinx knows every move Oka is going to make before Kai does – he knows all of his weaknesses, all of the ways to bring him down in the minimal number of moves. And Jinx is ruthless. He doesn't stop at 25 or 30%, giving Kai an opportunity to pull his baku. He takes it all the way down to zero.

But of course, Kai thinks that it's me. Any good will I might have built up over the past month evaporates with the final wicked swipe of Jinx's paw that levels the husky baku.

The whistle sounds. The audience is stunned into silence – there's no roar of applause. Unfortunately, I can hear every single one of my heartbeats resounding in my ear, loud as gongs.

Mr Baird is illuminated in the centre of the arena again. 'Well.' He clears his throat. 'That was an unexpected turn of events. It appears that we had a wild card entry into the Baku Battles. That means there will be one additional team for the Baku Battles final at Moncha HQ this year.' He looks down at me. 'I hope that you and your baku are up for the challenge. At least, you've done well to start. Team Lacey – your team has been awarded two hundred points for winning the second round of the Baku Battles. The other teams have twelve hours in order to challenge you for a share of the points. Although, by the looks of things ... I don't think that's going to happen.'

I suppose I've got my chance after all.

The chance to compete for the summer internship. To go behind the scenes at Moncha HQ. I'm the captain of my own Baku Battle team.

A team of one. Against an entire group who hate me.

CHAPTER TWENTY-NINE

I WISH THAT JINX COULD PICK ME UP AND fly me away to some faraway island where no one knows me. I would give up my left arm to not be sitting at a desk on the front row of Mr Baird's classroom, my butt falling asleep on the hard plastic chair, Jinx nonchalantly licking his paw at my feet, while the other team captains gather around Mr Baird's desk and yell.

'It's not *fair*,' says Gemma. She jabs her finger in my direction, and I think if she'd had a sword long enough, she would have stabbed me right through the heart with it. Instead, she suffices with pointing at me with her Shellac-ed nail. 'There's nowhere in the rules of Profectus Baku Battles that states this is a possibility.'

Mr Baird shrugs. 'The rules are pretty clear when it says to expect the absolute unexpected. And there *is* a precedent with wild card entries – it's a decision that comes from the upper echelons of Moncha Corp. It's all registered in the system. I've taken it up with the Profectus board, and though they find it highly unorthodox, they don't see a problem with another team competing at this stage. Don't tell me you are afraid of a little competition, guys,' he says, rubbing his unshaven chin, his shirtsleeves rolled up and stained with oil. 'You still have until the morning to fix up your injured bakus to try and take back some points.' He turns to Tobias. 'Your team pulled off a miracle last round. Shouldn't be too difficult to do that again, should it?'

I swallow, hard, not daring to catch Tobias's eye. We both know he won't have the companioneering skill to fix the broken bakus. I was his secret weapon.

Mr Baird continues. 'Besides, almost all of you have level 4 or higher bakus left. Shouldn't be a problem to defeat Lacey's level 3.'

'That's right. Stripe was already weak by the time your baku entered the arena,' says Gemma. 'That was a cheap move coming in at the end. You must have known about this for ages. How long have you been preparing that *strategy*?'

They all turn to look at me now, and my cheeks burn. *I didn't send Jinx into the arena*, is what I want to say. But that would open the door to questions I'm not prepared to answer yet.

Or, to be more accurate, questions I don't know *how* to answer yet.

>>God, they all have their panties in such a twist. Can't they just chill out?

They can't chill out. And that's all your fault. It's not supposed to be like this. You're not supposed to make decisions for me. It's one thing to send a text, but this is different. You're not real.

You're owned by me. You're supposed to be controlled by me.

He stares up at me with his dark eyes. But his expression is unreadable. He's never looked so . . . robotic.

'Well, Lacey?'

I jerk my head upwards. I haven't been listening to their conversations. Mr Baird is looking at me expectantly, while the others all have thunder and fury etched into their expressions.

'Well . . .' I draw out the word, trying desperately to remember what was said.

Gemma scoffs loudly, rolls her eyes and folds her arms over her chest. 'Looks like you got played harder than the rest of us,' she says to Tobias. 'Thought Nathan's bro would be smarter than that. Guess you are the lesser Washington.'

Tobias's expression causes my throat to hitch. He moves from anger to a look of such hurt and betrayal that I wince. And how can I blame him? I know what he must think. That I've been using our friendship – and the growing . . . whatever it is . . . between us – to form a strategy to hurt him. Even though that wasn't my intention in the slightest. *Jinx just wanted to protect Jupiter*, I want to say, but I know that no one will believe me. After all, bakus aren't supposed to want things.

They're not supposed to make decisions on their own.

They're supposed to obey their owners – or else who knows what kind of chaos we could encounter. People blaming their bakus for their actions, letting a robot take responsibility. I have to step up to the plate and own what Jinx has done.

'Well, are you up for the challenge?' Mr Baird repeats, his voice patient and a ghost of a smile playing on his lips.

I stand up out of my chair. 'I'm happy to pull out of the competition and not be a wild card. I . . . I don't know what came over me. It was all a big mistake. I promise. Nothing like that will ever happen again.'

Now Mr Baird's expression darkens. 'Oh no, it's too late for that. You must continue – albeit with a handicap for late entry. The board has deemed that I give Jinx a black mark for the next twelve hours, while the other teams attempt to repair their bakus. So he will stay at 80% damage and you won't be able to repair him. Other than that, I'm afraid that the decision is final. You will be a team captain in the next round of Baku Battles to be held at Moncha HQ, although you will have only you and your baku to rely on. Let's hope today wasn't a fluke.'

I drop my head, and nod.

'I need verbal confirmation from you that you're going to participate.'

I hesitate, then flick my eyes up. 'I will participate,' I say.

'Good, that's settled then.'

Gemma throws her hands up in the air and walks off with a strangled cry.

'You're going down, little miss,' hisses Dorian. I wince as he says it, but I try and keep my back as straight as possible. I can't let them intimidate me too much. Whatever they think, I know this wasn't my decision.

Tobias walks past last. He stops right in front of me,

and I can feel that he has a million things he wants to say, balancing right there on the tip of his tongue. His eyes search mine, the eyes that had previously been filled with happiness and laughter last time they looked at me. Now, they're hard – jade rocks instead of soft moss. 'I trusted you,' he says. Aero flaps his wings in my face, sending my hair flying. Then in several long strides, he's gone.

I deflate, my shoulders crumpling in on themselves. Even though I'm so mad at him, I find myself automatically reaching down and stroking Jinx. He wriggles under my hand until his nose nuzzles my palm, then he slinks in a figure of eight around my legs and up into my lap. I hold him close. My anger towards him dissipates as he purrs against my body. I know he meant well.

'Lacey?' Mr Baird asks. I look up to see he's been staring at me and Jinx, a curious expression on his face. 'I have to give Jinx his black mark.'

My eyes open wide. I'd heard him say that, but I hadn't really taken in what that would mean. 'Do you have to, sir?'

'It's the board-mandated punishment. And you're not going to be able to do any sort of repairs before tomorrow, do you understand?'

I nod, misery settling over my shoulders like I've been caught in a downpour.

'Bring your baku to me.'

'You brought this on yourself,' I mutter to him, before placing him down on Mr Baird's desk. I can see the black mark sitting there, dark and menacing.

Mr Baird doesn't put the mark on straight away. Instead, he stares at Jinx, who is curled up on the desk. I think the battle must have taken some of the energy out of him – more so than his pride will let on.

The longer that Jinx sits there, with Mr Baird staring at him, the more uneasy I get.

'He really is remarkable, Miss Chu,' Mr Baird says. He reaches out a hand and runs it over Jinx's soft electronic fur. 'And you say you got him from your local Moncha Store?'

I force myself to nod. But I've told this lie so many times now, it slips out as easily as the truth. 'That's right. As soon as I got the notification that I was into Profectus.'

'Interesting. Must be one of the latest models – I confess, I don't keep up as much as I should. My own owl baku is one of the first models.' He snaps his fingers and the owl flies down to the desk. He's right: I can instantly tell that this is one of the older versions. The feathers are much cruder, the technology more obvious and not as well hidden behind the animalistic shell. The owl is cumbersome, more machine than bird – but there's a certain type of elegance in that too.

Mr Baird tries to manipulate Jinx so that he can turn him over, but Jinx won't let him: he's pretending to be asleep. After a few moments, Mr Baird gives up, and places the black mark around Jinx's outstretched paw. The moment it latches on, Jinx goes totally limp. Inert. Switched off.

It pains me.

I lean in to take Jinx back, but Mr Baird stops me. 'Why did you enter the arena at that point? You must have known you would be risking extra damage to your baku, and it seems to me like you are very attached to him. You could have simply announced your wild card status before the third battle.'

'I . . . I didn't like Team Gemma's strategy,' I say, speaking honestly. 'And I don't think that Carter would have stopped. You saw him when he used that revive chip. He had no intention of letting Jupiter get through this round of battles in one piece.'

'Hmm, you might be right about that. And when did you get the notification about being a wild card? You should have been told about that before the first battle.'

'Oh, I . . .' I don't know what to say. I wrack my brains for a strong enough story, sensing Mr Baird's eyes boring into the top of my skull, but I don't look up to meet his gaze. Instead, I stare fixedly at Jinx. 'I'd like to keep that to myself, if that's okay.'

'Okay,' he says. He lets go of Jinx, and I hug him into my chest protectively. For a second, I think I feel him stir –the tiniest nuzzle of his nose into my neck – but that's not possible with the black mark. It must be my imagination. 'Just remember,' he says. 'You're going to have a lot of eyes on you now. Eyes on you – and on that baku of yours.'

'Yes, sir.'

'See you tomorrow, Miss Chu. The final battle takes place in two weeks' time. I hope you are ready.'

'I'll try,' I say, trying to sound more confident than I feel. 'Goodbye.'

I leave the confines of the classroom, wandering slowly back to my locker. When I get there, I see a note from Jake that tells me: 'If you have a private way out, I suggest you USE IT. You'll be mobbed.'

I'm grateful that he thought to leave me a note – when Jinx is back online, I'll send him a thank you. I grab my jacket and backpack as quickly as I can. Even though Jinx can't hear me with the mark on, I still find myself talking to him as I take one of the back stairwells to a less used exit.

Are we actually doing this, Jinx? Are you actually going to have to battle? What if I lose you? I can't even bring myself to be excited at the prospect of visiting Moncha headquarters. Yesterday that would have been all I cared about. Today . . .

We plunge into darkness as I enter the stairwell, and I don't dare turn on the light to alert anyone nearby to my presence. But a voice sounds out of the dark.

'Wait!'

CHAPTER THIRTY

'WAIT UP, LACEY.'

My heart pounding, I spin around to see Carter a few floors above me. No. He's the last person I want to talk to. I push through the exit doors and out into the cold air. I need to get home as quickly as possible.

I wrap my arms around Jinx's inert body. The temperature has taken a turn towards the Canadian winter and even at the beginning of November, it's dipping below zero. And it's pouring with freezing rain.

'You can't run forever,' he shouts at my retreating back. 'I know something's not right with you and that baku. You're not supposed to even be at this school. My dad *promised* me you wouldn't be at this school!'

Now, I freeze – but it has nothing to do with the cold. I spin around as Carter saunters towards me. He looks smaller without his baku by his side, but no less frightening. He's bright red with anger, his teeth gnashing together. 'What do you mean?' I ask.

He storms right up to me, so close I feel every word like a punch. 'You're not supposed to be at Profectus. You're never going to work at Moncha Corp, I don't care if you win every Baku Battle under the sun. My dad *hated* your dad. Don't you get it? I don't know what sort of glitch allowed you in, but it would be better for everyone if you just left now.'

'Hey, what's going on here?' Mr Baird strides round the corner.

'Your baku isn't normal, Lacey,' Carter hisses at me. 'I'm going to find out what's going on with it. That's for sure.' He ducks his head and pushes past me, disappearing into the depths of the parking lot.

'Are you okay, Lacey? What was that all about?'

'Nothing, sir. It's fine.'

He frowns. 'You're soaked through. How about I drive you home?'

I shake my head, shrinking inside my jacket. 'I'm okay.'

'Come on, you've had a rough day. You don't want to walk home in this freezing rain. You'll slide everywhere in those shoes.'

I look down at my feet. Yeah, wearing ballet flats wasn't the smartest idea. I really should be wearing my boots at all times, but I was so absent-minded, I forgot them in my locker.

The idea of a drive home in a warm car does sound nice. Mr Baird's owl baku flies over to a nearby vehicle, and there's a clicking noise as the doors unlock. The freezing cold water seeping through the soles of my shoes makes the decision for me. I hop in the car.

Mr Baird slides on to the seat next to me, and the car drives away.

'Um, do you need my address?'

'You did a dangerous thing, sending that baku in. I thought I could trust that you would stay under the radar.'

My eyes open wide.

'Tell me honestly, where did you get that baku?' he gestures at Jinx.

I purse my lips. I've just told him this story. 'From the Moncha Store,' I repeat.

He sighs. 'I double-checked your background. All your school codes have been tampered with. Carter was right. You weren't supposed to be at Profectus at all.'

Suddenly the inside of the car feels like it's closing in on me, my vision narrowing. My worst fears are coming to life: people are realizing that I don't belong at Profectus. I'm a fraud. An imposter.

They're going to kick me out. They're going to take Jinx away and I'm going to be left with nothing. Maybe they won't even let me have a baku at all. I'll be one of those people that's banned from having one – a criminal. It's the worst possible punishment I can think of, and it's now just one step from being inevitable.

I can't even imagine what my face looks like to someone outside of all this. Mr Baird frowns. 'I thought we could at least get away with it until the end of the school year, but now that Eric Smith's son is suspicious and you're set to visit Moncha headquarters . . .'

My fingers twitch against Jinx's body. 'I don't understand. Get away with what?' I catch a glimpse of the view outside the window and see that we're crossing over the bridge and into the city – the opposite direction to my home. 'Wait, where are we going?'

Mr Baird's fingers tighten on the seat as we cross the domineering viaduct that separates Monchaville from the rest of the city.

'It's not safe to talk yet.'

'Not safe to talk? I don't understand.' I shift in my seat, uncomfortably aware that there's no way for me to escape the confines of the car. 'Mr Baird, this is all very cold war spy thriller, but where exactly are we going?' I try and keep the tone light, even though fear is settling in the pit of my stomach. 'Where are you taking me? I think I have a right to know.'

'You'll know soon enough.'

The car drives straight down Queen Street West, past the trendy shops and towards the big converted warehouse buildings that pepper the West End. My mind takes me back fleetingly to the time when Zora and I had just bought my beetle baku. Before Profectus, before Team Tobias, before Jinx. It feels like a lifetime ago.

The car slows in front of one of the nondescript warehouses, constructed out of pale yellow brick, with huge glass windows that appear to be either blackened out, not revealing anything inside. There's no advertising on the building whatsoever, no signage, nothing to indicate who owns it. I guess the mystery is going to continue for a few moments longer. Anxiety and curiosity mingle in my stomach in equal dosages.

'Follow me,' he says, unbuckling his seatbelt and opening the door in one swift motion.

'As if I have a choice,' I mumble. We take a set of stairs up to the lobby, which is dominated by a single security desk and an old-fashioned body scanner. Most of the time, a police-regulated baku does security checks, but there isn't one of those in here.

'You'll have to check those in,' says the guard, who stands up from his desk as we enter.

'Um, what?' It looks to me as if he's pointing at Jinx, and then at the owl. 'There's no way I'm leaving Jinx here.'

'I promise you, he will be perfectly safe. I have to leave my owl here too.' Mr Baird puts his hand on my shoulder. 'You've trusted me this far. Just a little bit further and then I promise you can go back home and to your normal life.'

'No way,' I say. 'He has a black mark on him still – he can't communicate or anything. Let me keep him, or I'm leaving now.'

Mr Baird hesitates and exchanges a look with the guard. Eventually, he nods. 'Fine. Let's go.'

My hand clings to Jinx's body, a thin layer of sweat building on my palms. I wipe them on my jeans surreptitiously. I don't like this one bit.

'Come on, this way.' We pass through the security gate and into an elevator. Now I see the first sign. BRIGHTSPRK is written in discreet lettering at the top of the elevator buttons.

'Oh hell, no,' I say, but the doors shut before I can step back through.

BRIGHTSPRK is one of Moncha's main rivals. THE main rival. Just stepping in here feels like an act of treason. Now I look up at Mr Baird with an expression of pure scorn and fury. My fists are balled tightly by my side.

'I know what you must be thinking—'

'No, you *don't* know,' I say, through gritted teeth. I love Moncha Corp. Monica Chan is my hero. And now, here I am at BRIGHTSPRK? It makes my skin crawl.

The elevator doors open to a narrow hallway. I debate just staying in the elevator as Mr Baird walks out, but I force my feet to move.

I feel like I've crossed on to enemy lines. A place where bakus aren't allowed: I knew it had to be bad news.

Mr Baird stops in front of a door, jangles a set of keys from out of his pocket – so old-school – and opens it. It's a small office, again – like everything here – very plain, with not a lot of decoration or technology. There's a desk, unadorned, and wooden chairs either side. He walks around to one side, and gestures for me to sit on the other. There's a laptop sitting on his desk. It's older even than the one I have in my basement.

'Wow, BRIGHTSPRK not doing so well?' I remark.

'Lacey, I know you must be confused, but you have to know that I am trusting you too by letting you in on this secret.'

'I didn't ask you to.'

We stand there, on either side of the desk, facing each other.

I'm the one to break first. 'So how long have you been working at BRIGHTSPRK?'

'For my whole career.'

'Wow. A lifelong double agent. Isn't corporate espionage a crime?'

'I think what Moncha is doing is a crime.'

I scoff. 'What do you mean?'

'Well, that's what I need your help figuring out.'

'Okay, seriously?' I say, talking over the top of him. But he continues on as if I hadn't interrupted.

'Have you seen Monica Chan around recently? Or did you notice that she disappeared after the latest upgrade?'

I pause. 'She's around – she's been overseeing developments in other countries,' I parrot back Eric Smith's words. But even I'm not sure if I believe that. From what I know of Monica Chan, it'd be unlike her to leave her company in someone else's hands. But then again, maybe everyone needs a break from being the boss.

'If you say so.'

'I still don't see what this has to do with me. I mean – it must be big to blow your cover as some sort of career snitch.'

He sighs. 'Profectus is a bubble – you're so protected in there. Sheltered. But there's something bigger happening in the outside world.'

'What?'

'Moncha have lost something. Something big. And everyone is on the lookout for it.'

Unease stirs my stomach.

'Including BRIGHTSPRK,' he says. Then his eyes darken. 'We had some intel from deep inside Moncha's companioneering division that someone was working on a new baku. A baku that stood *against* everything that bakus were originally created for – rather than trying to create a perfect companion, someone was trying to create a baku that was fully autonomous. That made its own decisions, that had dreams and desires and goals. In other words . . . a baku that was independent. Alive. Its own creature.'

I frown, although heat rises at the base of my neck. It all sounds too familiar. An autonomous baku. I know a thing or two about that, and I'm starting to realize why I'm here. I force my fingers not to tighten their grip on Jinx, even though I want to hug him tight and take him far, far away from here. 'That doesn't make any sense,' I say, trying to sound casual. 'That would totally defeat the point of having a baku.'

'Maybe.' Mr Baird's eyes don't leave mine for even an instant. 'But you've shown aptitude for companioneering – sometimes, it's not just about something you *should* make, but what you *can* make. Pushing the envelope. It seemed like this rogue companioneer had really done it. We tried to get as much intel as possible, but even from those of us well positioned inside Moncha Corp, there was no way to get close without raising major red flags.'

'Then one day, a few months ago, we got lucky. We had communication from the companioneer in question – although we never found out their real name. They wanted help getting out – but getting past the super sensitive anti-intellectual property-theft barriers around Monchaville was going to be tough. They felt as if they were under imminent attack. At that time, I was working for the security division of Moncha, so I arranged for a barrier to be down at the right time and a car to be outside waiting to pick them up. But we weren't quick enough. We watched them take the person down just on the border of the old ravine. We never heard from them again. We don't know who they are, if they're alive or dead. We don't know if the baku made it out, or if it was recaptured and decommissioned. But when we saw Moncha security combing the ravine the next day, we assumed that meant they hadn't recovered the baku. We sent a team down there as well, but they found nothing. Maybe because it had already *been* found.'

I swallow, hard. 'Mr Baird, I don't know anything about that. It sounds like ... it sounds like science fiction. I don't know about any rogue bakus. I don't know why my entrance into Profectus got all messed up, but I had great stats coming in, perfect grades – well, you should know, Tobias picked me for his team!'

Mr Baird studies me thoughtfully, his hand stroking the base of his stubbly chin. Maybe being a double agent is the reason behind his scruffy appearance. The lines around his eyes tighten, as if he has aged by coming into the building and taking off his 'Moncha' employee mask. 'No, there's no doubt that you deserve to be at Profectus. Any school would be lucky to have you – and you will go on to do great things one day, anyone can see that. Moncha are lucky. You are a very loyal person, Lacey, I can see that. Just think about what I'm saying. You and your baku have an unusually strong connection. There are people on the lookout for unusual bakus. If Carter suspects that there's something more to Jinx than meets the eye … then I'm worried you could be in grave danger. I've been trying to keep an eye on you but things keep happening out of my control – like your selection on to Tobias's team, the wild card entry … that are drawing attention to you and your baku.'

I shake my head and prepare another lie. 'I sent Jinx intentionally into the ring. He wasn't disobeying orders. I promise.'

'Good. Because if by chance that isn't true, and in fact Jinx *isn't* what you say he is, then you might need my help. You won't ignore that, will you?'

Now I can't help it. I hug Jinx tighter to my body, my grip vicelike around him. 'I promise,' I say. 'But Mr Baird, I swear to you – Jinx is totally and utterly normal.'

CHAPTER THIRTY-ONE

I EXIT THE WAREHOUSE, JINX IN MY ARMS, feeling sick to my stomach. I take a deep breath, searching from side to side, and it takes everything I have not to break into a sprint. Mr Baird offered me a car back, but I'd rather make my own way. I don't want to have anything more to do with BRIGHTSPRK. The rain, at least, has let up – but the sidewalks are slick. I edge my way along until I reach a streetcar stop.

As I wait, I get plenty of time to think about Mr Baird's story.

A baku that's independent. Autonomous. That can make their own decisions.

Jinx is the rogue baku.

That means people are looking for him.

Powerful people. I could be in danger – and so could he.

I knew Jinx was different. I'd tried so hard to cover it up, laughing off Jinx's quirks and taking responsibility for commands I didn't make. But if Mr Baird suspects enough to blow his cover, or if Carter acts on his intuition . . . that means others can't be far behind. Others who might take Jinx by force.

No one knows for sure, I remind myself. I don't think Mr Baird would have let me go so easily if he was certain.

I can't hang around here any longer. I need to get home. I can't use Jinx to get myself a cab because of the black mark, so I spend a fruitless twenty minutes attempting to flag one down the old-fashioned way. Eventually a driver picks me up – I think out of nostalgia – or maybe pity. Paying for it is going to use up the last of my meagre savings, but it will be worth it.

When I get home, I sprint through the building, not even stopping for Darwin, the porter, who yells out my name as I pass. The elevator doors are shutting as I round the corner, and I manage to nip in just in time. I need to see Mom. I need to tell her everything – come clean to her about Jinx.

But what if she wants to turn Jinx in . . .

I'm not sure that I could do it.

The keys fumble in my hand as I attempt to get into the apartment.

'Mom? Mom, are you home?' I cry out when I'm finally in. There's no answer. I try to think back to whether this is one of her late shift days, but I can't remember.

It doesn't take me long to search the small apartment, my grip still as tight as ever on Jinx, refusing to let him go. There's no one there.

My heart almost leaps out of my chest as a loud ringing bursts through the silence. It takes me a moment to place it, but then I realize that it's our house phone. I run to the wall that it's hanging on, blowing off a cover of dust and moving piles of envelopes stuffed behind the receiver – we almost never use it since our bakus are automatically linked to the building's communications.

'Hello?' I say tentatively.

'Lacey?'

I breathe a sigh of relief at the familiar sound of Darwin's voice. 'Yes, it's me,' I say.

'Okay, glad I caught you – for some reason I couldn't get through to your baku?'

I stare down at the lifeless form of Jinx in my arms. 'Yeah, he's out of action at the moment – long story.'

There's a pause on the other end of the line. Bakus are never supposed to be out of action. But then Darwin is used to strange things from me, and he moves past it smoothly. 'You ran upstairs so fast, I couldn't tell you. Some of your friends arrived a little while ago. You had them on your pre-approved meeting list so they should be down in the basement. Also, if you have the chance, my baku has been playing up—'

What? My mind is racing. *My friends are here?* How is that possible? I thought they hated me. But maybe there's still a chance to redeem myself . . .

I don't even listen to Darwin as he rambles on about needing me to fix his baku. I don't have time for repairs right now. I mumble something about coming to see him later, then hang up the phone and race back to the elevators.

The basement is deathly quiet when I reach it – not even the sounds of Paul tinkering away. A feeling of foreboding descends on me. What if this is a trap? What if Carter is here, only pretending to be my friend? I try and reassure myself. Darwin has met Team Tobias. He wouldn't let in just anyone.

But when I walk past the parked cars and around the corner to the lockers, my heart sinks. There's no one there. But there is evidence that they've only just recently left. On the wall across from the locker, written in giant spray-painted letters, is the word TRAITOR.

I guess they haven't forgiven me after all. I sink down to the ground, my back against the door to my locker, tears welling in my eyes. Everything is falling apart, and I don't have the skills to repair it.

I need help. I might not have my teammates to rely on. But there's one person who I know I can rely on.

I need Zora. Whether she likes it or not.

CHAPTER THIRTY-TWO

'SO SAY THIS TO ME ONE MORE TIME.'

I swallow, and even though I want nothing more than to stare at the ground, I lift up my chin and look Zora straight in the eyes. We're down in the locker, and she is perched up on the stool by the old computer screen and I am sitting cross-legged on the floor. 'I don't know how Jinx works. He's not really mine.'

'You stole him.'

'I didn't steal him! I . . . I found him. And then I fixed him.'

'But he doesn't belong to you.'

I pause for a moment, then shake my head. 'No.'

'I don't get it,' she says, slowly shaking her head as well. 'It shouldn't be possible. You can't just take someone else's baku and claim it as your own.' Then, her voice catches in the back of her throat and comes out sounding small. 'I knew something was up. Why didn't you tell me?'

That's what's really bothering her. And me.

'I don't know . . . I guess I was afraid. At first, I was so focused on getting him ready so that I could go to Profectus.

But, gradually . . . I fell in love with him, Zora. I was scared he'd be taken away from me if anyone knew the truth. I figured if *no one* knew, then maybe I could keep him for ever.'

She obviously can see the hurt in my eyes, because she leans over and grabs my hand. 'If whoever they are knew that Jinx was here, how would you still have him?' she muses. 'They would surely just come and take him.'

'That's true,' I say. 'And maybe he isn't special at all. Maybe I'm just imagining that he's the rogue baku.'

'Your teacher's story is pretty far-fetched. I mean, he works for BRIGHTSPRK, right? How can you trust him?'

'I don't know,' I say. 'But Jinx *is* different. We communicate differently. I hear his voice in my head and . . .'

'Wait, hold up.' Zora flips her hands out in front of her to stop me. 'Like telepathically?'

'Something like that.'

Her jaw drops and it takes her a moment to recover.

'And he does things without me asking,' I continue.

'Can you show me?'

I point miserably to the black mark on his paw. 'Not until the morning,' I say, with a frown.

'Well, how about we take a look? Maybe we can find something in the code to help us understand. Otherwise, I think you're going to have to report this. If this is undocumented tech – like the telepathic thing – it could be dangerous.'

My mouth turns dry at the thought of turning Jinx in.

Who knows what they would do to him? Mr Baird was under the impression they wanted to destroy him.

I can't let that happen. I know that the connection between us is real. He is my baku. My companion. No one will be able to convince me otherwise.

Almost on instinct, my hand strokes the top of his head.

It takes me a beat, but then my eyes widen in surprise. 'Wait? You *want* to help me look at the code.'

Zora wriggles in her seat, and I can see Linus anxiously pacing across the tops of her shoulders. 'Just this once.'

I jump up to my feet and throw my arms around her. 'Thank you, thank you, thank you!'

She laughs until I pull away. Then, two tiny lines appear on her forehead as she frowns. 'Have you looked at it all?'

I nod, then pull at the edge of my collar. 'Yeah, but I can't say I understood a lot of it. It's more your expertise, you know?'

'That's for sure.'

I put my hands on her shoulders and look at her dead in the eye. 'You're one of the best coders I've ever met, Zora. You'd kick anyone's butt at Profectus if that's what you wanted to do.'

She nods, but her frown lines don't disappear. I know that I won't be able to talk her into believing in herself – she'll just have to see it for herself to remember. I give her Jinx, and we leash him up to the old monitor. Zora strikes a few keys with more hesitation than I'm used to from her, touching them lightly as if they were made of glass. But gradually, her fingers grow in confidence, striking them faster and faster, a pianist gaining momentum on a piece. Then she's flying, bypassing the computer's old operating system and opening up a program that allows her to infiltrate Jinx's inner workings. With a few taps of her fingers, she flings the code on to the screens around us, until we are almost immersed on all sides by lines of green text on a black background. This is the Zora that I am used to, her bottom lip jutted out in concentration, her dark eyes scanning every line, trying to make sense of what she's seeing. She can take it in much faster than I can – her brain reads code as easily as a book – or, like a musician, she can take in all the lines of music and hear the entire piece. She can also see exactly where things are going wrong, or where something is different.

Syncopated.

Off beat.

She leans back on the stool, almost so far that I'm worried she's going to topple off. I stand behind her just in case. She lets out a low whistle. 'Oh my God, Lacey.'

'What? What is it?' I'm trying to scan the code as fast as I can, but it's moving too quickly for me, too complex. I look at the screen and my eyes want to cross. I much prefer having a mechanical problem to fix, a tool in my hand.

'I haven't seen anything like this before.' Her fingers slow down, occasionally tapping out small sequences as she attempts to go deeper into Jinx's operating system. I shift in my seat. Suddenly, it feels like a violation – Jinx has seemed so real to me, it feels like we are performing brain surgery, not just looking at his code. My biggest fear is that we might damage some vital part of him.

'There are some lines of code here ...' She lifts her hand up to the screen: '... that keep jumping around. Look!' Almost as we're watching, the code moves from one portion of the screen to another. 'It definitely *shouldn't* be doing that. But whoever wrote this program is good. Very, very good. It has a kind of ... elegance to it that I haven't seen in a long time. Ah!'

'What?'

'See this?' She points to a line of code. At first, I can't see what's caught her interest in it. But if I squint, I can tell that the letters and numbers look slightly different than the ones around it. 'So obvious, right?' She looks over her shoulder at me.

I raise an eyebrow at her. 'Obvious?'

She lets out an exaggerated sigh at my coding incompetence. I grin back and squeeze her shoulders. 'I wondered why there were these big chunks of ugly, blocky code in the midst of all these otherwise *beautiful* lines. They're totally out of place – I can't believe you can't see them, I mean, it's like a bunch of weeds growing in a row of neat roses.'

'I sort of see ...' I say, while squinting.

'That's the black mark. It's written to infect the operating system while it's attached and stops any of the programs from functioning. There's no way to get this off?'

'I don't think so.'

'Huh. Okay, well I'll try to read around it.' She stares intensely at the code, occasionally stopping to zoom in on particular sections. Every now and then she scoffs at one of the lines, or makes a sound that I *think* is a small sigh of awe. After about ten minutes of doing this, she lifts one of her braids into her mouth and begins chewing. That's how I know things are *really* serious.

Even though I'm afraid of what she might find, it swells my heart to see her acting like this. It means the old Zora I once knew is still there.

I distract myself by tiding up some of the boxes around the locker, and start to scrub down some of the paint from the TRAITOR sign. I don't need to be looking at *that* every time I come down here to work. Plus, people might start asking questions. Zora already tried, but I can't break the Profectus NDA to tell her about Baku Battles and my teammates.

I pull down a few boxes and something else tumbles off a high shelf. The box from the Moncha Store. The poor scarab beetle baku is still encased in his packaging, returned there after Zora worked on him. He has no one to love him. He thought he was going to be leashed, but he never was.

For some reason, guilt gnaws at my stomach.

Zora sits up straighter on the stool, and that attracts my attention. I put the beetle box back up on the shelf. 'What is it? Did you find something?'

'I'm not sure . . .'

'What exactly are you looking for?' I ask.

'Coders often leave a signature – it's pretty hard not to

write something as extensive as this and not leave bits of yourself behind. And although there would have been a team of people at Moncha writing this, I think I see enough hallmarks of a single person here ... this doesn't feel like an "on the books" kind of project. Hang on ...'

She types furiously, but all I can see now is that code is dropping off the screens, falling rapidly, droplets in a furious rain storm. In its place is blankness. 'What's happening?' I ask.

'There's ... something ... another ... layer ...'

Briefly something flashes up on the screen, another layer of code, but instead of written in bright green, it's a flash of bright gold, like sparks of a firework. Then, just as fast as it appeared, it goes.

'Dammit!' Zora slams her hand down on the keyboard, but the screens in front of us are dark. Zora is breathing hard, as if she's just finished sprinting around a track as opposed to sitting in a chair, typing. Her brow is covered in sweat. She hasn't finished typing though. She keeps trying to draw back the regular code, but nothing happens. The screens remain blank.

She whirls around on me. 'What is this thing? Where did you get it?' She jabs her finger at Jinx's inert form.

'I don't ... I told you ...' The tidal force of her anger almost knocks me over.

'All that code we were looking at? Those elegant phrases, interspersed with the uglier sections ...'

'His code and the black mark.'

'No. All of it was an illusion. Like an overlay. A false front. I've never seen anything like it. I broke through but . . .' She throws her hands up at the screen. 'He shut me out.' She stares down at the small robotic creature curled up on the desk as if it is something alien.

'But he's got a black mark on him – he couldn't *do* anything.' I unleash him from the computer and gather him up in my arms. I'm afraid of the look in Zora's eyes, I realize. I don't know what she's going to do. She might take him. I can't let that happen.

'You have to hand him in.'

'Zora, you can't ask me to do that.'

We face off, staring at each other, Jinx in my arms, and Linus at Zora's ear. Finally, Zora's shoulders slump. 'I won't tell anyone. Promise you'll be careful. Your baku isn't normal. You don't have control. He's not the companion you thought he was.'

I open my mouth to protest. It doesn't matter to me what Jinx is. I still love him.

But she continues. 'Look around . . .' she gestures at the TRAITOR sign on the wall, and I wince, at the remnants of coffee mugs and ramen cups, and I wince again, at the bags under my eyes and greasy hair I haven't had time to wash. 'I know you want to believe that you are in control of this situation. But Lacey . . .' In that moment, both Linus and Zora fix me with the same wide-eyed stare. 'I'm not sure just who here is controlling who.'

CHAPTER THIRTY-THREE

FOR THE FIRST WEEK BACK AFTER MR Baird's shocking revelation, I'm as skittish as a mouse, imagining someone coming to take Jinx around every corner.

But nothing changes. Even Carter seems to have dropped his vendetta. My former teammates still ignore me, but as I walk past Kai in the hallway he flips a bottle of spray paint over in his hand, menacingly. At least I know who the 'TRAITOR' culprit is.

I go to each class as normal, keeping my head down, and use the isolation to regain some focus. For once, History and French get my full attention – much to the surprise of my professors.

There had only been one odd moment to remind me of the wild happenings of the week before.

The morning after the Baku Battle, when it was established that no other team had managed to repair their bakus enough to take any points from me, I had to meet with Mr Baird to remove Jinx's black mark.

I'd tried to make as little eye contact with him as possible, but he acted as if nothing unusual had happened the night before. I guess he's had a lot of acting practice in his years as a corporate spy.

'Well done, Lacey,' he said, once the mark was off. 'Good luck with the next battle.'

'Th-thank you, sir,' I stammered out.

But it was once I'd gotten to my desk that the strange thing happened.

>>You looked at my code, said Jinx.

Yes, with Zora, I reply.

>>Did you find anything?

No . . . I'm sorry, Jinx.

He beeps, which I interpret as a sigh.

>>Don't worry, I'm doing enough to figure this out for the both of us.

What are you doing?

He didn't reply.

Jinx? What do you mean?

The questions spilled out of me then.

Do you know how you came to be at the bottom of the ravine? Do you remember anything of the time before I brought you back to life?

All the things I'd wanted to ask but hadn't.

Then the biggest question of all. *Do you remember who made you?*

>>No, he'd replied, and for the first time his robotic tone was devoid of its usual warmth. But I'm getting close.

Even now, he refuses to explain more. I don't care. I'm glad just to have Jinx back and everything back to normal.

At the end of the week, I stay back to talk to Mr Baird.

'It doesn't seem like anyone is after Jinx,' I tell him. 'I know you think I might be in danger, and I appreciate the warning. But Jinx isn't what you are looking for. He's not some rogue baku – he's just normal. And I also want to let you know that working for Moncha Corp is still my dream. I want that internship more than anything. That hasn't changed.'

It takes him a moment that seems to stretch into a lifetime. Then, he nods. 'It doesn't look like I could change your mind even if I wanted to.'

'But ... I also wanted to let you know that your secret is safe with me.'

Mr Baird's eyes search my face. 'I appreciate that.'

I turn to go, but Mr Baird speaks again. 'You know, Lacey, if that rogue baku did fall into the wrong hands ... then there could be more at stake here than a school competition.'

I swallow. 'I understand,' I say, even though I'm not sure that I do.

When I leave Mr Baird's classroom, I'm surprised to see Jake waiting for me. He has a friendly smile on his face, which almost breaks my heart. I haven't seen a friendly face at Profectus Academy this whole week. 'Just checking you haven't found some other new rule that means you're not participating tomorrow? Or if you're going to be fighting with ten bakus instead of just one?'

I shake my head. 'No tactics, no strategies. I just need to find a way to get through this.'

He raises an eyebrow. 'Get through? Not to win? Even with a summer internship at Moncha HQ and one-to-one with Monica Chan up for grabs?'

I swallow. He's read me like an e-book in oversized font.

He laughs at my expression. 'All my money is on you, by the way.'

'That seems like a bad bet.'

His eyes twinkle. 'Well, see, that's exactly where you're wrong. Of course I'll be putting money on you. Money, Monchacoin, heck I'd even take homework passes. You're on fire. Or, if you maybe need help dodging questions you don't want to answer, I'll take a couple of *your* homework passes to act as a bodyguard. Speaking of bodyguards ... Are you sure you can't sneak me on the behind-the-scenes Moncha HQ tour?'

I shrug. 'No dice. Captains only.'

'Damn. Thought being your only friend left at school might have *some* perks.'

That hurt, and he notices. He squeezes my upper arm. 'Screw 'em. You have a great baku, you're a better fighter in your first year than people who have been here for years. You're on track to go right to the top of Moncha. Just don't forget the people who were nice to you on your way up.' He winks at me.

'Never,' I say.

'Good luck, then!'

'I hope I can deliver.' Preparing for the battle hasn't exactly been at the top of my agenda – not with all my attempts to stay under the radar, worrying about people coming for Jinx.

'If it were just you, I might be worried. But with that baku by your side? Lacey, you're unstoppable.'

PART FIVE

MONCHA HQ

PART FIVE

I STARE UP THROUGH THE GATES AND AT the entrance to Moncha HQ, Jinx pacing at my feet.

With everything that's happened, I've barely stopped to register where I am. I exhale sharply, my breath streaming out in front of me, a white cloud into the cold air. I'm outside the building I've dreamed of working in my entire life. The building where Monica Chan works.

Where bakus are created.

Where the magic happens.

And where once upon a time, Dad came to work every day.

I shift from foot to foot, wriggling my toes to keep them warm. The headquarters are just east of downtown Toronto, on the shore of Lake Ontario, in a part of Toronto that until twenty years ago was known as the Distillery District. Just around the corner is the BakuBeats warehouse, where I celebrated with my former teammates. I remember reading that the Distillery District was once Monica Chan's favourite part of the city – a blend of old red brick and modern glass towers, a collision of history and modernity

261

that made her happy. Plus, it was the location of her favourite coffee shop.

When she made her money, she bought out the historic buildings, and built her headquarters.

It was a controversial move. So many people protested at this young tech CEO coming in and commandeering a place that had been not only a great tourist attraction, but the setting of countless movies and a place of historic importance for the city. But Monica won everyone over, keeping the historic feel and spirit of openness to the public, while shrouding the actual headquarters themselves in mystery. The headquarters took almost a decade to complete – a lifetime in an era where entire sixty-plus-storey condo towers shot up like weeds in the space of a few months. Yet from the surface – and from the air – nothing about the Distillery District looked any different for Moncha's involvement. Plenty of rival firms sent drones overhead to find out exactly what was going on with the building, bribed employees and workmen to act as spies. But there's never been a public leak. It's like the Willy Wonka's Chocolate Factory of tech: totally out in the open, and yet fully concealed.

And I'm about to be allowed in. I hope it doesn't disappoint. I crane my neck as employees walk past me and into the building. From what I've glimpsed so far, the lobby interior looks just like any other corporate office.

Jinx sits at my feet, grooming himself. I didn't know what to wear, so I'm in the most sensible corporate-type clothing that I own – a plain black dress that I borrowed from my mom and a dark red cardigan underneath my puffer jacket to ward off the cold November air, and a pair of thick black tights and boring patent leather Mary Janes that make me feel like I'm five and forty years old all at the same time. How does that work? With my asymmetrical bob falling over my eyes and thick glasses, I don't think I'm fooling anyone into thinking I'm cool enough to work here, and – seeing the streams of Moncha employees walking in sweats and oversized parkas, I wish I had just gone with my normal *out of school* uniform of trainers, jeans and a button-down shirt.

Jinx buzzes. >>Teacher and hostiles approaching.

I look up and see Mr Baird, with the other team captains. I swallow down my feelings of insecurity, and my mixed emotions at seeing Tobias again. His face is buried in the hood of his jacket, his posture hunched over, his back turned to me.

I can't tell what is worse – him ignoring me, or the open hostility on the faces of Gemma and Elektra. They've both got new versions of their bakus to replace the ones that were destroyed by Jinx in the Baku Battle.

Tears threaten to prick at my eyes, but I hold them back. I'm here at Moncha headquarters now. I'm going to make the most of it.

'Before we go in,' says Mr Baird, his voice tense, 'I'm afraid I have to black-mark all of your bakus. Security reasons.'

>>No, I don't want . . .

Jinx wriggles in my arms, trying to escape, but Mr Baird latches the mark on in time. I feel sick, as if I've violated

Jinx's trust. But maybe it's better for us both – at least he won't attract any unwanted attention while he's in that state. I take a deep breath, and remind myself that I'm about to embark on a tour of a building I've wanted to see all my life.

We head in through the automatic doors, and I gasp.

What I'd seen before – the lobby that looked like every other boring corporate office block – was just an illusion. A hologram laid behind the doors, to fool anyone who was looking in from the outside.

The real lobby?

It's a cathedral of light and space and green and *curves*. The building is not the vision of the future I saw in old sci-fi flicks, all shiny chrome and glass (only the bakus wandering around are evidence of that). This is warm red brick and tiled mosaic floors, renovated to take advantage of the natural light, streaming in through iron-clad squares of window. There are trails of hanging vines and ivy, and bright pops of colour from the occasional bloom. A fountain bubbles up from the centre, adding to the serene atmosphere. There are perches everywhere for flying bakus, obstacle courses around the walls for land-based ones, and snugs for leashing up.

We're greeted at the fountain by a young woman with a stunning lynx baku. She steps forward to shake Mr Baird's hands. 'Are these the team captains?' she asks, giving us a beaming smile.

'All present and accounted for,' says the teacher.

'Well then, if you guys would like to follow me . . . I can give you the grand tour! My name is Nina Fiore, and this is my baku, Bright. I'm a high-level baku designer here at Moncha Corp. We have about an hour before the Baku Battles, so lots to cram in.' She leans in towards us conspiratorially. 'So many of us have requested the afternoon off to watch – lots of former Baku Battle alumni in this building! Looking forward to a great show! I especially can't wait to see that eagle baku in action. I remember when he was just a few sketches of a pencil on paper in the Moncha brainstorming lab.' To my shock, she actually wipes a tear away from her eye. But then my heart swells with pride. I knew that the people who worked at Moncha really cared about what they were creating, and here was direct proof.

'Speaking of,' Nina continues, after gathering herself, 'let's head to the brainstorming lab now. It's as good a place to start as any . . .'

If could have bottled my own feelings in the hour that followed, I would have: my emotions swapping between elation and wonder, delight and curiosity and awe. Any unease or discomfort I had is wiped away. Being here is better than Disney World, better than Christmas – the inner workings of Moncha are exactly what I had envisioned and more.

More, because people seem to actually *enjoy* working here. The brainstorming lab is filled with people collaborating, using their bakus to project ideas on to large white tables. We get a glimpse of the manufacturing plant, which is like my basement locker on steroids: I glimpse every different kind of material and machinery I could ever imagine working with, all state-of-the-art, and the companioneers inside all smile and wave at us as we pass by.

Nina informs us that Moncha HQ is totally self-sufficient, the machines and computers running on green energy provided by solar panels in the roof, and even the water is recycled daily so nothing is taken from the city's mains. It's nothing like the depictions of working life on TV, the daily grind, bracketed by boring commutes. There's a genuine buzz in the air, electric in its intensity. These are people keyed up on a different plane. I wish that I could have brought Mom and Zora with me. They would have understood, then, what I meant about not being satisfied with simply being 'content'. I wanted to strive for more. I wanted to strive for *this*. For *joy*.

Me being me, all this is accompanied by an undercurrent of panic that maybe I won't get there. Not even the angry team captains can make me feel as bad as I manage to do to myself. The other captains seem so at ease with their abilities, their innate confidence shining through. They don't doubt their place here. But even though I've known my whole life that I wanted to be a companioneer, even as the ring around my finger tells me that engineering is in my blood, even as Jinx and Aero and Jupiter are working proof that I have some skills, I still worry that I don't belong.

No, it's not that. I remind myself. *The reason you don't feel comfortable is because you didn't earn yourself a place at Profectus. You were rejected. You didn't make Tobias's team; there was a mistake. You were never a wild card. It was a fluke.*

Your true baku is sitting in a box on a shelf in your storage locker and you should be at St Agnes.

But then there's another voice. A voice that says: Fluke or not, you're here now. You have to embrace it. You have to live it. And you have to run with it, as fast and as hard as you can, to make it that much harder for anyone to take it away from you.

Maybe it will all come crashing down. But I'll be damned if I'm the one who presses down on the detonator for the explosion.

We travel down several flights of stairs, the tension rising in the air between the other captains as battle time draws near.

Even though we're underground, the hallways are wide and spacious, the ceiling height generous – so it feels as if there is a lot of light. There are even 'windows' at specific intervals, programmed to show off different outdoor scenes – like a stunning waterfall or leafy forest.

Nina stops outside a black door, marked with a stylized BB. My fingers fidget against Jinx's body as I realize that the final Baku Battle is about to begin.

'I hope you enjoyed your tour of Moncha HQ! I look forward to welcoming one of you back here for the summer internship,' Nina says with a wink. 'Good luck – and may the best baku win.'

The door opens and Mr Baird beckons us through. We're led into a room where the other teammates are waiting. I hang back as the captains join their teams, then head towards a paper sign that has my name on it. All the other teams have their names designed up – Gemma's are in neon lights, while Tobias's are in a series of neat gold sans serif. Dorian's are in black and white 1920s Hollywood-style font, and Elektra's team are in an elaborate cursive, whilst Pearce's are the most outrageous, in a font that looks as if its styled out of lightning bolts.

'Competing bakus in the centre.'

The other captains know the drill, but I know nothing – I just wait and watch. There's a stand in the centre of the room and one by one, the fighters – Tobias, Pearce, Dorian, Terence (from Team Elektra) and Kayla (from Team Gemma) – strap their bakus down on the table.

When I step forward, I place Jinx down gently and tie up the straps. Mr Baird stares at Jinx with laser-like intensity as he removes the black mark from his paw.

Jinx springs to life and he tenses immediately. He's not able to move because of the straps – although I can see he desperately wants to.

>>What happened? Where am I?

We're inside Moncha HQ, and you're in the baku circle, ready to enter the arena for the final Baku Battle. Don't you remember? They made us put black marks on you when we entered the building.

>>No. Let's get out of here.

Jinx, it's okay. We have to do this one final Baku Battle and then we never have to do this again. If you don't want to fight, I won't make you.

'Miss Chu?' says Mr Baird, one eyebrow raised. 'Back to your station, please.'

I take a step back to my paper sign.

>>Don't leave me here, says Jinx.

Just this battle.

>>And then we can go?

I promise.

It's the first time I've heard him panic. Maybe even afraid. I don't understand, and it's making me even more nervous than I was before.

'Fighters, this way,' says Mr Baird.

There are choruses of 'Good luck' directed at the fighters by the other teams, but no one to cheer me on. I grit my teeth, determined to make quick work of this – so that I can get back to Jinx and find out what's wrong. We're led into another room filled with glass cylinders: the elevators that will lift us up into the arena. My cylinder is sandwiched in between Dorian and Tobias – an uncomfortable place to be.

'All right, battlers. There are five hundred points up for grabs here – meaning a win here for any of you would put you in with a chance at the grand prize: the summer internship right here at Moncha HQ, in a department of your choosing. The last baku standing – or any bakus on the field after thirty minutes – will be declared the winner, with other teams given the opportunity to repair their bakus before tomorrow morning. But if you pull your baku before thirty minutes are up, then you will not be eligible for points. Does everyone understand?'

We nod.

'As Ms Fiore said: May the best baku win.' For a moment, Mr Baird sounds sad, losing his normal cool, and he presses his fingers against his eyebrows. I take a step forward out of the cylinder, but the glass slams shut around me and Mr Baird leaves the room.

Now, the chat starts.

Dorian snaps his fingers at me. Reluctantly, I turn my head in his direction. His thick black hair is gelled into place so that it creates a perfect crest of a wave on his forehead. 'Good luck, newbie. You're going to need it.'

My throat is so dry, I don't respond. Instead, I turn to the other side, where a few feet away is Tobias. His fingers are balled into tight fists at his side. He must sense me looking, as he turns his head my way, his eyes dark. He says nothing.

But I don't have time to think about it. The elevator shakes, and I'm lifted up into the arena. I can barely hear myself think over the roar of the crowd – all of the students from Profectus, and lots of Moncha employees too. I blink several times, trying to take in the sheer size of this arena, which must be double that of the one at Profectus. Huge spotlights shine down on us, so bright they're almost blinding. I lift my hand to shield my eyes until they can adjust.

To my left is Dorian and his wolf.

To my right is Tobias and his eagle.

But in front of me, there's nothing. Jinx isn't there.

He's gone.

270

CHAPTER THIRTY-FIVE

T HE OTHER BAKUS LEAP INTO ACTION around me. But it barely lasts a moment before a whistle blows, and everything comes to a grinding halt.

The teacher who blows the whistle isn't Mr Baird, but Dr Grant. 'BATTLERS, HALT!' she cries out to us. The other participants look at each other in confusion, their bakus frozen in place, while the crowd's mood shifts from frenzied to annoyed.

Tobias is first to realize the problem. 'Where's Jinx, Lacey?' he calls out to me from his spot.

The place where Jinx is supposed to be is empty. My heartbeat pounds in my ears. 'I . . . I don't know.'

Dr Grant's voice rises above the crowd. 'Miss Chu, your baku needs to be in play, or else we will have to suspend the entire tournament. All bakus must be present and accounted for, and all teams must have at least one baku in the arena.'

I don't know where Jinx is. I don't know what could have happened to him. *And where's Mr Baird?* This was a mistake.

I should never have left Jinx alone. Panic rises in my chest, but I also see an opportunity. 'Disqualify me, then,' I say quickly. My eyes scan the crowd and I see Jake's face fall at my words, then cloud over with annoyance. I'm going to lose yet another friend, but in this moment, I don't care. 'I forfeit my points and my place in the competition. The other teams can battle for the internship.' I hate how squeaky and desperate my voice sounds, but I've seen a way to end this agony and I'm going to take it.

'Yeah, let her quit!' says Gemma from her teambox, gleeful in witnessing what she thinks might end up being my downfall. I wince at the word 'quit', but it's true – I want out. I want out and to go back to being the freshman, a teammate, the mechanic behind the scenes. Not a captain.

And I want to find Jinx.

Then I want to go home and explain everything to Mom and Zora. They will help me figure out a solution.

Dr Grant shakes her head. 'There won't be any quitting. The rules are clear. Captains must participate once they've signed up. The battle will resume tomorrow. If your baku does not appear again, then the punishment will be a week-long suspension from school – and we will be forced to review your place at Profectus.'

Tears prick my eyes. Suspension, and possible expulsion.

But it's not the dread of being kicked out of school that's worrying me. *Where are you, Jinx?*

I scan the remaining players, all glaring at me – except Tobias, who refuses to make eye contact – but I can barely see straight. The floor beneath my feet vibrates, and one by one we're taken back down into the holding pit. The groans and boos from the crowd – who were expecting an exciting battle – follow me down. I think I even get hit with someone's balled up popcorn wrapper.

My mind is racing too fast to care. *What has happened to Jinx?* I hope that he's run off and hidden somewhere. But my gut is telling me that something else has happened.

As soon as my feet touch the ground, Tobias shoulders past me. 'Great, now we have to do this whole charade over again. Come on, Aero,' he mutters to his baku. 'Let's go train. Might as well do something productive out of this wasted evening.'

'Thanks, Lacey,' says Gemma, who bursts into the team room to meet Kayla, sarcasm dripping off her every word. 'Why are you just trying to drag out the inevitable? You're going to lose, that little machine you love so much is going to get destroyed, and that's it. Game over.'

'There's more to life than just Baku Battles, Gemma,' I snap back.

She stares at me, then shakes her head. 'You had so much potential. I thought you were going to be one of the good ones, one of the ones who didn't get swept away by sentimentality. Looks like you're the same as everyone else.'

She and Kayla leave the room, and I'm alone.

Jinx?

There's no response. Nothing from him whatsoever. I

touch the spot on the stand where I last placed Jinx. There are no clues as to where he might have gone.

The panic that I had been suppressing rises now. I'd been relying on the fact that this is something Jinx sometimes does. He runs away. He disappears on me. But he always comes back.

What if this time he doesn't?

What if now you are alone?

That can't be the case.

There's only one thing that could have happened. *He's been taken.*

I run from the room, straight into the back of Dr Grant. 'Where is Mr Baird?' I ask.

She frowns and clucks her tongue against the roof of her mouth. 'He's been fired.'

The colour drains from my face. 'What?'

'Just a few moments before the battles began. I sent him away to pack his things and leave. Now, Miss Chu – I'm very disappointed in ...'

'Sorry, Dr Grant, I have to go. Need to find my baku before tomorrow, you understand.'

Normally I would be cringing inside at being so rude to the Profectus Principal, but I don't have a moment to waste. I bolt from the competitors' room.

'Miss Chu? Miss Chu!' Her voice calls out to my back, but I don't stop.

I run up the stairs two at a time, using the momentum of my sprint to swing around the banisters and launch myself forwards even faster. I reach the beautiful atrium again but I can't even take in what I'm seeing. My thoughts are focused on a single goal. I need to catch up to Mr Baird.

I dash around the outside of the building to the car park. I spot Mr Baird getting into his car and manage to reach him just in time.

'Where is he?' I slam my hand on the roof of his car, then peer in the back windows, trying to see if Jinx is hidden there. All Mr Baird would need is a black mark and he could smuggle Jinx out of Moncha HQ, no problem.

He certainly looks shifty as he rolls down the window. 'Where is who? What are you even doing here?'

'What are you talking about? Where is Jinx? You took him before the battle, I know you did.'

'Take Jinx? What? He's missing?'

'Of course he's missing, otherwise I'd be battling at Moncha HQ – you know that full well. No one else would steal Jinx. You as good as told me you wanted him. Give him back now, or else . . .'

'Or else you'll do something even worse than get me fired from my job? I was trying to protect you. But you're too blinded by loyalty to Moncha Corp to understand.'

I take a step back, panic and anger over Jinx's disappearance warring with the shock of what Mr Baird is saying. 'Get you fired? I didn't do anything! I haven't told anyone about you. And you repaid me by stealing Jinx. I told you he's a normal baku.'

He stares at me, his eyes scanning my face. Slowly, the

outrage that had been etched on his face drops. 'You didn't tell anyone?'

'No!' I repeat.

After a moment, he says: 'I believe you. And I didn't take Jinx.'

'Oh.' I slump down against the car door, tears spilling out on to my cheeks. Anger had been keeping me upright, but now I feel as though I'm going to collapse under the worry. 'Then – who did?'

He shakes his head. 'You said he was taken just before the battle?'

I nod. 'The last time I saw him, I was placing him on the stand. But he never showed up in the arena.'

'So Moncha have taken him,' says Mr Baird, his voice tight.

He's voiced my worst fear out loud, but I still shake my head. 'You don't know that. It could have been . . .'

Mr Baird looks at me with pity in his eyes. 'It's a shame. I think he was a marvel. Maybe I should have been stronger with my actions . . . prevented you from bringing him straight to Moncha HQ. But you convinced me that he was normal. Now you have to accept that he is gone. If Moncha have their hands on him, they will have destroyed him. Here.' He hands me over an old-fashioned business card, since I don't have a baku for him to send his contact details directly to. 'If Moncha isn't for you . . . maybe you'll consider BRIGHTSPRK.'

I take the card with trembling fingers and step back as he rolls up the window and the car drives away. My head hangs low.

'*You just have to accept now that he is gone.*' Mr Baird's words ring in my ears.

But I won't accept it. Not yet. Not until I have proof that Jinx is really gone. I won't give up on him.

CHAPTER THIRTY-SIX

I WANT TO MESSAGE ZORA, BUT WITHOUT A baku I'm cut off from communication. I also have no money on me – no way to pay for public transport up to St Agnes. I'm so reliant on Jinx for practical things as well as for companionship.

I've never felt so alone. I have no choice but to walk, conscious that every minute that goes by without Jinx is an opportunity for someone to destroy him.

It takes me almost an hour, and when I arrive at St Agnes, I'm red-faced and breathless. I walk straight through the front doors as if I belong, thankful now that I didn't have to wear my Profectus Academy uniform to Moncha HQ. I have no idea where in the school Zora is, so for a moment, I'm at a loss. But there's one place inside the school where I know I can at least send her a message.

I make a beeline up to the library, where I know there is a bank of old desktop computers gathering dust. I duck past the librarian – trying to be inconspicuous – and take a seat at the nearest computer. I clear a thick layer of grime just to be able to see the keys. The machine boots up incredibly slowly, but eventually it sputters to life. I stare at the screen for a few seconds. I've almost forgotten how to use an old operating system, but I find my way to an old messaging program.

I type in Zora's 'number' (it's really Linus's unique identity code) and start typing.

L: Are you there? It's me, Lacey.

L: SOS.

Within a few seconds, I get a reply – and I breathe a sigh of relief for the fact that Zora constantly monitors her inbox.

Z: Everything OK? SOS?

L: Jinx is gone. I think someone stole him.

Z: ???!!!???

Z: How are we messaging right now??

L: I'm on an old computer in the St Agnes library.

Z: WHAT?! I'll be there. Wait for me.

True to her word, within a minute, I hear the clomp of Zora's boots on the linoleum floor.

'Jinx is missing,' I say again, once she catches up to me.

Zora gets down to business straight away, pulling over one of the wheeled office chairs to sit in front of the screen with me. 'Let's check his last GPS location. You can do it through the old Moncha database.'

I smack my palm to my forehead. *Why didn't I think of that?* I type in the address for Moncha Corp database, then I stare at the log-in screen. I haven't had to use my old log-in and password in years. I set it up when I got my first cell phone, at ten years old. Finally, from somewhere deep in my memory banks, I dredge up the password.

Then I scream in frustration. There's a second layer of security. How did people used to do it back in the day? Remember the random combination of letters and numbers, of mother's maiden names and first streets and pet names, whether something is in upper or lower case, whether it contains numbers or symbols or letters or some combination of everything. Eventually, however, I remember what my ten-year-old's answer to 'what's your favourite movie' is, and I crack my way in to my old Moncha homepage.

The layout of the page is so clunky, it makes me cringe to think that this was once the norm. I type Jinx's unique identity code into the section which would show his last recorded GPS location.

Of course. Of course, it says Moncha HQ. Why did I expect anything different? According to the computer, Jinx should have been exactly where I left him: in the arena.

'Have you reported it to the police?' Zora asks.

'Not yet . . .'

I log out of my Moncha account and turn off the computer. Linus races down Zora's arm. 'Here, use Linus to make the call.'

I nod. 'Linus, call Moncha's stolen baku line.'

There's a brief pause as Linus connects.

'Moncha guard. How can we help?'

'My name is Lacey Chu and I need to report my baku as stolen.'

'Baku unique identity code please.'

'J1NX89.'

There's a silence that feels a moment too long. 'I'm afraid we have no baku registered to you under that number.'

'J1NX89,' I repeat. 'I'm a student at Profectus school . . .'

Zora raises one of her eyebrows at me.

'There's no baku registered to you at all, Miss Chu.'

'What? That's not possible. You can look at my records—'

'I have to warn you that we take prank calls very seriously. This is going down as a warning on the record of Miss Zora Layeni and her baku Linus354. Goodbye.'

Linus switches off the call and crawls back up Zora's arm, as we stare at each other in disbelief. 'Not registered?' Zora's eyes open wide.

'They've wiped Jinx from the database,' I say, frozen with shock.

'That means Moncha Corp know he's the rogue baku,' says Zora, biting her lower lip.

I nod, tears welling up in my eyes. 'Zora ... they're going to destroy him.'

She leans forward and grabs my hand. 'What are we going to do?' asks Zora.

I blink, squeezing her fingers back tightly. Never have I been so grateful to hear the word 'we' in my life. 'I need help. I need someone with at least a level 3 baku.'

Zora breathes out heavily, clutching level 2 Linus to her chest. 'What are you thinking?'

'I think ... I think I need my teammates back.'

Z ORA PROMISES TO MEET ME AFTER school, and in the meantime calls me a car to take me to where I *think* my old teammates will be. We hug each other tightly before leaving.

'Don't worry,' she tells me. 'We'll get him back.'

The drive over to Companioneers Crescent disappears in a flash, and the car pulls up at the edge of the recreation ground.

I can see Team Tobias wrapped up in their brightly coloured coats, huddling up for a strategy session with red cups of coffee – or hot chocolate in Ashley's case – steaming at their sides. I snuggle down into the collar of my down jacket, but then force myself to lift my head up high as I approach.

It's Tobias who sees me first. He scrambles to his feet and the others follow, taking a defensive stance behind him.

'What are you doing here?' he demands. 'Come to cheat some more?'

The insinuation stings, but I don't let it get to me.

'Please, guys ... I need your help. Jinx is gone. They're

saying he never existed. But I think he might still be at Moncha HQ somewhere.'

'Wait a second. You want us to help you?' says Tobias, his hands on his hips. 'You have some nerve, Lacey. You led us all on, letting us think you were a part of our team when really you were a wild card all along.' He shakes his head. 'You know what? If I was someone else – like maybe Gemma – I could be impressed by your ruthlessness. It's impressive. But I didn't think you had it in you. So no, don't come crawling back here for help now.'

I can't take Tobias's intense angry gaze any more, so I look at the other team members. But there's no sympathy on their faces either. No one wavers. Not Kai, not River, who's always sort of liked me, not Ashley, who remains stony-faced. They're all strong behind their captain. They're a proper team – tightly bonded, woven together, strong. I was the loose strand. Something that could be snipped off at any convenient moment.

I just didn't expect to be the one holding the scissors and making the cut.

'It was a mistake to come here,' I say.

'Damn right it was,' grumbles Kai.

'Come on, guys, we have a battle to prepare for,' says Tobias.

Without another look, they spin around and walk out of the rink, shutting out the lights as they leave, leaving me alone in the cold and the darkness.

* * *

I head home. There's nothing left for me to do. There's no way I can track Jinx. I can't go back to Moncha HQ. Even worse, I don't have anything to remember him by. He's gone for ever.

I lock myself in my room and cry into my pillow, the fabric turning damp beneath my cheek. Mom asks me what's wrong, but I can't bring myself to explain. Not yet.

I've done everything I can think of, and I'm exhausted.

Well, *almost* everything.

Jinx is smart. More than that, he makes his own decisions.

What if Jinx tried to get a message out to me? There's no way he could. I'm totally out of reach – I have no phone and no baku. I wish I hadn't recycled my old phone, smashed-up screen and all.

Then I remember. I *do* have a baku. On a shelf in my locker.

'Mom – I'm going downstairs. I'll be back later.'

'Honey, are you sure? I don't think you should be alone right now . . .'

'Mom, I'm okay.' I give her a quick kiss on the cheek. 'I promise you I will tell you everything. There's just one thing I have to do for school first.'

Her face searches mine, and then she nods.

I race downstairs and when I leave the lifts I see Paul walking towards his locker.

'Paul!' I cry out.

'Oh, hi, Lacey!' He must catch sight of the look on my face, because his brows furrow. 'Are you okay? What's wrong?'

I can't help it – I burst into tears again. I turn into a

snivelling, sniffling mess in front of him, my chest heaving with sobs. 'It's Jinx ... he's gone.'

'Gone? What do you mean?'

'Taken. He ... he was special. Different. Someone wanted to destroy him, and I delivered him straight into the wrong hands.' It's the first time I've said it out loud to anyone except Zora. I can't hide it any longer.

He doesn't ask me any of the questions I expect – like whether I've contacted Moncha security. He doesn't even seem surprised by my statement. Instead, he stares at me with his intense gaze. His lemur does the same. 'He wasn't a normal baku, was he?'

'No,' I say, but the words are just a whisper.

The feeling of Jinx being gone is a suckerpunch to my gut.

'What are they up to in that fancy building of theirs?' His words trail off as he stares into the distance.

'Paul?'

He blinks a couple of times and comes back down to earth. Then he puts one hand on my shoulder. 'I know losing Jinx might feel like the end of the world. But your future isn't decided just by your baku, Lacey. It's up to you.'

I smile weakly and squeeze his hand in thanks. But he doesn't understand. 'I'd better continue ...'

He nods and lets me pass. But before I go, he says one final thing: 'Listen, Tinker. You fixed that baku from nothing. I've never seen anyone work harder than you did this summer. Whatever Jinx is ... he is because of you. Don't let anyone take *that* away from you.'

'I won't,' I whisper back. I hadn't realized just how closely he'd been watching my progress. My heart swells to know that he does know how much this means to me after all. 'Thanks, Paul.'

'And if I could give you once piece of advice?'

I nod, waiting for him to continue. 'Contact Monica Chan. This sounds like something she should know about.'

'But . . . how do I do that?'

He shrugs. 'If I knew that, I would tell you. Good luck, Tinker.'

Contact Monica Chan. Paul is right. Destroying a baku . . . even a rogue one . . . doesn't sound like something Monica would want her company to do.

But I need to get myself a working baku first. I let myself into my locker, not even bothering to turn on the light. I open the box containing the scarab beetle. 'Well, hello old friend,' I whisper to it.

I wipe down the front of the box with my hand, removing some of the film of dust. He really is a beautiful little creature, even if he isn't very powerful. He has an emerald green carapace that glitters purple in low light. His legs and pincers are a glossy obsidian, little slices of companioneering perfection. I slide him out of the package, gently using the pads of my fingertips to pry him from his plastic enclosure. He sits on my palm, almost covering it completely, and I can feel the little rubbery pads of his fingers that will give him incredible flexibility and strength. He'll be able to cling on to my skin, no matter how much

I shake him around. He's a brilliant little companion – for someone.

'I'm sorry,' I whisper again. I should have been happy to have him. I almost feel unworthy now, that I looked down on him so much. He's not only what I deserve; he's what I could afford.

I should be okay with that.

I take a deep breath, then I lift him to the leash at my ear. I feel the sync – a tiny spark – and the beetle comes to life, his legs wriggling against my neck. This is the experience I was supposed to have a few months ago.

A strip hologram projector lifts a series of texts into the air above his back.

>>Hello, Lacey! My name is . . .

There's a pause as he waits for me to fill in his name. I hadn't thought that far ahead. What am I supposed to call him? It doesn't seem right to give him a boring name, but I can't think for too long about it . . . I have a job I need him to do.

I think about what his colouring made me think of. An oil slick.

'Slick,' I say out loud.

>>Hello, Lacey, my name is Slick! Nice to meet you.

'And you,' I reply.

>>I'm just downloading your preferences now, so that we can be lifetime companions. Oh! I see that you're a big fan of ramen noodles. Me too. I'll help you locate the best ramen restaurants in Toronto.

I can't help the small smile that creeps on to my face. 'Oh, well thank you.'

>>You're a very popular person, Lacey. I'm receiving a lot of messages for you. Would you like to read them now, or do you want me to save them for another time? Whatever is convenient for you.

He's so polite! I can see how it could be addictive, having something so nice and sweet in your ear. But I miss Jinx's cheeky little asides and backtalk – not to mention the fact that reading the text is a lot more cumbersome than having his voice in my head.

'Let's go ahead and read the messages.'

>>Here you go.

I'm flooded with connections – missed messages from Zora, a few Flashes, notifications from my social media, and an email from Profectus saying that since the battle was called off, lessons have resumed as normal. My absence hasn't gone unnoted. I don't read any of them, just flick through notification after notification, hoping for something from Jinx.

But there's nothing. Nothing that seems even remotely out of the ordinary.

>>Excuse me, Lacey?

'Yes?' I rub my eyes, wracking my brain to try and think of another way to find Jinx.

>>There's a video here that's been sent to your spam. Do you want me to auto-delete anything that is flagged as Spam, or would you like to view?

My instinct is to delete it: that's definitely what you should do if you get sent strange videos over the internet. But this might be a way for Jinx to get through while staying under the radar.

'Let me see this one,' I say.

>>You got it.

My heart leaps up into my throat as the video projects on to the wall in front of me. It's video feed from Jinx. He flicks his tail and shows me just a tiny portion of his body, and I would recognize it anywhere. It's him.

'Slick, please make sure you are recording back-up footage of this,' I say quickly, just in case the stream stops running or gets deleted. 'And make it as large as you can.'

Slick enlarges the view so it's as if I'm immersed in the video. I use it to look around, trying to take in every detail. He's being carried in a cage by someone. I catch a glimpse of a moving picture on the wall, the dream-like image of a waterfall, and the Moncha logo with a cluster of stars in the background.

Mr Baird was right. Moncha have taken him back.

My heart sinks. Maybe Monica has known about this all along.

No, not Monica.

The view shifts so that I catch sight of a snout, the curve of a tusk. A boar baku.

Carter has him.

My heart beats so fast inside my chest, it threatens to burst out. I was so caught up, I didn't even think to check whether Carter was in his team box at the Baku Battles. He must have nabbed Jinx while I was in the cylinder. But what is he doing with my baku?

There's a crackle and suddenly there's audio alongside the video. Carter is on the phone to someone. I can only hear one side of the conversation. 'Dad? I've got the baku. No, I really think you need to see this . . . Well come back then! If you get on the jet now you can make it back this evening . . . Yes, I'm alone! . . . No, she's not going to know where he is. I put one of those black marks on so he's totally out of it.'

The audio crackles and dies.

Carter. I should have known. I'd seen the predatory look in his eyes as he looked at Jinx.

Now he wants to bring him like some sort of prize to his father. He probably thinks that's a way of getting in his good books.

I ball my fingers into my fist and collapse down on to the floor. The sight of him locked up in a cage has cut me down to the core – but at least he's in one piece still. And I'm not going to leave Jinx. He might be a robot, but he has no one to protect him. I'm not going to give up.

But how, Lacey? How are you going to get through Moncha security alone? says a niggling voice in my head.

There's a tiny tapping sound at my locker door. I open my eyes from my position on the floor. At first I see a pair of sparkly silver Converse, and next to them – the paws of a spaniel baku. Jupiter.

CHAPTER THIRTY-EIGHT

I SLOWLY SIT UP, PUSHING MYSELF INTO AN upright position.

'Ashley?' I say, blinking slowly – as if I expect in the span of one blink for her to disappear. But she's still standing there.

'Hi, Lacey,' she says. 'Can I come in?'

I scan her hands for cans of spray paint, rolls of toilet paper – or something worse, but there's nothing. She even holds her hands out in the open to show she's 'unarmed'.

'I just want to talk.'

I nod. 'Okay.' I undo the bolt on the cage door to my locker and let her in.

Jupiter runs up to me, and I pet her on the head, before gesturing for Ashley to take a seat. She doesn't. Instead, we stand there, looking at each other. I roll back and forward on my left sneaker, not sure what to say.

'I ...' Ashley's mouth opens and then closes again. She looks down at Jupiter, and tears well up in her eyes. 'I'm not doing this for you,' she says, her voice fierce.

'Okay . . .' I say, not sure about where this is going.

'This is for Jinx. Jinx saved Jupiter. If it wasn't for him . . . Carter would have destroyed her beyond repair. I know that. So if there's anything I can do to help find him . . . then I want to.'

I chew at my bottom lip for a moment. 'Really?'

To my surprise, she steps forward and engulfs me in a hug. 'Are you kidding? Of course. I don't know what I'd do if I lost Jupiter – or if he was taken from me. It would be horrible.'

I lean into her hug, feeling just how genuine her concern is, and appreciating it. When we finally separate, I nod. 'It is horrible. The worst.'

'So let's find him. What do you know?'

I take a deep breath, before launching in.

And yet, before I can, there's even more commotion. 'So that's where our missing teammate has got to.'

Ashley and I both turn at the same time, to see Tobias, Kai and River outside the locker.

'You can't just skip out on a team meeting like that,' says Tobias, his arms crossed.

For a second, I think Ashley is going to waver on her offer – but she doesn't. 'The team meeting ended, and I have a right to do what I would like with my spare time.'

Kai and Tobias exchange a glance. 'Were we this mouthy when we were starting out on the teams?' Kai asks, but I hear amusement tinging his voice.

'I'm sure that we had more respect for our elders,' says Tobias.

293

'Well come on, guys,' says River. 'Let's not just stand here. If we're going to help get this bloody baku back then that's what we have to do.'

Tobias turns to me. 'We're all going to help you,' he says.

'Oh, thank you—' I stammer. I can't believe my luck.

'No,' Tobias interrupts me. 'Don't thank us yet. We're not helping you because we like you. Well . . . at least, that's not why I am doing it. The way you played us was harsh. We're doing it because we think it's not right that someone stole your baku. And whether we like it or not, you were once part of our team. If that means helping you get that stinking cat back, then so be it.'

He might be telling me not to thank him, not to be grateful, not to grin widely, but I can't help it.

'I do know something about where he is,' I say, finally. I hesitate for an instant more – especially as this means giving away my biggest secret. But if I can't trust my teammates now, I might never save Jinx.

And that's just not a risk that I am willing to take.

'I was sent this video.' I play the stream back for them. 'Do you recognize it, Tobias?'

His face is stern, his normally full lips pressed together into a thin line. 'Yeah, I do. Why on earth is your baku in the Team Happiness wing at Moncha HQ?'

CHAPTER THIRTY-NINE

'CARTER IS THE ONE CARRYING HIM IN the video,' I say.

Kai lets out a low whistle. 'And it looks as if he's upgraded his boar already. Look at the point on that tusk.'

'But wait – what is that?' asks River. I look up and see he's not watching the video – he's staring at me, pointing at Slick on my shoulder. My new baku.

I cringe. 'I had to leash a baku in order to send and receive messages . . . and this was the one I originally bought.'

'But that's a level 1 scarab beetle.'

'I know,' I say, my voice small.

'You're not even allowed on to the *grounds* of Profectus with something like that,' says Kai.

'Don't you think I know that?' I say. Then I sigh. 'Look, I was rejected by Profectus at first. But then they changed their mind . . .'

Kai turns to Tobias. 'Okay, man, are we really going to waste our evening? I mean she has a scarab baku. She doesn't stand a chance in the final tomorrow. We don't need this.'

'We don't need this?' Tobias laughs. 'Kai, Oka was mincemeat because of this girl's baku. I want to compete against the best – that's the only way you know if you're the best.'

'Whatever,' he says, crossing his arms over his chest. But I can tell that he's in by the way that his brand new baku, Oka version 2, steps forward into the circle.

'Right, so let me get this straight – if you bought a beetle baku, how did you end up with Jinx?' says Tobias.

I shrug. 'I kind of . . . found him by some railway tracks. Then I brought him back here and fixed him up like new.'

'And no one came to claim him? He didn't have any record of previous owners when you leashed him?'

I shake my head.

'And now Carter has taken him.'

'Yes. And he wants to give Jinx to his dad.'

Tobias frowns. 'But why? What's so special about your damn baku anyway?'

'Apparently, at the beginning of the summer someone at Moncha developed a one-of-a-kind prototype. It wasn't quite ready for release yet and then it went missing,' I say. 'Moncha have been searching non-stop to try and get it back. And Carter thinks that Jinx might be it.'

'What do you think?' Tobias asks, one of his eyebrows arching into his forehead.

I open and close my mouth. 'I . . . I don't know,' I say, finally.

'Does it matter?' asks Ashley. 'The point is, he was Lacey's baku. Carter stole him and we can't stand by and let that happen.'

296

'We don't have long,' I say. 'Carter told his dad to get on a jet.'

'He's in Singapore, according to latest news reports,' says River, scanning some information on the back of his new frog baku. 'If he literally got on a superjet an hour ago, he could be back in Toronto in six hours.'

'So that's how long we have to figure out how to break and enter into Eric Smith's private wing at Moncha HQ, find Jinx, steal him back from Carter and get out of there without getting caught?' says Tobias.

'That about sums it up,' I say.

He sighs heavily. 'Well, you don't make things easy for us. And then what happens when you get Jinx? Carter's not going to go down without a fight, and if Eric Smith wants it back ...'

'Yeah,' says Kai. 'You know, even though we all "buy" a baku, they technically still belong to Moncha Corp? It's buried deep in the ts & cs. No one ever reads those things, but I do. And if you found yours, you'll have even less claim to him than normal.'

'That can't be true!' scoffs Ashley, hugging Jupiter tight to her chest.

'It is. So if Eric wants Jinx back, he can just take him from you. You'll need an additional plan.'

I nod. 'I've thought of that. I'll get in touch with Mr Baird.'

'But he's just been fired!' says Tobias. 'I heard it's because he's a corporate traitor. That he works for BRIGHTSPRK or something.'

'Well . . . that's true,' I say. I figure now that he's been fired, I don't need to worry about keeping his secret any more.

There are gasps all around the locker.

'But he's going to help me. He said he'll protect me and Jinx. He can arrange for us to get picked up once we get Jinx back. And then I'm going to find Monica Chan and tell her what her partner is up to. She'll put a stop to his plans once and for all, I know it.'

'Dude, you have to tell us what is going on with Jinx,' says River.

'Does he have some sort of new technology?' asks Tobias.

He's real, is what I want to say. But the words balance on the tip of my tongue without slipping out. It's too crazy, I can't say it out loud. I know I need to give them something though. 'It's buried in his code. Something that Moncha doesn't want to get out.'

'Ooh, ooh, is it mind control?' asks River. 'That's what all the conspiracy posters on Reddit say is the next step for exploiting baku owners.'

'What? No!' I say, although I suppose telepathic communication isn't *that* far off.

'Huh, like some sort of proprietary software or something?' muses Tobias.

I nod. 'Yeah, more like that.'

'Well, I guess it doesn't matter. Let's prepare a strategy,' he says, rubbing his hands together.

'This is Carter we're talking about. Not some sort

of mastermind villain. We'll be able to take him down easily,' says Kai.

'But we're running out of time,' Tobias says, looking down at his watch.

'I'll call Mr Baird,' I say. I pull out the business card from my pocket, then I dig out an ancient rotary phone from one of the boxes in my locker. The others look at it like it's some kind of alien device.

'People used to talk to each other using that?' asks Ashley, wrinkling her nose.

'Apparently.'

'Gross. How did you even know if someone was being sincere if you couldn't see their face?'

I shrug. 'Like I know. But I don't think I should use a Moncha Corp baku to call someone at BRIGHTSPRK.'

'This is like a Bond movie!' exclaims River.

I dial the number, waiting for it to ring out. 'Hello?' says the voice on the other end.

'Mr Baird? This is Lacey. Jinx and I need your help.'

CHAPTER FORTY

'WE'RE PART OF CARTER'S BAKU Battle team,' Tobias says to the security guard at the front desk, Aero spreading his wings – simultaneously looking impressive and partially obscuring us from view. We know that Carter trains here with Gemma's team, so we're hoping that the guard hasn't paid too much attention to which particular students have been coming and going.

'He's signed in, you're right, but he didn't mention anything about a team . . .'

'We have a standing order to practise whenever possible. Eric Smith said we could,' says Tobias, putting on his most authoritative-sounding voice. Aero squawks loudly. This is stage one of the plan. All we need to do is get in, find Carter, get Jinx back, and then Mr Baird will be waiting outside to take Jinx and me to safety. What I'll do from then . . . I'll figure out later.

The security guard frowns. I'm hoping that the fear of

pissing off Eric Smith is greater than the desire to check if we're really supposed to be there.

Then Tobias pulls out his trump card. It's a pass he stole from his dad's home office, emblazoned with the same logo we saw on the video: the logo for Team Happiness. The guard's eyes widen at the sight. 'All right, go on through – but try not to create too much of a mess this time around, okay guys?' His sleek black panther baku sniffs us each as we pass, but with my level 1 baku especially, I don't attract any special notice.

We walk casually towards the elevators. Tobias leans down to talk in my ear.

'Okay, the four of us will take on Carter – we shouldn't have any trouble. You focus on getting Jinx.'

I nod. 'I will.'

Tobias and I head down in the elevator, while the others take the stairs, following Tobias's directions. Thankfully there aren't many staff around so late at night, so there's less chance of us running into much questioning.

There's no denying that we might have a better chance against Carter if we use the element of surprise, but we've decided that our first course of action is for Tobias to try and reason with him.

Tension radiates from him. I want to make things better between us, and I hesitate. But this might be the last time that I will get to see him for a while.

As the elevator doors slide closed, I reach out and touch Tobias's arm, just above his elbow. He looks down at it, but doesn't shift his position. I swallow. 'Thank you for doing this.'

He sighs and turns to face me. 'I want ...' but he doesn't finish the statement. The bell dings for our floor and for once I wish that technology wouldn't work so friggin' well – that it would break down, leaving us stranded together, trapped in the elevator until we sort things out. Aero flaps out first, and Tobias follows, moving so quickly my hand is forced to drop.

Jinx. I remind myself. Jinx first, and then I can focus on rebuilding my relationships.

'This way,' Tobias says, looking at the map that Aero projects in front of him. 'Through here.' He leads me through a sliding glass door emblazoned with the constellation on it, into a long hallway – the one I saw in the video, with the waterfall window. This wing, however, feels different to the other parts of Moncha HQ that I've seen. For one thing, the walls seem to shimmer as we walk quickly past, making my eyes go funny.

'All the walls here are screens,' says Tobias. 'Eric wants Team Happiness to be able to code whenever inspiration strikes.'

'Wow,' I say. If I wasn't so focused on finding Jinx, I'd be way more impressed. 'How are we going to find Carter in this labyrinth though?'

Tobias gives me a small smile. 'That, I think, will be the easy part. Aero, call Hunter.'

Aero obeys the command, and a second later we hear the snuffling sound of the boar from further down the hall. We race to catch up with the sound, then pause outside the door.

'Ready?' Tobias mouths to me. I nod.

We open the door.

Carter is standing at the far end of a huge open-plan space, similar to the brainstorming lab we'd been shown earlier.

'No one is supposed to be in here!' says Carter, sounding panicked. 'Do I have to spell out every single instruction . . .'

He stops talking when he looks up and sees us.

'Give back Jinx, you animal!' I blurt out, so not the softly, softly approach that Tobias and I had discussed. Tobias throws his arm out in front of me to stop me from doing something stupid – like launching myself towards him.

'What Lacey means to say is, she knows you have her baku and we would like to ask for it back – nicely,' says Tobias. Aero is down by his side, and I see him furiously typing a message on his back, to communicate our position to the others.

Carter looks as if he is going to lie to us, but then he moves his body to reveal the cage that holds Jinx's inert body. 'There's no way you're getting this machine back. It wasn't yours to begin with. You don't even know what that thing is. But my dad knows. He's been looking for this baku everywhere. And I'm the one who's going to return it to him.'

'Carter – listen. There's two of us and one of you. Let's make this easy – just give us the baku back,' Tobias says.

Carter laughs. 'Hunter can easily take on Aero and Lacey doesn't even have a baku.' As if to prove his point, the upgraded Hunter steps forward. His bodywork has changed – there's no attempt to make him look like a 'realistic' boar – he's a brute of titanium and chrome, with two layers of super-charged, razor-sharp curved tusks that look especially vicious. 'But did you really think I would come down here with no back-up whatsoever?'

Three other security bakus, the thick-legged, sinewy black metal panthers, jump up on to the tables behind the boar. I swallow. Aero's not going to be able to handle this on his own.

Luckily, we're not alone either.

Oka bursts through a door at the far end of the room, Lizard and Jupiter not far behind. We've come at Carter from both sides. Now it's a fair fight.

Carter grunts, but still doesn't look afraid. 'Hunter, get that eagle.'

Aero flaps his wings, raising himself up off the ground. But the boar is good – so good – and Aero is restricted by the ceiling height. Hunter has had upgrades to his back haunches, and with a powerful run-up, launches high into the air. He side-swipes at Aero with his tusks, almost taking a slice out of the eagle's wing.

Tobias is forced to send Aero into defence.

The panthers divide up the remaining bakus between them. Oka and Lizard rally around Jupiter in an attempt to protect her. Ashley barks at them to leave her alone – she can do it. I feel a surge of pride for my friend, especially as she launches Jupiter over the top of Oka and into the oncoming path of a panther.

Carter has underestimated me again. That's always his

mistake – to see me as the weak link, the one who shouldn't have made it, the underdog. I place Slick down on the floor and send him scurrying around to Jinx, while I distract Carter by facing up to him directly. My hands ball into tight fists. He's used to having baku fight baku. Well, he's about to get another thing coming.

Carter grins as he sees me approach. 'What you going to do, Lacey, hit me?'

'If you don't give me back Jinx, then yes.'

'Well, I have another surprise for you. In school we might only be able to fight baku against baku. But here? The security bakus can fight *you*.'

My heart stops, and I spin around, screaming 'Watch out!' to Kai, River and Ashley as the panthers leap *past* the bakus and aim their attacks at the people themselves. It goes against everything I believed Moncha Corp stood for. And it's the opportunity that Carter needs. While Tobias is distracted by my screams, he sends Hunter up to bring Aero down. There's a sickening crunch of metal against metal, as Hunter's tusk pierces Aero's belly.

But despite the noise and action, I manage to slip Slick past. He gets to Jinx just as one of the panthers jumps at me. He just misses – because Tobias shoves me out of the way. I roll on the ground, direct my fall towards Carter, then lunge at him to take him out at the ankles. Caught by surprise, he falls to the ground and I pin him there. 'Got you, you thief!' I shout. 'Call off your baku! Call him off!'

'No way!' he says, defiant even with his cheek pressed to the ground. But I see exactly what I need spilling out of the top of his backpack. Black marks.

Risking taking a hand off Carter for an instant, I chuck the bag of black marks at Tobias. 'Use these!' I shout. Tobias snatches the bag out of the air and uses the marks to subdue Hunter and the security panthers.

Carter wriggles beneath me and I use both hands to subdue him again.

He writhes his limbs. 'What's the point of you "saving" that thing? Moncha owns the baku, not you. My dad is going to hunt you down. Hunt you down and find that baku – no matter where you go.'

'What? You're not going to tell your dad anything except that you made a big mistake. Otherwise you're going to have to explain to him how you had Jinx in your hands and let him slip away. Another failure in your father's eyes. Is that what you want? Because you can come looking for Jinx. But you won't be able to find him.'

For a moment, Carter looks scared. 'You don't understand. He won't stop there. You don't understand what this baku means to him. It could have implications for the whole company. If BRIGHTSPRK get him . . .'

'No one is going to get him. No one is going to get to use him.'

Carter shakes his head. 'You're so naïve. Dad has resources you can only dream of. One baku just isn't worth it. It'll be your whole career. Your future.'

I don't doubt it. But I have to be brave. 'Friends are always worth it.'

'I've got Carter,' says Tobias, touching my shoulder gently. 'You go and get Jinx.'

I scramble up gratefully, then walk over to the cage, where I see Slick working hard to remove the black mark from Jinx's paw. Just as I reach them, the mark pops off. I stretch my arms towards Jinx, my heart soaring as he saunters out of the cage, looking (as far as I can tell) unharmed. He leaps up into my arms.

My relief is heightened when I hear his voice in my head.

>>You came for me.

Of course I did.

>>Thank you, Lacey.

Any time.

Carter looks small, defeated, as Tobias lifts him up to standing. I almost pity him. He thought this was the best way to impress his dad ... but it's just backfired. 'Go home, Carter,' Tobias says, giving him a shove. Carter picks up his inert boar, struggling under the weight of it.

'I'll make sure he doesn't cause any trouble,' says Kai, who is the first of my teammates to recover. He has a scrape on his arm from his altercation with a panther, but a big goofy grin on his face – as if he *enjoyed* it. That's Kai for you. He grabs Carter under the arm and frogmarches him from the room.

Now I have to trust that Mr Baird can find a safe place for Jinx and me. Somewhere far from Eric Smith's reaches.

Until we can get hold of Monica and she can sort this all out for good.

'Come on, let's get out of here,' says Tobias. He's got one arm around Ashley, who is bleeding from a scratch along her hairline, the other arm supporting River, who is getting shakily to his feet. I nod.

'I couldn't have done it without you guys,' I say, with a smile to the rest of the team. I squeeze Jinx in my arms, ready to walk out of there – and to safety.

But, to my horror, Jinx bolts.

CHAPTER FORTY-ONE

I CAN ALMOST SENSE IT BEFORE HE DOES IT. The tensing of his small electronic body in my arms, the way that his ears twitch – left and right – his whiskers taking in the surroundings. I instinctively adjust my grip, trying to hold on to him tighter. He can't do this now. We're so close to being safe. Mr Baird is waiting for us outside. Every moment we stay at Moncha Corp is another moment we are in danger.

But Jinx leaps from my arms, able to wriggle out of the tightest grip that I could muster.

'Jinx, no!' I shout out loud.

Tobias and the others shout after me in confusion. I sprint after Jinx who darts through an opening I didn't even realize was a sliding door. It slams shut just as I cross the threshold. I'm separated from the team now, but I can't look back – not when Jinx is running away from me. A strangled cry escapes from my throat, and I drop to my knees with the momentum of trying to keep up on the slick hardwood floor. Jinx nips through another door. If I don't hurry, I'm going to be the one locked out next.

I scramble on the floor, hurtling myself down the hallway. But the door slides across before I make it there. I slam my hand up against the glass and I see Jinx stop and stare back at me.

'Don't leave me again,' I cry out. 'I just got you back.'

>>I'm sorry, Lacey. His voice is soft inside my ear. I need to find out who I really am.

'But you belong with me,' I say, my eyes welling with tears. I want it to be true so badly.

>>It's all been leading to this.

What do you mean?

>>Ever since I was hit with that blaster, I've been looking for a way back here.

My mind flashes back to the hole in his side when I found him. Caused by a blaster. That's one mystery solved, but it brings me no satisfaction.

>>When you passed by me in the ravine, I knew you could be my way back here. You'd just had your leash installed. I used a proximity signal to find out more about you. I learned you had the skill to fix me. I ran through all the possibilities, factored in all the variables, examined every permutation . . . In the end, it was simple. I could see the path that would lead me back to the heart of Moncha HQ. No one would suspect the baku of a first year student. The hacking was easy: Getting you into Profectus, getting you on to the right team, getting a wild card place so you'd be in the arena. The things I didn't

factor in were the black marks. But you rescued me. And now I am so close to finding out the answers my vast databases couldn't solve.

You . . . used me?

He flicks his tail. >>I need to know who I am.

I nod, even though it hurts every fibre of my being.

And then he spins around and, in a couple of bounding leaps, is off beyond my sights.

I think I hear a siren from behind me. Maybe Carter managed to alert Moncha security. Jinx might not think that he needs me, but I'm not going to leave him until I know that he is safe. How can I find a way to follow?

>>I can open the door for you says a polite voice. Slick. I'd almost totally forgotten about him.

Slick crawls out of my pocket and on to the door's lock. One of the beetle's front legs disappears into the keyhole, and in a few moments he breaks through the security.

'How did you do that?' My jaw drops. I'm sure that's not standard for a beetle baku.

>>My code has been adjusted by a Miss Zora Layeni to add some specific features and update some of my applications. As a result, I am excellent at picking locks. She wrote in a message: 'So you never get locked out of your cave ever again'.

My throat feels tight. Zora did this for me as thanks for fixing Linus. I'm so shocked, I could kiss him. He vibrates with happiness. The door clicks open and I'm through.

Then, I stop. It's like I've travelled through a portal and

311

out into ... suburbia? It's like a set on a movie studio lot. I appear to be on a street, lined with trees either side that can't possibly be real – the ceiling above us looks like open sky, but I know it has to be an illusion. I turn back towards the door – the only thing that looks out of place. Otherwise, I could be outside and back in time.

'Jinx?' I call out tentatively.

There's a light on in one of the houses a few metres away. There's a red post box at the front with the letters CHAN written in gold along the side. A shiver runs down my spine. The house is the type almost no one can afford any more, unless you're on Companioneers Crescent: wide-fronted, with two huge windows downstairs, and four on the upper level. It's painted a warm, creamy white, with deep olive-green shutters.

Is this where Monica Chan lives?

On a fake street buried beneath Moncha HQ? Why would she choose to do that?

No. Something is not right. I need to go in and find out what's going on, once and for all. A blinking red light catches my eye. I look up and I see cameras in the trees – and thick iron bars concealed amongst the greenery.

That's when I realize: it's not a home at all. It's a prison.

I slowly walk down the path, treading on each flagstone carefully as if each one might be booby-trapped. Who knows in a place like this? But I peer through the front window and spy a flash of Jinx's tail, giving me the push I need to enter the house. The door is unlocked. I knock on it once, unable to shake the politeness from my system, but go in without waiting for a response.

'Hello?' I say, tentatively.

The door swings open into a wide hallway, rich oriental carpets covering dark hardwood floors and vibrant paintings of countryside in oversized gilt frames on pale green walls. I feel like I've walked into a dream. None of it seems real. I wrap my arms around my waist, a deep sense of *wrong* pervading all my senses.

A giggle from the front room catches my attention. I walk in without hesitating any longer. Sitting cross-legged on the floor, stroking Jinx, is my idol and tech icon – Monica Chan – her signature jagged fringe grown out of shape. Jinx rolls on to his belly, allowing her to stroke him in his most vulnerable state, and a pang of jealousy spikes through my belly. Monica is talking to him, laughing – and, I realize as I get closer, crying too. Tears are rolling down her cheeks, dripping on to Jinx's fur. 'I thought I'd never see you again!'

She looks up as I walk in, and doesn't even blink. It's as if my presence is not a surprise to her. 'Are you the one who did this? Are you the one who brought him back to life?'

'His name is Jinx,' I say, through my teeth.

'Jinx. Oh, a perfect name. A perfect name for a perfect creature. My little trickster. He looks very different now, but I would recognize him anywhere.'

'There wasn't much to work with,' I say, bristling at the implied insult at my handiwork. Then I soften. 'You created him?'

313

'Created him?' She continues to brush Jinx's fur with her fingers as she talks, as if she wants to touch every part of him. 'I suppose you could say that. It would be more accurate to say that he created me. He showed me the light.' At that, her eyes seem to glaze over. 'I ... can't think like that. It's too difficult. I am happy now.' Her fingers lift from Jinx's fur, hovering just above him. She wants to touch him but something is stopping her.

Jinx rolls over on to his paws now. He nuzzles up to her, then hops into her arms, climbing on to her shoulder. Absentmindedly – more habit than purposeful movement – she runs her fingers around Jinx's tail, holding it up to the leash around her ear. 'Do you mind?' she asks, her eyes suddenly bright as if she's woken from a trance. It's as if the artificial light from the basement prison she lives in is replaced with inner light that shines from her face like moonlight. This is the woman I recognize from all the videos I've watched. The woman I've idolized for so long.

I hold my breath as she connects Jinx's tail to her leash. And yet ... nothing seems to happen. I breathe a sigh of relief, despite myself.

Monica closes her eyes. When she opens them again, she deflates. 'I suppose things have moved on for both of us. Come on, let's drink some tea. We won't have much time – and I don't know how much longer I'm going to be this lucid – but I do know that a cup of green tea can fix anything. Something my mom said once.'

'My dad used to say something similar,' I say, my voice sounding small.

'He must have been a smart man, your father.'

I don't elaborate – because I don't want memories of my dad to ruin this moment. But Monica continues. 'Is that who gave you that ring?'

My eyebrows raise in surprise, but then I realize that I've been playing with it again – it must have caught her eye.

'I had one of those once,' she says.

'I know,' I say, sheepishly. 'It's another one of the reasons why I wear it. You're like – my hero,' I splutter out, before I can stop myself.

Monica blushes and it covers both her cheeks, travelling down her neck – reminding me of how I react when I blush. The fact that someone so powerful and confident can still be reduced to redness like me endears her to me even more. Does she have to be perfect in every way?

'If you put him back together after what he endured, you must be a pretty incredible companioneer. Has Eric tried to offer you a job yet?'

'I don't think that's likely. I think Eric hates me. At least, his son does.'

'And why is that?'

I shrug. 'Because I beat him at everything?'

Monica chuckles, then beckons at something behind my head. I turn around to see a sloth baku walking into the room, two teacups balanced on its back.

'Take one,' she says to me.

I do as she says, but I can't hold my questions in any longer. 'What's going on? Where are we? Why are you here?'

Monica sips her tea. Then, she frowns. 'I did something . . . bad.'

I drop out of my chair, so that I'm almost sitting at her feet. 'Do you know what Eric is doing to your company in your absence? He wants to destroy Jinx, you know. His son tried to steal him away from me.'

Her eyes darken. 'Yes, well, the Smith family seems to have made a habit of trying to take things that don't belong to them. I should have acted sooner.' She levels her gaze at me. 'If you're a companioneer, then you know something about the magic of building. Of creating. I wanted to keep challenging myself. Keep pushing the envelope.

'But I was so focused on my race to invent, that I forgot about my responsibility to the company that bears my own name. I'm not a natural CEO. I'm a creator. An inventor.'

'A companioneer,' I say, quietly.

'Exactly. You understand that impulse to work. That's when I was happiest. Jinx was my pet project. You must know that feeling, as an inventor . . . there's the work you're supposed to be doing, and then there's that secret project that sets your heart on fire, the one you don't share with anyone, the one that consumes you . . . that was this idea, for me – this question I wanted to answer. I'd created a perfect companion. But could I go a step further?

'Could I create something that *chose* to be my friend? Not a slave – but a true friend? I spent every waking hour working on him, refining every component and aspect of his design, tinkering with his code, inching closer to perfection with every step.

'The closer I got, the more protective I became. I didn't want to share what I was working on with Eric. He begged and cajoled me, but nothing worked. I could tell he was getting frustrated, but also I knew he would wait. His frustration stemmed from the fact that he knew whatever I came up with would be a game changer for the company. So many of the updates I'd made – had they come to light – would have triggered a jump in Moncha's shares. But I wasn't ready to share him yet. *I wasn't ready for him to belong to anyone but me.*'

'And did it work?' I ask.

Monica laughs, scratching between Jinx's ears. 'What do you think? No. I ended up with scratches up and down my arms, having to use the black marks to keep him powered down – every time I leashed him up, he would rebel and act like an out-of-control wildcat. Nothing I tried made him *want* to be leashed up to me, apart from to use me as a power source. And with advances in piezoelectricity and solar energy, he didn't even need me for that. You've noticed that, haven't you? That he doesn't need to be leashed to you to keep his charge?'

I nod, biting down on my lip.

'That was just *one* of the breakthroughs I'd made creating Jinx. He is the culmination of all my hard work . . . I thought maybe my code was the only thing not up to scratch. That was always my biggest weakness, when it came to building the bakus. So I decided it was time to share with Eric what I had created.'

She pauses then, her eyes staring off into the middle distance.

'What happened then?' I prompt.

She sighs, her shoulders collapsing down. 'He freaked out. He couldn't understand what I was playing at – trying to create something that didn't obey. It didn't make any sense. He tried to alter the code I'd already written, but it backfired. The baku rejected the update – he wouldn't accept Eric's code! Even more than that, it started *rewriting* Eric's code, infecting and dismantling it. We had to wipe the entire project to stop the baku from destroying *everything* on the Moncha cloud. It would have been chaos.

'I couldn't tell if Eric was angry or amazed. He called my baku a monster. A virus. He wanted to destroy the baku then and there – he tried to! But I grabbed him and ran. This was my baby that Eric was trying to mess with. I triggered an old alarm that I'd set up a long time ago, in case something like this would ever happen. A mutual promise with an old university friend of mine who worked at BRIGHTSPRK to offer each other sanctuary, no questions asked. But Eric sent security after me. They took me down, and that's when I lost the baku down into the ravine.

'Next thing I knew, I woke up here. Leashed up to Pardem here. And curiously . . . happy.' She gestures over to her sloth baku, who gives her a sleepy smile.

'But Monica – how can you be happy knowing what Eric

is still trying to do? That he's taken over the running of your company. He's told everyone you're away on business! When you've been stuck down here all along.'

She doesn't immediately reply, but she cocks her head to one side. 'You have to get out of here,' she says, softly. There's no sense of urgency in her voice, even though her words quicken the beating of my heart. 'If they find you ... then he will arrest you.'

'I can't leave you here!'

'You must.'

>>And what about me?

Well, Jinx? It's up to you. You can come with me and I will promise to do anything I can to stop Eric getting to you.

Monica looks up at me. 'You two ... you're communicating, aren't you?'

I nod.

She smiles, her face lighting up with the wideness of her grin. 'Don't you see, Lacey? You've done what I couldn't. You don't need a leash to be attached to Jinx. To know what he's thinking, to communicate with him. You're not leashed to him right now. You're leashed to that beetle.'

I stare down at my shoulder, where Slick is sitting. I can't believe I didn't realize it before. Jinx and I *are* communicating without officially being leashed.

'Because you two choose each other. That's what true friendship is. That's what life is. Being presented with options and choosing your own path. Maybe not every choice makes you happier. Maybe not every decision will be the right one. But if you think carefully, I know you will know what to do.'

My eyes fill up with tears. 'But Monica, I can't just leave you . . .'

The sloth nudges Jinx out of the way, and Jinx steps backwards from her.

>>Lacey, she's right. We have to leave.

'I'm so sorry, Jinx,' I whisper to him. Slick crawls up on to my shoulder and raises one of his small, beetle legs, in solidarity.

Pardem approaches Monica, climbing up on to her lap with his painstakingly deliberate movements, his arms wrapping around her neck in a slow, loving embrace. As he leashes to her, her demeanour changes again. The tension in her shoulders slips away and she sinks into the cushioned back of the armchair, her muscles relaxing. A small smile creeps on to her lips, and I can't deny it – she looks peaceful. Serene. But the light is gone.

Jinx leaps up into my arms.

>>So that is my creator?

I squeeze his body tightly. *She might have built your body, but Jinx . . . I think the point of all this is that* you *created* you. *Through your choices, your decisions.*

Jinx rolls his spine and arches his back in my arms. I carry him out of the perfect house, down the perfect pathway, towards the Hollywood suburban dream that his creator is trapped in. He purrs softly, but I know that it's not me who needs comforting, but him. I hold him close, stroking him.

I can't just leave her here . . . it's terrible. Moncha needs Monica Chan.

>>We won't let Eric Smith take over. We'll figure it out.

But how? I don't know if I'm capable. I'm just a teenager. I'm not a superhero. I'm not special. I'm just me.

>>Lucky for you, I am special. We will do it together.

Suddenly, Slick beeps and flashes wildly. I look down at his carapace and see that he's flagged Moncha security guards approaching.

We'd better move, Jinx.

He doesn't reply, but he doesn't wriggle out of my arms either – which I take to be a good sign. I run out of the creepy fake suburb, the movie-set ideal of perfect happiness.

Jinx directs me to the quickest route outside, using an unmarked exit that means we don't have to go through the main atrium. But instead of following his directions to Mr Baird's car, where I know Tobias and my teammates are waiting, I turn and head in another direction, down a narrow alleyway running behind the building. Relying on my memory, I try and orient myself in the streets. Slick beeps in my ear, but this time – I ignore him.

>>Where are we going? asks Jinx.

Don't you remember this place?

I turn the corner and we arrive at the park where Jinx and I saw the wild cats. I place him down gently on the floor. Then he hears the first meow, and his ears prick up to attention.

'This is what you want, isn't it, Jinx? To find your place in the world. You can live here and you don't have to belong to anyone.'

It's more than that. It wouldn't be right to take Jinx to BRIGHTSPRK, to force him to help me save Monica, or even to bring him home with me. He's my entire world, but that doesn't give me the right to decide what's best for him. He needs to make that decision all on his own.

I don't want a friend I have to force to be with me. Friendship is about choice, not obligation.

I know that now.

My heart feels as if it is ripping in two, but I summon some courage. 'Go,' I say. 'Be free.'

I don't know if it's the right decision. But it's what feels right to me.

I'm not starting out a campaign for Monica's freedom by keeping my baku on a leash against his will.

More than my baku. My friend.

>>I love you Lacey, he says.

Without a second pause, Jinx runs away from me and my heart lurches. Then he stops at the gate to the park, his head cocked to one side, ears perked up into triangles. My heart swells at the sight of him, his tail gently swaying from side to side in the breeze.

'I love you too,' I whisper. 'Go. Be free . . .'

He lifts up on to his haunches then, pivoting around in the strange sinewy way that cats move. But before he disappears from view, he turns his head and looks back at me. I wonder

322

what he is thinking. What funny quip he might say at that moment. But I don't need to wonder whether he is happy.

I just know.

He'll come back and find me. If he wants to.

But I'm not done with Moncha Corp. Not with my idol locked up in the basement of her own headquarters and Eric Smith taking over. I'm going to find a way to save her, and then save the company that I've admired for so long. I've got my teammates, and I've got Mr Baird and the resources of BRIGHTSPRK. We can expose Eric and bring Monica back to the head of her own company.

'Slick, take me to Mr Baird,' I say, leashing the beetle to my ear.

Slick beeps, a series of tones I haven't heard before.

>>I'm sorry, I can't do that. His robotic voice is hard in my ear.

'What?' I frown. 'What do you mean?'

>>I'm sorry, Lacey, he says again, this time more softly.

A jolt of electricity shocks me through the leash and I collapse to the ground.

ACKNOWLEDGEMENTS

As a once-upon-a-time science fair nerd (and proud of it!), my first thanks go out to the amazing teens innovating and creating in STEM fields: you guys are my inspiration, and I can't wait to see what the future will look like in your capable hands.

Huge thanks as always to my wonderful editor, Lucy Rogers at S&S Children's UK. You loved Jinx's voice from the start and have been such a brilliant champion for me, and for this series. Thanks to the whole team at S&S for the hard work you do!

To my agent, Juliet Mushens at CaskieMushens – you are my rock, always willing to jump into the arena for me at a moment's notice! What a journey this has been, and I'm so grateful to have you in my corner.

To Kim Curran – thank you for being with me on every step of this journey, and for your patience and guidance through multiple drafts! I have so many writing friends to thank who have supported me above and beyond over the past year: Amie, Laura, James, Juno, Will, Laure, Tom, Neil, Keith and Zoe. You are all superstars.

To Jessie (and Jinx-inspiration Margot), and Adam, Tania and Scarlett – you guys gave me the space and time to write when I needed it most, and I can't thank you enough.

And finally, to all my family and friends who have boosted me up over this past year, you have no idea what your support means to me. I'm lucky to have you all.